Embellish

R.L. Sloan

Outskirts Press, Inc.
Denver, Colorado

This is a work of fiction. The events and characters described herein are imaginary and are not intended to refer to specific places or living persons. The opinions expressed in this manuscript are solely the opinions of the author and do not represent the opinions or thoughts of the publisher. The author has represented and warranted full ownership and/or legal right to publish all the materials in this book.

Embellish

v2.0

Cover Art designed by Javin Alexander.

Outskirts Press, Inc.
http://www.outskirtspress.com

Paperback ISBN: 978-1-4327-4032-0
Hardback ISBN: 978-1-4327-4033-7

Library of Congress Control Number: 2009926078

PRINTED IN THE UNITED STATES OF AMERICA

This book is dedicated to Lee, Jean, Linda, Joe, Linda-Jean,
and last but certainly not least…to Bear
I love you all so very much!

Acknowledgments

Giving thanks to our savior, I am so grateful for being blessed. Thank you, Father. I would like to thank my friend, Antoinette Franklin for all the support she gave me. She has been wonderful. My best friend also played a huge role in this project, and I am blessed to have her.

A wonderful Thank you to my sister for all of her support; I love you.

Outskirts Press was the wonderful publishing company that believed in me and made this happen. Thank you so much.

I'd also like to thank my loving husband, Joe, and my wonderful little pie-faced daughter Linda-Jean I love you both dearly.

1

...As the little girl was being dragged away, she could taste dirt as pieces of the earth made their way into her mouth and down her throat. Salty tears stained her face as she thought about how ugly she felt as three boys tore her dress and called her a fat pig. The boys laughed as she cried for them to stop. The boys finally came to a stop, and she was thrown to the ground. The sounds of belt buckles clicked and clanked followed by zippers, and eventually clothing dropping to the ground made her scream even louder. The oldest boy took his hand and covered her mouth, making it difficult to breathe.

"Please, please!" moaned the little girl as the oldest boy kneeled on top of her, and eventually lay his body on top of her. "Why do you hate me so much?"

"Shut up, you black pig!" She saw his "peepee thing." She lay on her back as he tried to put his peepee between her legs. He tried and tried but was unable to put it in. Her chubby little legs stopped his peepee from going in. In his frustration, the oldest boy began to curse as the two other boys laughed and taunted the girl for being chubby...

I awoke clammy with sweat in the dead of a hot April night. Why do I keep having this dream over and over again? I have told others about it, but I never confessed it to my mother before she died. How was I supposed to tell when every day I was made fun of for being a fat black girl? I was the only little black girl on my street living on the deep Westside of San Antonio, Texas. This area of San Antonio was primarily hispanic, and children that looked like me were scarce. Waking up every day was not exactly the most joyful thing for a six-year-old little girl like me. I picked up a Hispanic accent in hopes of fitting in, but it was no use. My accent did not work.

After being taunted by neighborhood children every day for nearly five years, and surviving what I now know was a deep depression from a gang rape, I finally made friends in the sixth grade. I couldn't wait to get to school to play with my friends.

One morning, I awoke to get dressed for school, and I went to wake my mother up to dress my sister. I called to my mom and continued my routine to catch the bus. I was on my way out the door when I was confronted by my stepfather.

"You aren't going anywhere!" he said.

"What's wrong?" I said, confused and angry. He was definitely one of the demons in my life, making communication with my mother strained and always in question. Not only was I hated by neighborhood children, but I was also hated by my stepfather and his mother. I had confessed to my mother that after my stepfather had awakened from one of his drunken stupors, he asked me, "What would you do if I had sex with you?" My mother was confused and didn't know what to believe, so I was labeled by my stepfather and his mother as a "peace breaker." Once I knew how they felt about me, I was unable to tell my mother about the rape.

"Mama, what's wrong? Please wake up! I love you—don't you know that? Please wake up!"

I reached for her and held her in my arms. I touched her face and tried to give her mouth-to-mouth resuscitation. I know what death tastes like, cold and lifeless. I realized her mouth was blue, and her eyes were cloudy and distant. She lay still. She lay silent as all the love I had for her and all the joy I had for her as my mother cracked and crumbled. No more me. I am nothing…After my mother's death, there was no way of knowing that from that moment on, life for me would be like waking up naked in a foreign country and having people stare at you because you are exposed.

My maternal grandparents were left with the painful task of raising me. Totally clueless to the fact I had already had more unpleasant sexual experiences than lightweight porn stars, they never new all of the rendezvous I had in high school with my high school sweetheart, Matt. I was totally out of control. Matt provided physical warmth and security.

Matt and I were always meeting up to indulge our bodies in ecstasy until I found out he was cheating on me with some tramp that was as big as a cow. He left me begging him not to breakup with me. I confronted him about him giving me "coochie critters," better known as "crabs" for the slow to process. His country bumpkin ass will live to see the day he regrets that move. I hate him!

College was a different story! I actually survived not getting an STD that didn't have an antidote. How about that? Just lucky I guess, or blessed with a guardian angel. I eventually got a shot at seeing just how low I could actually go. By the way, my name is Solis Burkes! Not giving my name when I first meet someone is an extremely bad habit I have. Guess I just don't have faith in people anymore. So what's the use in getting all personal when they are just going to pass through your life?

Anyway, college was on! Sexy guys, poon hound dogs, and oh yeah, hoes with deadly hair weaves. You know the girls that think they are better than everyone else? I eventually got past them, thinking that I am just as good as any one of them and could get any guy I wanted to. I was subtly attractive. I had pouty full lips, full swivel hips, full breasts, and a small waist. I had an hourglass figure. Shoulder-length curly black hair, almond-shaped eyes, and a beautiful beauty mark on my right cheek described my physical beauty. I could pull the guys in when I walked by.

Eventually, I lost count of how many guys I had tried to have a relationship with. When I suddenly realized I didn't remember their names—that was when I knew I had hit rock bottom. I let my body be used as a doormat.

I thought I was having fun doing it, but I wanted someone to call my own to love me. I knew it was risky to say the least, especially after my father called me from prison and told me that he was HIV positive. Damn, can this get any worse? I mean, my dad and mother broke up long before she died, and he didn't raise me and all, but come on, this is not good!

I guess history repeats itself to some degree. My dad's mother died when he was only two years old. He spent time at St. Peter Claver's orphanage. His father worked long hours, often forgetting he had three sons who were grieving the loss of their mother.

"I told Daddy that I had cancer," my dad said over the phone as he recalled breaking the news to his father and stepmother.

"Cancer?" I said.

"Well, I just told him that, but uh, I tested positive for HIV," my dad said.

I cried all night. The hot and salty tears I cried were for the fact that not only had my dad spent what I tabulated to be at least thirty-three years of his fifty-eight years imprisoned for what could only be antisocial behavior from a heroin addiction but for the fact that I felt I was going to lose him immediately. This cannot be happening to me!

With all this in the back of my mind, I continued to long for someone to call my own. After all the heartache, regret, and earth-shattering anger, I still longed for something; I didn't know what it was, but I hoped to find it someday.

Life continued, and I had decided to keep on pushing until I made myself into someone that my mother and grandparents could be proud of. I refused to fail as so many people thought I would, since I grew up without my parents.

I ran the street with a fickle crowd of girls that were from high school. We all seemed to have the usual ups and downs, booty calls, wanting to be pretty, wanting to be accepted, money, and getting to class on time. I was doing alright at San Pedro High, better known as San Antonio College or SAC. It got the nickname San Pedro High, because it was a junior college, and if you didn't get a scholarship to go off to a huge Ivy League university, you would attend SAC along with several other friends that were in the same boat. This made it seem just like being at the high school you graduated from.

"Are you going to class?" Elbithea asked. "You know you have an exam coming up soon."

"Yeah, I am going, but I can't wait to leave. I am ready to start the weekend," I said.

"What's up for the weekend?" she asked. "Are you and Affinity going to the NCO club tonight?"

"Hell, yeah! Girl, I got the cutest way-too-tight freak him dress that I plan to strut in on the dance floor. Are you coming with us?"

"Naw, I have penciled in a booty call, with Orriseil tonight."

"Hey!" I said as she gave me a high five, and we went our separate ways. She was headed to English and I was headed to biology.

The hallway didn't have too many students in it, and just as I had wandered onto the threshold of the stairwell, I felt a warm sensation that seemed to cover my lips. It felt like an invisible kiss, gentle, delicate, and wet. I was held in this kiss for what seemed to be an eternity. It felt so good, but at the same time, I thought I was losing my mind.

There was no one around me that was touching me. I looked a

bit stupid standing there as people tried to get around me to get to class. I stood looking dumbfounded trying to figure out what had happened to me. This was a kiss, or at least it felt like one, but there was no one around.

I went to class trying to put it out of my mind, but the desire that had been unleashed within me at that moment made it impossible to push the incident into a corner of my mind.

I made it to biology class. I found a seat as far away from Professor Porterfoy's spitting ass as possible. I can never understand how someone can talk so loudly and so long, and not feel that they have some leftover food and other unknown particles flying out of their mouth, and pretend to be clueless? Then if you happened to be unlucky enough to have one of those particles make contact with your face or land somewhere else on your person, someone like Professor Porterfoy had the nerve to get pissed at you for actually wiping it off!

As Professor Porterfoy lectured on and on about blood alleles with which I was familiar from watching crime scene investigation programs, my thoughts lingered on the invisible kiss and my response. I wanted more of it; how weak am I? Sitting there not knowing if aliens had landed, I had a ghost after me, or if I was having an out of body experience. All I knew is that I wanted more of that insatiable feeling that I was experiencing. I couldn't shake the feeling.

I had always imagined that there was someone in this world who was made just for me. Our bodies would be made to satisfy each other. Our souls would be one. We would not be able to exist if we were apart from each other.

Yes, I knew that a love like this existed just for me, but I did not know if and when I would ever be able to experience it in this lifetime; but could I be wrong? What just happened in the hallway? I often imagined that the love of my life would travel across time for what nourishment my love would provide to his soul. Has his journey ended? Has mine just begun? These are too many questions for the end of the day! I am now in party mode.

I left campus in my old beat-up Mustang and headed home. I couldn't wait until I got my own place. One of my mother's younger siblings, Chase lives at home as well, and he sure can act childish. He was always teasing me and calling me names.

"Lou, Lou! What are you doing Lou, Lou!" Chase said. Okay, I got this nickname, because my middle name is Louisa, or so they tell me. Personally, I think they named me after a character on TV with the last name of Hogg. I hated that nickname!!!

"Nothing, Chase, what do you want?" I said.

"Let me use your Pointer Sisters tape. I'll bring it back!" he said looking so innocent, knowing he had already conned me out of eight others. Chump!

"Nah, nah, bring the others back first, fool!" I said just as my grandma Olvignia turned the corner and started in.

"Alright now, watch your mouth, and don't start that shit! The Dallas Cowboys are playing tonight, so take that shit out of here! Chase! Why don't you get your ass somewhere and sit down and leave that girl alone?" she said with a beer in her hand ready to relax.

"Punk," I mumbled under my breath as I went down the hall to my room. As I shut the door, I lay across my bed, looking up at the ceiling. I started to wonder what my mother would be doing if she were here right now.

That was silly. I had these thoughts every day. I guess it's just a way for me to keep her near me. Some days are better than others, meaning some days I still grieve so badly that I don't even want to leave the house. It's as if her death just happened last week. Other times, I can say her name without literally falling apart.

I wondered what kind of plans God had in store when he took

her home. "Taking her home" is what Grandma calls my mother's death. I think it must have been awful to leave behind loved ones. It's unbearable. Sometimes I wonder if I am angry at God. No, it is wrong to be angry at God. I never want anything like that to happen to me, especially if I have children. I would never want my kids to make the mistakes I've made. I don't want God to punish me for being angry with him. I just don't know what to think.

One thing I can't seem to get over is how lonely I felt. Hours would pass by, and I would not leave my room. Just being away from everyone makes me feel safe, but at the same time, I longed to be close in some way to someone.

Just then, the phone rang.

"Hi baby," I said. It was Kyle Haskins. He and I have been seeing each other off and on for several months. He and I are going to the movies tomorrow. Kyle had rich, dark-brown skin. He was tall, thin, and built like a track runner.

"I've missed you today," I said. "What's going on?"

"Hey, uh, I'm still at work," he said, "but I am getting off soon."

"I can't wait to see you tomorrow. I have already got my new outfit out and ready to go. What time are you coming through?" I said.

"Look, uh, I'm not going to be able to make it. I am going to roll out with Nick, and we are going to the football game," he said. Just then, I could here the phone ring in the background at his house, and his brother Brian mumbles that Lisa wants him on the phone. He tells me to hold on and comes back to the phone.

"Hey, that's Nick on the phone, let me call you right back," he lied.

"Kyle what kind of game do you think you are playing?" I said. "Bastard—you are not slick. Why are you lying?" I said, pissed to the max now. I heard you tell her to hold on. So is she the famous 'Nick' and 'football game' you are going to? You think I am that stupid?"

"Look, I got to go!" he said, scared and busted from being caught in a lie.

"Yeah, go straight to hell!" I said as I slammed the phone down hard as I could.

Seems like, we always end up breaking up and then dating again. I don't know why it hurts so much each time as if I hadn't already been through this with him. Before I could begin my usual dramatic cry, the phone rang again. This time it was Affinity.

"What's up, girl?" she said.

"Nothing, I just got through slamming the phone down on Kyle's 'short yellow bus riding' ass," I said. The short yellow school bus is for the special needs children, and he acted like he was definitely special needs.

"Some girl called while he was on the phone with me, and he lied and whispered to his brother in the background to tell her to hold on," I told Affinity. "He tried to whisper, but I could hear his 'can't whisper quietly' ass. How stupid does he think I am? What time are you coming to pick me up?" I asked.

"I'll be there in an hour," she said as music blared in the background.

"You sound like you are getting hyped up already!" I said as I began to feel the rush of anticipation of hitting the club and dancing the night away, and dancing away all the "boy blues" that came with finding a mate.

"I am getting hyped, and I am ready to cruise the night away," she said, and I heard her tell her sister to stop turning the radio station from her song that was playing.

"Alright," I said. "I will be ready when you get here."

"Cool, alright, bye," she said and hung up the phone.

Suddenly, my mood shifted back into the party mode I was in before

I came through the door to the house. It felt good having something to look forward to, and this was it. I couldn't wait to get outside of the walls of the house.

I went ahead and put on that sexy little red dress I had bought at Judy's boutique. It was too cute. I had a set of black pumps that had spiked heels that made my legs look shapely and toned. I looked good.

I carefully applied my makeup, and then slid a layer of lip gloss across my lips. I quietly opened my door and slid up the hallway, careful not to alert Chase. He had a bad habit of trying to see what I was wearing to alert Grandma. His duty of being self-appointed warden was wearing on my nerves. As soon as he heard my footsteps, there his face was in the frame of his door.

"Lou Lou what are you wearing, Lou Lou?" he crowed. "I need ten dollars so I can get some gas—you got some money?" Blackmail, of course, but I didn't care—I just wanted out.

"Here, Chase!" I said. "Now shut the hell up or I will tell the next girl that calls here you went to the clinic for results. 'Results' sounds bad, Chase—so don't push me!" I whispered.

"Alright, I'll be quiet," he said as his face quickly retreated back into his darkened room. I confidently continued up the hall, and I had just about made it when…

"Where are you going, girl?" Grandma Olvignia said. "Damn!" I mumbled.

"Affinity is coming to get me, and we are going to the movies," I quickly fired back.

"You're dressed like ya'll are going to ride by the movies and stop the car at a club; so quit that lying—quit that lying!" she echoed as I was trying hard not to melt from embarrassment.

"Grandma, I just want to go and hangout with my friend. We will be back before it's too late," I said, trying to negotiate a way out the front door.

"Well… you go on, but be warned. Something strange is moving through here. I don't quite know what it is, but its close. I can't tell if it means well or if it has bad plans, but you be safe, child, you hear?" she said as she continued to flip the remote and sip slowly from her can.

Grandma said "something moving through." I can only imagine what she is talking about. She has the gift of foresight. Grandma's family has deep spiritual voodoo roots planted in San Antonio with relatives that go all the way back to freed slaves that first came here after the Emancipation Proclamation that freed the slaves in Texas. Her ancestors were big followers of the voodoo religion.

Grandma Olvignia's people were slaves from the northern tip of Africa. She often told us stories that were passed down from generations about how life was "back home" on the mother continent. She spoke of how her family owned many acres of land and was able to keep their families together. She explained that she came from a long line of women who were able to tell when trouble was near, when a baby was going to be born, or, when death was near.

Grandma explained that her mother spoke of a woman that was as beautiful as she was powerful. Her name was Priestess Auldicia, and she lusted after one of the men in our family known as Oded. Oded was a strong warrior who was a newlywed and loved his new bride as no man had loved any woman before. He would never succumb to the seductive allure of Priestess Auldicia.

Grandma Olvignia explained that Priestess Auldicia was insulted and angered by the fact that she could not enchant Oded with one of her intimacy spells. She soon conjured a spell to awaken some of the most evil blood-lusting demons known to go forth and rape the man's new bride. Priestess Auldicia did so by having the demon possess one of Oded's enemies. This enemy had been lusting after the women in Oded's family long before Oded became a man.

The priestess was smart, and she knew how to cover her tracks for such a vile indiscretion. She knew if she were ever caught, she would be damned to the doorsteps of hell for causing a war between the two families. Grandma Olvignia explained that the other women in the family knew of the wickedness that Priestess Auldicia had within her, and soon drove her out of the midst of the community. The women in our family vowed to pass the knowledge of spells and voodoo within our bloodline for survival. My grandmother remained true to her matriarch gift, and when she had her own children, she noticed instantly the gift from two of her daughters.

Grandma was a strong, special woman. She had to be a strong woman to parent six children and still keep her sanity.

Grandma Olvignia was sick with her own illnesses though. She had fought ovarian and breast cancer and she had won. She was a borderline diabetic, and over three fourths of her arteries were blocked, yet she continued to enjoy her life. She had been a devoted wife to my grandfather, Leonine.

Grandma Olvignia explained to me that when my mother was younger, she used to play with the Ouija board. My mother and my aunt used to sit in their room and sniggle and giggle like little ones do, chant protection hymns, and step dance to protect their house and their other siblings.

My grandmother explained that my mother and my aunt Etienne were allowed to play with the board until, one day, the board spoke to my mother. The Ouija board warned my mother that she was going to die very young. The same board told my aunt that she would be successful in her lifetime. Grandma Olvignia explained that when my mother told her of these things, both my mother and my aunt were forbidden from going near anything to do with magic or the sight.

While my mother was alive, her interest in foresight and dark magic continued. She sought after anything to do with the art of spells, magic, and children of the underworld. My mother had continued in her quest for knowledge of voodoo, more so after she married my stepfather. The night she died, the emergency medical response team found a small vat with crushed residue in it that she appeared to have ingested. It is unclear if she killed herself or if my stepfather had given it to her. Well, here I go again insinuating something that has left me wandering in and out of grief.

To this day, no one knows what the circumstances were that surrounded my mother's death—only that my stepfather ran off with one of her friends who turned out to be a sorry bitch dog! No one has seen either of them since. It just might be better that way, because I can't honestly say what I would do if I were to see either of them today.

Nevertheless, I believe my grandmother watches me so closely to see if I will have the sight or the knowledge of voodoo. She often tells me I have a lot of anger within me. Sometimes I believe what she is saying to be true. Other times, I just feel like I am misplaced and wandering through life. I never feel sure of myself, always second-guessing decisions. I have often been told that I present as a much older person than what my chronological age is, yet my birth certificate says differently. I guess you have to experience heartbreak that pierces your soul for you to appear to have a more mature persona.

"Grandma, I will be alright, and don't wait up, okay?" I said.

"You just hear what I said, child. Be careful," she said.

And with that, Affinity rang the doorbell right on time to save me.

"What's up, girl?" I said, quickly reaching for the door to leave.

"Nothing, are you ready?" Affinity asked as she stood outside on the porch, too nervous to let Grandma Olvignia see what she had on, because we would have been busted for sure.

"Let's roll. I can't wait to hit the dance floor," I said. And with that, I called a quick good-bye to Grandma and coasted out of the neighborhood. Dancing was one way for me to shake the woes of dating and, for sure, to shake off the crap that Kyle was dishing out.

This night held something exciting in the air, and I could feel it. The feeling was like hot wattage on a dangling wire.

2

As we pulled up to the club, you could smell all kinds of cologne and perfume in the air as people got out of their cars and walked up to the door of the Fort Sam NCO Club. I was already having a huge adrenaline rush when I heard the beats from the bass bumping from the dance floor as the deejay played the hits. That mess with Kyle only lasted for a little while. My mood had changed, and I was happy to be out. I continued in my quest for love, but I was finding only false glamour for my wanting eyes to see instead of seeing all the deception and evil in what searching for love truly was.

Affinity and I were looking good! We had on the tightest ass-cupping dresses you could find in the club. We had on heels that looked like tent spikes, and Raunch perfume was our fragrance of the day but smells like funky pesticide now. Oh yes, we were on the hunt for attention, affirmation, and adoration. We struck poses in every corner of the room, with absolutely no luck. No glances at all from any men in our direction. I looked up, and I zeroed in on a worthwhile specimen.

"Girl, look at him," I whispered to Affinity. "Damn, he looks good!"

"He looks like a wildebeest in the face—don't you see his nostrils flared?" Affinity said as she smirked and nearly spilled her drink.

"He has a beautiful chest. Oh, here he comes!" I said as the light-skinned guy, with the extremely buffed chest, bowed legs, and dimples walked slowly towards us, or so it seemed. He came and stood right by us, and before another moment could pass, he opened his mouth to reveal a gaping hole that appeared to have once been occupied by an incisor and a canine tooth.

"Oh, hell no!" I said in protest. His teeth are missing! No wonder he keeps his lips wrapped around the straw of that drink and not talking to anyone. Yuck!

Affinity laughed out loud nearly getting us busted by the guy. I mean, surely he had to know that we were laughing at him. I could tell Affinity was beginning to buzz from the drinks that she was downing. I have no idea where that girl gets the stomach to swig down so much alcohol and still keep standing. I turned from Affinity and began to walk to the ladies' room when I suddenly felt a cold, wet mist encircle me. It brought a tingle down my spine that was a sensation that could only be described as needles, ice, heat, and exhilaration all at the same time. The wet embrace was so soothing that it brought me to a complete standstill.

The mist tickled my earlobes as I closed my eyes and felt it continue to work its way around my fingertips and down to my calves. I forced myself to continue to walk towards the ladies' room.

As I approached the ladies' room, I looked down the hall and caught a glimpse of what looked like a flicker of candlelight moving in one of the empty dining halls down from the club where the deejay was. I followed the flicker of light, actually drawn to it like a magnet. I couldn't stop following if I had wanted to. I approached the door of the dining hall and stepped in. The room was dark with only a small candle lit in a far corner at the very back of the room. As I approached the light, I heard a voice that was as smooth as satin speak words that entranced and serenaded me closer to the source.

"Welcome, I have been hoping to speak with you before the night was over," the voice said. "I have been waiting for you, watching you, and wanting to feel you close," the satin voice continued. The words were pronounced in an accent that wasn't the usual dialect that locals preferred as they greeted and socialized with each other. It was melodic, serenading me closer to it.

In the candlelight and lingering mist stood a figure that towered an estimated 6 feet 7 inches tall. The man's form was beckoning with muscles that rippled through his chest underneath his skintight shirt. His shirt was stretched across his chest that made the material look youth-sized.

As he stepped from the shadows that were thrown on either side of the walls of the room, his magnificent thick, silky-black, shoulder-length mane cascaded down his back with every movement he made. He stopped, just breathing distance from me, with a smile that seemed to further illuminate the room and complement the moonlight outside.

"Who are you?" was all I could manage to let slip from my lips. As I stood there, I realized that my heart was racing, my legs wanted to turn and retreat to where my friend was, but all the while, my curiosity was nagging me to the point of proceeding with the conversation. I didn't know this stranger, yet I continued to stand in the midst of his presence, and it could have meant if I was going to live or if this was my last living night on earth.

"Pardon me, I am Nacio. I have been intrigued by your eyes and your lips all night," he said as he reached for my hand and gently kissed it. When his lips touched the skin of my hand, I felt the soothing mist and desire that had led me astray from the ladies' room and into this room to begin with. As I looked into his eyes, which seemed to be a shade of every color that is known, I noticed he possessed the most beautiful thick black, highly arched eyebrows that seemed to be the keepers of naughty thoughts and desires that were unspoken.

"Me?" I asked, with quivering lips and voice quivering to a whisper. "Why me?"

"Only you," he said as he studied me with the eyes of a child, unblinking and eager. His skin was as cool as frost breath on a fifty degree morning, yet as soothing as a warm towel. His words rolled from lips like that of a morning tide on a shore. Of course, they did, because each word he spoke washed me into a sea of desire that had no end or beginning. As I stood there, I felt that familiar cool and warm stillness that had introduced itself to me earlier that day in the hall before class. It was him.

"Forgive me if I have startled you, Solis. That is not what I wish to do," he said as I couldn't take my eyes off his lips as he spoke. His words mesmerized me so lovingly.

"How do you know my name?" was all I could manage from my verbal captivity.

"I know that you have been looking for what only I can provide for you, my love. You will solve the mystery of that in the near future. Just know that I will love you like no other, nor will you want any other," he said as he reached his perfect hand for my neck. He pulled me in close to his chest and slowly glided his tongue over the muscle and pulsing vascularity that warmly established my life force within me.

At that moment, I felt the tips of what I could only interpret to be sharp peaks of teeth graze my skin. He kissed my neck, slowly and then more desperately. I ached and moaned with such a hunger for his touch that I began to realize that I was just as cheap and trashy as other girls I talked about, because they would screw guys they just met. But, my goodness, I couldn't help myself! He hadn't even undressed me, but the desire had my hips responding and my thighs a wet mess. Somebody help me!

"Yes, I am the man who will love you like no other...but not tonight!" he said. At that moment, a cool whoosh of air blew over my shoulders and he was gone. I was left standing in the candlelit room alone, confused, and extremely stimulated, and that felt gross when I walked.

What in the heck just happened? I stood in the middle of the room calling out to him. "Nacio, Nacio, where are you?" I called, but no response. I started walking back towards the hallway and hastened my pace to a jog hoping to find him in the crowd. As I reached the ladies' room, which had been my initial destination, I saw Affinity standing at the front door of the club. I hadn't even realized that they had "last call for alcohol" over 30 minutes ago, and the military base MPs were shutting the club down.

"Affinity, you cannot drive. You are too full," I said as I watched her stand there swaying back and forth to an imaginary lullaby in a drunken stupor. The music had long since stopped, and there was no telling what beat Affinity's mind was entertaining her with.

"I can dri', I can dri', I got my lizenze!" Affinity slurred as she was shaking the keys at me. I quickly snatched the keys and started to guide Affinity's totally inebriated body to the car, all the while still anxiously looking around for Nacio. The desire for him was still burning like a wildfire. Oh well, guess he's just another jerk that likes to play games with females that he meets, and then he drops them after a while.

I have gotten so used to the fact that this happens over and over again, but, oh well. I guess I'd just better hurry and get Affinity home, because I hadn't realized that in a few hours, the sun was about to come up. If Affinity hadn't been so wasted, we could have gone and had breakfast at Debbie's. That girl loves alcohol more than she loves food. My goodness!

When I got home, I had the darnedest time getting Affinity into my house. She was just going to have to take the heat when she got home the next day. I knew I was going to have a lot of explaining to do to Grandma Olvignia, because having friends over to spend the night was something that was not allowed here at home. Grandma said that "it was easier to keep trouble out of your home if that rule was followed." Anyway, I was too tired to try to weigh the pros and cons. I changed out of my clothes and put Affinity in the twin bed in my room. I got in my own bed and drifted off to an alcohol-induced slumber, and the dream began again.....

...this time, as I lay on the ground with dirt on my dress and hips, I see the face of my cruel and heartless rapists. His name was Klein...I can't remember his last name. One of them kept taunting me and calling me names. I cried and cried, and all he did was laugh and call to his sister, Childress who helped hold me down along with the other two boys whose names I couldn't recall other than Justice. The boys took turns making fun of me and penetrating me. Once they were done, they all left running in different directions. They left me there in a pile of dirt, degraded and humiliated...

I awoke the next day, shaking. I was able to remember more and more details of the rape that had occurred when I was a child. I hope once I can recall the details from that incident that I can put it all behind me forever. Well, no sense in harping on it now—I had to face Grandma this morning. I went to make myself some coffee, and when I looked up, Grandma had come into the kitchen; so the admonishment began.

"What is that girl doing still here?" Grandma Olvignia, said as she stirred her coffee at a fierce pace.

"It was late, Grandma, and I didn't want Affinity to drive home alone," I said in her defense; but as I had mentioned, Grandma had foresight and was aware of all happenings in her environment.

"Stop that lying, stop that lying! I already know what happened last night, child," Grandma said as she postured her hands on her hips, her knees hyper-extended and locked. This stance of hers was better known as her Battle Mode.

"What'd I tell you about folks staying over? Now I got to burn some white sage for cleansing the atmosphere in this house," she said as I stood there and felt like I was the one who got caught with my hand in the cookie jar.

"That girl was drunk last night. I could smell the stench off her as soon as you let her slither in here. When she is going home?" Grandma inquired.

"She is going this morning, Grandma. I just wanted her to be safe," I said, trying to look as humble as possible. One thing was for sure, you didn't want to cross Grandma Olvignia. She was tough and could make life a misery if a person did not make amends with her.

"Did you meet him?" Grandma asked with her coffee in grip pulled up to her lips. "I knew you and he would cross paths soon enough."

"Who are you talking about Grandma?" I asked, confused and a little shaken by her accurate inquiry.

"Quit playing with me, Solis. What did he say?" Oh man, Grandma was tough, and she knew I had met Nacio. The thing was I was not sure what to tell her or where to begin. This was especially difficult because my desire instantly began to smolder once more, but I was angry because he left me in a state of response to him that was totally out of control.

"Yes, Grandma Olvignia, I met him. He scared me at first. I have so many questions for him. He says that he knows me. The strangest thing happened to me yesterday when I was going to class. It was if he were there in class with me before I met him last night. How could he have done that?" I said, looking rather dumbfounded. Grandma was looking for any hint that I might be holding back on her.

"Child, he does know you. I would be lying to you if I said that I did not know what he was here for, but I would rather you find this one out on your own. I don't believe he means any harm, but there are things that only he can tell you. You go with caution, child," she warned. "There are things that he is going to show you that you have been waiting to know—but be careful. Be careful what you wish for, child. Sometimes it is not always for the best," Grandma warned again.

"Grandma, why can't you just tell me instead of saying things like that," I pleaded.

"Because, Solis, you deserve to live your life," she said as she reached for the lighter and began to burn the white sage just as Affinity was walking into the kitchen facing me. Behind her back, Grandma mouthed, "*Get her ass out of here.*"

"Affinity, you ready to go?" I said nervously as Grandma began to walk through the house with the sage burning in a small dish as she murmured a chant up and down the hallway. Grandma felt like too much alcohol brought bad spirits to your doorstep, and the spirits needed to be driven away.

"Yeah, girl, I'm gone. Thank you, Grandma Olvignia," Affinity said as she left. Grandma just cut her eyes in Affinity's direction after she got an eyeful of the dress, which looked twisted in the early morning light.

Anyway, the weekend continued to roll by. I couldn't shake the lingering thoughts that I entertained about Nacio and the soft, pulsating kisses he planted upon my neck as I stood agonizingly so in his embrace, longing for more. I was also pissed, because he left me aching for him. I wanted to tell Affinity about him, but I wasn't sure just how much to tell her. Plus, would she even believe me?

I let the idea of telling Affinity about Nacio mill around in my mind a few more minutes, and then decided to put that thought on hold and get ready to go to the library to do some studying for my biology exam. I was just about ready to go when my phone rang. It was Kyle's confused ass, trying to start a fight with me.

"Hey, what's up, girl?" he said, sounding like nothing had happened at all. I saw you last night at the NCO. So are you trying to hook up with someone else?

"What do you want, Kyle?" I said as I took a bored breath, listening to him about to beg.

"You don't have to get all snotty with me. I just asked a question. You know I only went to hang out with Nick."

"Whatever, Kyle, you are not the only guy that finds me to be cute, and quite frankly, I don't have time for your shit anymore. Go play your young head games with Lisa. I'm sure she would understand your insecurities," I said as I once again slammed the phone down as hard as I could. It felt good to do that! It might have been childish for me to do, but I was beginning to feel a newfound confidence that was starting to make me feel alive. It made me want to start regarding myself with some value, and not be pushed around or taken for granted anymore.

I glanced over at the clock by my phone and realized that I needed to get to the library. I have a biology assignment that I need to get completed before Monday. I also wanted to be alone to continue to daydream about Nacio. Just thinking his name sent a hot jolt to my groin that caused hot steamy humidity to accumulate there as it did last night. I need to slow my thoughts down about this man. I still know nothing about him. I mostly wonder what Grandma's link to him is?

I jumped in my car and headed downtown to the Central Library that was closest to San Antonio College. I drove through an old neighborhood and noticed how run-down it looked. The houses looked like condemned shacks, with the roofs dangerously collapsing and jagged beams sticking out of the ground.

Trash lined the edge of the poorly tended yards; the yards didn't seem to have a beginning or end. Old cans of baby formula and soiled diapers deliberately lay in the middle of the road to turn the stomach of any visitor to the neighborhood.

There was the strangest graffiti written on the sides of old buildings and the houses, with symbols that were circular and were written in dark black spray paint. There was also a symbol that had what looked like a star, a pentagram perhaps. The pentagram was drawn over a pair of evil cat-shaped eyes behind another symbol that looked like some sort of dagger. Out to the side of the graffiti were the initials C.T. This felt truly creepy. I noticed that some of the graffiti was written at the very top of some of the buildings that were at least ten stories high. How could anyone have possibly gotten up that high to tag?

I don't know, maybe it was some sort of crazy gang initiation, but it still doesn't answer the question of how it was done. Come to think of it, I saw some of the same graffiti written on expressway signs that stood at least twenty-five feet in the air stretched across the expressway itself. Being able to do that would be impossible for a human, but yet here I am looking at what looks to be graffiti that has a whole different language. There were some names that were written and had been crossed out on the sides of the houses. I certainly didn't understand it. Oh well, I just hope that whoever is doing it stays out of my neighborhood. From the looks of the writing, anyone would instantly know that it signified trouble.

I finally arrived at the library. There were only a few cars in the parking lot. That was good; that meant I would have any study station I wanted, and I could be free to roam between the towering vaulted shelves of books at will. I zeroed in on my favorite study station. As I walked towards it, the librarian gave me a friendly glance as she continued cataloging returned books.

I sat down, put my backpack down, and started to wander through the several shelves on the hunt for information about blood-typing. I had found the book that had the information I needed. I reached for the book—and there it was again, that soothing, fantastic sensation that had cloaked me at the club last night. The sensation was more overwhelming than before. I closed my eyes for a moment to steady myself; when I opened them, there before me stood Nacio. He was sexy and regal looking as if he had just stepped out of the pages of one of the medieval novels on the shelf. Nacio's eyes were a magnificent gray color at that moment. His eyes did not blink nor did they move from mine.

"My love," he said. "I couldn't wait to see you once more."

I watched his lips say those words, and all I wanted was to put my lips with his and suckle his breath. At that moment, I ignored my desire and unleashed my fury.

3

"You left me last night," I said. "You left me confused and very angry!"

"Forgive me," he said. "I was about to lose control of my desire for you. I felt an emotional surge within me, and the feeling is truly overwhelming; I felt that it would not be the most appropriate moment for you."

"But you left me. Oh well, I know nothing about you anyway, so I guess no harm done," I said trying to pretend as though what he had done didn't matter, but it did. "Why would I believe that you would be any different than any other guy I have met?"

"Again, please forgive me. The last thing I would ever want to do is hurt you, Solis," he said, eyes unblinking and moving so dangerously towards my personal space. He moved as fluidly as a school of minnows leisurely exploring their underwater environment.

"Yeah, whatever, I don't have time for your boy games," I said, trying to be confident and nonchalant. As I turned and spun on my heels, he was once again in front of me, and this time, his face was close enough to kiss mine. I jumped back.

"Whoa! How in the hell did you do that!" scared and dumbfounded, I said, and at this point, traveling backward away from him. He continued his fixation on me, with his eyebrows arched high and his lips turned upward in a smile that could illuminate the darkest of night skies. Man, he was so beautiful, and I was so weak and quickly losing my battle to resist his enchantment.

"Solis, there is so much I feel at this moment for you, but I don't want to scare you away. Right now, I think I am scaring you, and I would like a chance for you to get to know me. I would cease to exist if I couldn't be near you, please. Please get to know me," he said, extending his hand and waiting for me to accept his gesture.

"You are right. You are scaring me, Nacio. How are you able to move like that?" I said, totally freaked out, yet not able to break free from his captive gaze.

I took his hand and was amazed at the coolness and the clammy surface of his skin. I wondered why I hadn't noticed this last night. Maybe it was because my body was as hot as a furnace. I had never felt this way about anyone before. He responded to me in a way that made feel as though he felt the same.

"Look, I have an assignment due, and I have to complete it today; so unless you want to help me write it, please let me work," I said. Before I could get another word in, he took my notes from my hand and sat me at my study station. He then proceeded to go into a section at the library that had the medical stacks. He came back with a thin book with an extremely withered spine that appeared to have been used often. He handed the book to me.

"Here you go," he said. "This should tell you all you need to know about blood alleles and blood-typing."

"How did you know what my assignment subject was?" I said, looking at him curiously.

"Well, my dear, to be honest, there is very little I do not know about you," he said, and there went that smile again. This was no fair! He couldn't keep doing this to me. He would melt me from the inside out every time he smiled. "Do your assignment, and I will tell you about ***You***!"

I completed my assignment in what seemed to be twenty minutes. My haste was driven by the anticipation of finding out all I could about my newfound admirer. I wanted to know all I could about him, since he claimed to know so much about me. I wanted to know how he knew all that he knew so far.

"Alright, I'm done. So start talking! How do you know so much about me?" I said with my gaze fixed on him, trying very hard to beat him at the "no blinking game," but again losing my battle.

"Well, I would like to just cut to the chase about me," he said. "Uh, how can I put this? I am a vampire and have been for the last two hundred and fifty-seven years."

Immediately, I snickered and laughed. Then I let out a sidesplitting belly laugh that got me a roared shush from the librarian at the customer service desk. I laughed for at least ten minutes.

"You expect me to believe that?" I said, still searching for my composure and watching Nacio. As I did, he smiled his smile. Slowly I noticed that his smile became crowned with pearly white fangs that looked lethal upon contact. I continued to deny the point he was trying to make—no pun intended.

"My love, I am happy you find what I am telling you so amusing, but it is true. I have no reason to lie to you," he continued to plead his case. I continued to deny every word.

"Nacio, this appears to be a nice parlor trick, but I am not buying this sales pitch," I said, trying hard not to laugh, yet becoming annoyed. I was beginning to take his words as arrogance.

"Dear, how would you explain my cool skin? Do you think you and I met for the first time last night at the club? I first kissed you yesterday afternoon," he said, still smiling and rather smug.

I instantly had to catch my breath, because I knew that I had indeed felt a presence before class yesterday. "So are you stalking me then? I still don't believe you," I was still in denial. "So you are telling me that you were that wet mist?"

"Solis, you are in a library. Go and look up the undead, the night walkers, children of the night, or whatever this century has termed my kind—but go with caution; you might see a picture of me next to one of the terms. And yes, I am the mist that you have been experiencing," he said as he licked his tongue across those lethal-looking choppers.

So I began my quest to disprove this beautiful creature that sat before me, smug, sexy, and beguiling. I went from stack to dusty stack in the library reading all the myths and terminology for what Nacio had described himself as being, still not wanting to believe him.

There was folklore on vampires not casting shadows, being cold-blooded, not liking garlic, not having a pulse, not being able to travel in sunlight, shape-shifting at will, being killed by a wooden stake, cringing at the sight of crucifixes, and last but not least, killing for blood. If I did believe him that meant that I am attracted to a two-hundred-and-fifty-seven-year-old corpse. Now, that sounded awful and quite disgusting, yet here I sat. My attempt at trying to disprove what he was saying went on for the next few hours.

The library was closing, and the librarian had begun to shut the lights off, clearly an indication that it was time to make a move. As I gathered my things, he immediately took my books and put them in my backpack.

"I don't want you holding anything in your hands. I like watching you walk and don't want anything hindering your range of motion," he said as his eyes scanned me and eagerly looked for any response that his flattery might have yielded.

I was eating this up. This attention felt so good. I had never had any guy study me the way that his eyes scanned me. It was as if he could not get enough of me. We reached my car and put my backpack away, but I did not want the day to end. Not yet. It was only 5 o'clock, and I was not ready to be without him again.

"Let's walk," I said. As I took a few steps ahead of him, I turned and looked behind me. Nacio was standing motionless looking at my hips. He stood there looking at me and smiling.

"If I didn't know better, I would think that you were looking at me like a meal," I said teasingly.

"Solis, I am only admiring you and trying desperately to understand the hold you have on me, believe it or not," he said, matching his pace to mine. "Only Father Time would truly be able to answer that. I have been looking for you through lifetimes."

"How did you come to be?" I said, now slowly accepting what he had been trying to get me to comprehend throughout the day.

"Well, I guess I should start from the very beginning," he said as he looked down at the ground and walked at an enjoyable pace. We were headed to an entryway to the River Walk and soon were passing underneath Market Street. The river curved along a none-too-crowded pathway. The San Antonio River walk is one of the city's most attractive attributes with its seductive allure for lovers and thrill seekers alike.

"My name is Nacio Galvazio De Puente. I am apart of race of people that was once known as North African Berber inhabitants, the Canary Islanders," Nacio said. "I was brought here as a slave in the mid 1730s. We were a mixed breed of people consisting of Black-African and Spanish heritage. We owned land and cattle on the northern tip of Africa. I was very happy in my youth, back then. The world seemed so new," he said, and there went that smile once again. Gosh, he was so gorgeous!

"Go on," I said, becoming more and more entranced as I entertained the thoughts of the northern coastal tip of Africa, the seashore, birds flying over, and the inhabitants of his little village.

"All was going well in my village until several of us were captured just inland on shore. Several members of my family were sold into captivity and brought here to San Antonio," Nacio said, and his eyes became fixated and changed from a light blue-gray to tornado black as he revisited the pain of his existence.

"Once we arrived here, the governor purchased my family and me. We were forced to build this city. Well, actually, it was a township back then," he said as he stopped in front of a brick in the wall not too far from the beautiful river theatre.

"I put this very cobblestone in this wall; and though I was tired from the labor and digging this River Walk to its current greatness, I have great pride in its magnificence," Nacio reflected as he slowly ran his hand over the jagged cobblestone. We continued to walk around another of the river's bends. "This orange cobblestone was put here by my brother," he said.

"You mean you actually dug the river's trench and built it from the ground up?" I said, totally overwhelmed and trying desperately to put in perspective all the things Nacio was saying to me, which, at that moment, were truly overwhelming.

"Yes, my love! I did these things. My family and I worked under the fierce hand of a slave owner named De La Juan Arguno Puente. Master Puente demonstrated the power of his whip like a lightning strike, slicing pain upon the surface of one's skin like razors," Nacio winced as he reflected upon the feeling of his skin peeling open and oozing a steady stream of blood mixed with sorrow.

"Do you have marks from your bondage?" I asked now looking upon his face innocent and childlike.

He turned his back to me and glanced over his left shoulder as his hair cascaded forward over his right shoulder, giving me the look of approval to proceed underneath his shirt. There, underneath the stitching of his silk shirt, lay the aged lines of what once looked like keloid markings from whippings upon his skin. The lines were mere mesh markings that lay beneath the surface of his skin and now looked like old veins.

"It is true, time heals all wounds, as the saying has been phrased," Nacio said as he looked at me lovingly. "I have seen much sorrow in my lifetime."

"Please, go on. I'm listening," I said fascinated at the composure he demonstrated after telling me of his pain.

"Life as a slave continued here under Master Puente. I went on to continue to dig the river from the beginning in San Pedro Spring in San Pedro Park," he said as he began to move closer to me.

"You began digging the river from San Pedro Park?" I said still aghast at all the information I was taking in.

"Yes," he said. "Now close your eyes and I will show you." Just then, I did as he said, and I found myself in his strong grip.

"Don't open them until I tell you to," he said as I heard the wind speed pick up. "Open them," Nacio said.

At that moment, when my eyes opened, we were standing next to a dome-sized oak tree that was clearly hundreds of years old.

"How did we get here?" I said shocked, listening to the leaves crunch under my shoes.

"Well, my dear, one thing I can do as a vampire is what my kind calls being able to *teleport*, moving from one point to another unheard and unseen by the human eye," he said with a nickel-slick grin.

"Alright, Nacio, this is freaky," I said feeling my chest, legs, and head making sure all was accounted for. "I asked you earlier how you came to be. You know, how you became a vampire."

"Yes, dear, I was getting to that. Life under the whip of Master Puente continued for the next few years. My family was captured, brought here, and sold into slavery, but we were followed by an enemy of ours. The evil voodoo Priestess Auldicia appeared here shortly after our capture. Legend had it that she was driven there from afar for evil deeds that she had done. Priestess Auldicia had dealings with demons that had cursed her with the evil of sexual lust and bloodlust alike. Priestess Auldicia, tracked my family and me to the home just south of downtown where Master Puente owned land. During my youth, she ambushed me one night in an attempt to seduce me. She transported me to a location that I was not familiar with. She tortured me by cutting my whip wounds with her finger nails. Although I was in pain, I would not give in to her demands," he said, clearly reliving the pain with every word he spoke.

"She began to feed on me, and did so until she satiated her appetite. In doing so, she left me near death, yet undead. Over the next several months, my transformation into the undead continued. I had no idea what was happening to me. The ache that I felt each night was indescribable. My veins would squirm and crawl under my skin at night. I felt my teeth begin to sharpen and grow until I bit my lip, and tasted blood. Little did I know soon, blood would be my only sustenance for my existence," Nacio said, exhibiting what looked like a remorseful expression.

"As my bloodlust continued, I knew I could never return to my family in my condition, and because I would not give in to her, she annihilated my entire family. I was alone and left to fend for myself. I was desperately trying to understand what was happening to me," he said.

"As the months passed, I began to notice that my hair grew longer and thicker. I began to watch as my flesh became more dense and solid. My coordination allowed me to become more agile and graceful, gazelle-like. My motion and speed were like that of a cheetah. My skin became elastic and as strong as the earth itself. My regeneration and healing ability was unlike that of any living creature, increasing my ability to be unharmed. I began to spend lots of time alone, and in doing so, I discovered the ability to teleport from one point to another simply by concentrating on my destination.

"My transformation also increased my bloodlust to the point

that I became a monster, and I hated myself for it," Nacio said as he clenched his fists. "Years passed, and I continued my transformation to what I am now. The sun was no longer painful as years passed, which enabled me to go out in the daylight, giving me the ability to adapt to each century as needed. During my travels, I discovered others that were like me. I came across a vampire named Armando Caraway. He explained our existence, and said that our death could be caused by beheading with a silver knife or by sword and fire. Without either of these, we would remain immortal throughout time," Nacio said, shifting his weight and now leaning against the tree he claimed he planted hundreds of years ago.

"As I said earlier, I took great pride in watching the township grow and would continue to complete work late at night on the river to help relieve some of the sorrow of slavery and to enable the other slaves to rest and recuperate from a cruel day's labor. I found myself feeding on criminals that stalked and raped women during the night. San Antonio, eventually, became the home of several young female prostitutes that were orphans due to slavery and the plague that had left them parentless," he explained.

"Those females were often on the streets at night, making themselves easy prey to savage men. I would often follow them during their trysts to make certain that they survived the interludes. Some of the men that were with the females were soldiers. By this time, General Santa Ana had descended upon the township to siege the Alamo. The State of Texas was trying to win independence from Mexico. General Santa Ana could not figure out why so many of his men would come up missing just before the dawn's early light, and often figured them for deserters. To make certain that Santa Ana's numbers continued to decline and there was no trace of the remains of the soldiers, I would entomb their bodies in graves located far outside of the township," Nacio continued as I listened with awe.

"Eventually, slavery was abolished, and I continued to live in the southern part of downtown—what you know as the King William area. I kept my master's name, and my love for masonry and architecture soon led me to invest in projects that led to the Puente Masonry and Architecture Empire. That is my day job, my dear, and what keeps me busy while you are busy learning about blood alleles," he said as it just dawned on me what he had said.

"You own the Puente Masonry Company?" I said, thinking that my jaw could drop no further from so much information but was now dangling dangerously close to my lap. Puente Masonry is one of the elite and flourishing construction and architectural firms in the San Antonio metropolitan area. The city is firm on maintaining its historical flare, but any new skyscrapers that enhanced the city's horizon were birthed from the Puente Masonry Company.

"Indeed, I do," he said. Why won't he stop smiling? I keep asking myself.

"Do you still feed on criminals now?" I asked, changing the subject and trying to control my desire to reach out and touch him.

"Only if I feel that something is about to happen and I catch them in the act. I don't kill them if that's what you are concerned about. There is a blood bank, a few blocks up from here. I am able to teleport in at night and get my supply of plasma," he said. "Yes, it's alright if you want to touch me. I want you to," he said, and there he goes again, fixating his eyes on me as though I am all that matters in this world. Instantly, I blush and look away. He immediately reaches for my face and lures my eyes to his.

"I can hear you and feel you," he said as my heart felt like the size of a pumpkin and was beating like a base drum.

"You mean you can read my mind and know all the self-talk I do?" I said, feeling real stupid at what was beginning to happen inside of me. I was definitely on the edge of something that was truly dangerous.

"You were born to Lisa Sharon Henderson and Raymond David Burkes on August fourth. Your mother has been deceased since you were eight years old, and your father has been in prison since before then. You have been living with your maternal grandparents since that tragic episode in your life. This morning, you were desperately trying to get your grandmother Olvignia to have some mercy on your friend Affinity to no avail. You have been angry with me since last night, and you actually wanted to wound me for leaving you. You also wanted to kiss me and do other things that couples do, but you have been shy about that. Does that pretty much sum you up?" Nacio said, looking as smug as a Cheshire cat.

"Are you joking with me?" I said, wanting a bus to come and accidently run over me for being so embarrassed right now. If my face could have exploded, now couldn't have been a moment too soon.

"My Grandma Olvignia," I began to say when Nacio abruptly cut me off.

"...is extremely gifted with foresight and has been expecting me," he said as I stood there with my mouth totally agape, and unable to move. "Your grandma's ancestors were apart of a family that were friends to my family. Your grandma has told you that she was a slave descendant as well, correct?" he said.

"Yes, and she has gone into great detail about the slave ships, and her family's existence," I replied.

"You ask how I know so much about you," he began. "Well, shortly after I was bitten by Priestess Auldicia, I overheard her talking to her evil minions. It appeared she had a long bloodline of evil ancestors, who were as treacherous as she was."

"Many of her family members had been cursed with the lust for blood and sexual intimacies," he said. "Priestess Auldicia was beautiful, but deadly. Any man that had any type of attraction to her in the beginning was seduced and sacrificed to Satan in an attempt to keep her power on earth. The price she paid for her contractual agreement with Satan was her curse of being a vampire," Nacio said as his eyes once again displayed the tornado black hue that was instantly terrifying.

"Priestess Auldicia?" I said. "I know that name. You are right, that name is pure evil. It is the name of evil that my grandmother has described as the evil that has to be contained and kept away from loved ones. Grandma described this Priestess Auldicia as a woman who disturbingly thought ***all*** men desired her, but this was not true. So in her mind, she approached all men that became the object of her desire, and then ended their lives when they would not give in to her."

"Those unfortunate souls that did fall prey to her desire in hopes of saving themselves, or the woman they were betrothed to, still found a tragic end to their lives and the lives of their loved ones," Nacio explained with pain in his eyes.

"Did Priestess Auldicia kill someone you loved?" I asked slowly and cautiously, because the pain I saw in Nacio's eyes brought an awful pain that settled in my stomach.

"No, not exactly," he said. "After Priestess Auldicia transformed me into a vampire, she went into hiding. Legend had it that she angered Satan himself, lost her reign on earth, and was condemned to hell, fulfilling her contract to Satan. Her ancestors continued to roam the earth, spreading evil throughout the corners of the globe," he said.

"After completing a foundation job one night at a new home subdivision site, I heard the screams of a young child coming from an empty model home," he said, speaking slowly and intensely. "I followed the sounds of pain and pleading to what stood before me: three young boys and a young girl that were standing over a naked younger girl. I transformed into a heavy mist driven by a strong wind to scare the children away. I walked over to the young child that lay on the ground, humiliated and frightened. That child was you, Solis," he said as he reached his cool hand over to put my hand with his. "It was at the moment that I saw one of the children that I knew they were descendants of Priestess Auldicia. The children evidently had the curse of their ancestor upon them. I am not sure that they are aware of their family history. It could mean destruction for them should they ever take on the power their evil ancestor had. Those children appeared to have the curse already manifesting within their souls by the cruel act I caught them in," Nacio explained.

"I watched the children fearfully retreat, and then you were able to collect yourself and walk home," he said. "I wished I could have done more for you at the time, but I did not want to further frighten you," he said. "I vowed from that day forward to watch over you and protect you. Over the past few months, you have been lying in bed robbed of precious sleep because of this negative experience. Some of the thoughts that manifest in and out of your dreams have been centered on that horrible night. This is what made me finally come forward to give you the answers to the questions you seem to seek the answers for. Also, I could no longer control my desire to stay away from you. I honestly had to wait for you to grow into adulthood, and I have prayed that you would find yourself as deeply in love with me as I am with you," Nacio said, appearing statuesque and seductive.

Having said that, Nacio leaned over, took me into his arms, and kissed me with his cool lips; but all it did was make me realize how hot my lips were and how I wanted him to continue to kiss me until I could barely breathe. And he did.

"Nacio, you said that you were there the day I was raped. I can't seem to remember the names of those kids that did that to me," I said, still feeling intoxicated from the passion of his kiss.

"As I said, she had descendants that are alive in this century throughout the globe. Those perpetrators that did that to you are from her bloodline," he said as he continued to hold me close. The worst of the four children is the ringleader, Childress Treemount. It is highly likely that her brother, Klein, was solely acting upon directives given to him by his sister, Childress.

"Treemount of course!" I said. "That was their horrible last name. They made my life a living hell, each day being worse than the last. Now it is all coming back to me!" I said, clearly angry and ready to strike.

"For so long, Nacio, I have lived in terror and self-hatred for what they did to me on that day. At one point in time, I did not even feel worthy enough to live, all because they made me feel like filth," I said, fighting back the sharp sting of tears in my eyes.

"Do you know where she and her awful family are today?" I asked, clearly in "fight mode" now. "That episode in my life was so traumatizing, I actually had blocked out pieces of the event. I had totally forgotten their names. Maybe that was a good thing because I probably would have tried to hunt them down," I said, now shaking and starting to pace.

"No, sweetheart, you would not have!" Nacio interjected. "Childress and her brothers, Klein, Justice, and Erland are truly no good. The evil that flows through their veins is bewitched with voodoo magic that makes them a deadly enemy to all who cross them. Childress has disappeared, but her brothers are still at large. There has been lots of criminal activity in the city lately. Several murders have occurred over the past few years. The style of killings reminded me of how their ancestor, the Priestess Auldicia, would kill willfully and without remorse," he said, with his gray eyes dangerously near tornado black.

"I have not sensed them near in several years, but I would imagine that they are well versed in ancient voodoo magic now that they are adults. They could be 'under the radar,' which encourages me to be cautious," he said, moving close enough to my face to share my air.

"Oh gosh, look at the time! I have to go," I said, hating to end the night. "When will I see you again?" Just then, Nacio grabbed me up in his arms, and the wind picked up speed again, transporting us back to the library parking lot next to my car. I got in, and Nacio stood outside of the driver's side.

"Actually, I am right outside your window each night. I have been for awhile, but I won't come in, because, well, you know your Grandma Olvignia would know instantly," he said, snickering a bit as he continued to hold me close.

"Well, let's plan to see each other every day at two o'clock. This way, I will be done with class, and we can meet at a different place each day?" I said, looking doe-eyed with excitement.

"Yes, I think that could be arranged, and I have the perfect place for our next interlude," he said. "I will meet you at your car tomorrow, and we will go to the Japanese Tea Garden. Sound okay?" he said as he kissed me. I agreed and drove home…again, a wet mess.

Childress Treemount

4

"Hello, I am Dr. Kross Malveaux, and you are…let's see here," Dr. Malveaux said, looking at the file in his hands. "You are Childress Treemount, state inmate number 1097816. You've served a ten-year sentence for capital murder, and you've completed that sentence. Now you are currently completing a three-year sentence for aggravated sexual assault of a female. Is this true?" Dr. Malveaux hummed.

"You are the one with that paper there, cher; what are you asking me for?" Childress spewed back, with her jade-green eyes narrowing at the corners. "Why don't you come a little closer here, cher, and let me rub on you some. I can make a man like you feel real good, don't you know?"

Childress was very beguiling. She had supple ivory skin that contrasted with her green eyes. Her lips were full and a playful pink color. Her teeth were straight and pearly white. She had a splash of freckles that gave away her mixed heritage. She had short-sheared, curly blondish-red locks of hair that were at least an inch long and able to be coiled around her unusually long fingernails. Each of her nails was at least three inches in length and was as straight as a sharp knife. She was of medium build, full breasted, and stood 5 feet7 inches tall with full hips and thighs. Her calves were bowed at the knees, which made her appear to walk with her butt stuck out, with motion in her hips. Her physical appearance was the preference of, and lure for, many darker-skinned African American men, which often sealed their tragic fate.

"That's a real mean New Orleanian accent you got there. Where are you from Ms. Treemount?" Dr. Malveaux replied, curious and treading dangerous waters.

"Jefferson Parrish, cher. Why are you going to take me back there?" Childress said, draping one leg over the couch and slowly delaying the other leg in an exaggerated motion that seemed to go on forever in Mr. Malveaux's mind.

"Why don't you tell me how you got back in this mess of being locked up again?" Dr. Malveaux said, peering over his glasses. "I have to give an assessment on you to see if you are capable of not coming back in here again, and if you can be a suitable citizen. Can you do that, Childress?" Dr. Malveaux asked, continuing to look at her.

"You want to know if I can keep from going back to jail," Childress said. "Well, are you going to come see me when I'm out?" Childress said, eyes fixated and unblinking on Dr. Malveaux's crotch.

It was as if Childress's gaze sent forth a heat straight to the seat of Dr. Malveaux's pants, because his response was to cross and then re-cross his legs to hide the obvious erection that was starting to come forth as Childress had willed. "Uh, Ms. Treemount, please take your eyes off me. I'm a married man and want to continue to be so when I get home," the good doctor said.

"Well, cher, what do you want to know?" Childress said, slithering back in her chair, lips turned up in an "all too satisfied with herself" smile at Dr. Malveaux's lengthening erection.

"Start out at your childhood, Ms. Treemount," Dr. Malveaux said, with his laptop now covering a clearly defined bulge underneath his flat-front khaki pants. "And try to be honest."

"Alright, let me be honest about the nice package you have under those pants, cher. I would like to visit with it someday soon, don't you know?" Childress explained with words like wine to Dr. Malveaux's ears but poison without the antidote. "Let's see, yes, I went to one of the Louisiana State penitentiaries for ten years for murder. But that was long before Hurricane Katrina blew through and took with her all the life force my family had," she said as her eyes glazed over, reminiscing on life back in the wards.

"I was born in New Orleans. My mother's name was Frances Treemount. She was Creole, and she had four of us. We each had a different Creole daddy. I have three brothers, Klein, Justice, and Erland. My daddy went to the Pen for killing Klein's daddy and Justice's daddy. Erland's daddy left the state before my daddy could get to him next. My daddy killed both of them in one night. He told my mama if she had another child by another man, he was gonna kill her, cut her up, and bury each one of her limbs in a different state," Childress explained, sitting motionless.

"After my daddy cursed my mama with a spell of fear and misery, we moved to San Antonio, Texas, for a while. I hated that damned place. The people used to piss me off just because they were always so nice, everywhere you turned. The men, well now, the men were a different story. My mama was a beautiful woman and never had any problem getting a hold of another man. She found some awful ones, let me tell you," Childress said, shaking her head in denial.

"She found one man named Lewis Ordinand. He was a sorry drunkard. He came in one night and forced himself on my mama. He left her bleeding and crying on the floor, and he went and got some more to drink. As my mother lay on the floor, she got up and crawled to the bed. She found strength enough to make it to the bathroom. She cleaned herself up. I stood in the doorway of the bathroom and watched her as she took some of the pubic hair from the washcloth she had used to clean Lewis off of her. My mama kept wax voodoo dolls handy at all times. She practiced spells all the time and knew how to deal with people that crossed her path too sharply," Childress said, staring straight ahead.

"Mama worked all night carving that wax voodoo doll. She was skilled at making the wax figure in the exact image of the person she cursed. By the time she was finished, Lewis was just waking up from sleeping off his liquor. Mama took the pubic hair, some chicken bones, a chicken neck, and some chicken blood, and poured it all in a bowl. The wax doll was put in the middle of the bowl. Mama picked up a long sewing needle and stabbed the doll in its crotch," Childress said, making a stabbing motion with her right fist.

"Dark-red blood ran out of the hole that was now in the doll. By this time, Lewis had stumbled out of the bedroom and into the bathroom. Blood was oozing from the front of his pants. His knees buckled and he fell on top of his bottle of bourbon, shattering the bottle inward and stabbing him in the heart, killing him instantly," Childress explained with a sinister smile stretched across her face.

"Once Lewis's body shook one last time before Death put its scythe in his back, my mama turned and looked at me, and said, 'Never let a man disrespect your body, cher…ever!' and with that, I began to slowly hate any man that looked like Lewis," Childress said with her eyes narrowed back and angled into slits.

"Is that why you killed that poor man all those years ago?" Dr. Malveaux hummed, "because he looked like your mother's boyfriend Lewis? "What is it that makes you think that you can take someone else's life and not have consequences for it, Ms. Treemount?"

"Nah, I killed him because I gave him my number, and he shoved it in his pocket and walked away, then dropped it out of his pocket while he was reaching to answer his cell phone to talk to another female. Mama said never let a man disrespect my body, I felt he had disrespected me, and I could not have that, cher," Childress slithered restlessly in her chair.

"You see, Dr. Malveaux, you must understand that what scares the average female doesn't scare me. I've had to eat baked rat for breakfast, fried frog legs for lunch, and fried alligator for dinner. I grew up in an environment where the elements were my natural habitat. So putting an end to someone's life is ...natural," Childress said, licking her lips as if she'd just finished a meal.

"Uh huh," Dr. Malveaux said. "What about this woman you sexually assaulted? What led you to attack her in the manner you did, Ms. Treemount?"

"Well, cher, she thought she was cute. She was looking in the mirror and bumped into me, and she didn't say excuse me. By the time I got through whipping her, they called it a sexual assault because I ripped all that girl's clothes off. I wanted to embarrass and humiliate her the same way she embarrassed me!" Childress said, with a frightening glare in her eyes.

"Do you have any remorse at all for the transgressions you have committed towards others, Ms. Treemount?" Dr. Malveaux inquired, again treading dangerously with a now defensive Childress.

"Why sure, Reverend!" Childress said, being facetious. "Guess we all got to ask for forgiveness for our sins and all, cher."

"Why don't I believe you?" Dr. Malveaux said. And what did he say that for?

"Look here, man, don't test me!" Childress exploded and lunged for Dr. Malveaux's face. "I'll turn that little package you're hiding in them khaki pants into an inside belly button that you will never see again—you hear?"

Just then, Childress reached and wiped off Dr. Malveaux's shoulder and collected some loose strands of hair that lay so innocently on his shoulder. "Now, see there, ya'll done made me get angry and things. Let's me and you play nice," Childress crooned with her lips curled up at the corners in a guilty smirk.

"Uh, Ms. Treemount, please assume your seat," Dr. Malveaux said, a bit shaken at the explosive behavior that Childress displayed. "Please resume your story."

"Alright, Dr...Malveaux," Childress said gnawing on his name like a neck bone. "After Lewis came up dead under the suspicious circumstances like he did, Mama packed us all back up, and we went back to New Orleans. My brothers were no different from me. They all spent time in and out of jail, cher. Erland and Klein held up the First National Bank of New Orleans and led the Louisiana State Police on a high-speed chase that made CNN news, heeheeeheeeheee," Childress chuckled as she recalled seeing the news bulletins interrupt regularly scheduled programming on the television that night.

"They tore up many cars and trucks in that high-speed chase that crossed two county lines! Those boys are tough! Mama sure raised them to get what they want!" Childress bellowed.

"So after your brothers served time for that armed bank robbery and high-speed chase is when ya'll came back to San Antonio?" Dr. Malveaux inquired.

"Nah, man, we moved back after that bitch Hurricane Katrina blew our home down and washed some of us out to sea!" Childress shouted and jumped to her feet. "Mama did a step dance and spell to try to ward off that storm, but Katrina came anyway."

"That storm blew in before daylight one night in August 2005," Childress explained. "We had already been sent to the dome football stadium and were all trapped inside. The wind whipped over the dome, the electricity went out, the sewage backed up, and the toilets overflowed. We were living in there like dogs! People started turning their anger on one another in there. Nighttime in the dome was awful. There was moaning and screaming to the point that let whoever was listening know that it was possibly their last night living. There were fights, rapes, and some killings that went on in there. The days after the storm blew in were the worst," Childress responded in a low whisper.

"After nearly dying of thirst from not having any running water and food, Mama went into a diabetic coma. She was airlifted to the nearest major city, Houston, Texas. Klein, Justice, Erland, and I later followed a day later in a bus. We had no contact with Mama until we looked her up on a hospital list at the Astrodome in Houston. She was at Hermann Hospital. She was then transported to the Wilford Hall in San Antonio, Texas. That is where our new life began at a makeshift shelter at Kelly USA," Childress continued to whisper.

"Again, dogs lived better than we did. Many of us continued to chant, and do some praying as the news of New Orleans being totally underwater made us curse the name of Mother Nature. We slept on cots next to other criminals and motherless children. Families were torn apart, women had their periods with no sanitary protection, some had babies in the shelter with no birth records to follow up; and when we finally got to bathe, we were herded like cattle into communal showers with little dignity to be found," Childress said as she began to weep.

"Mama worsened as the days turned into months. We were trying to get a hold of some money and a place to live in San Antonio, but FEMA kept giving us the runaround," Childress said as she started to pick at the trash that had accumulated under talon-like fingernails.

"After living in that airplane hangar that FEMA called a shelter at Kelly USA, I needed a place for us to stay. I found a cohort in crime that helped me come up on some money to get a place to live. Her name was Believa Beaushanks," Childress stated, grinning from ear to ear as she continued to narrate.

"Believa and I had us a good scam going. We started off snatching expensive leather purses out of these mall stores. Once we hit one or two malls, we would rent a car and go up and down the highway between San Antonio and Austin stealing purses, and then reselling them. We also wrote hot checks to cover some of the travel expenses. Once I got enough cash, I was able to put down on a little house for Mama. We stole at least once a week at different malls, and then ventured further north. We had all kinds of purses, and things were going real good. Believa and I were real tight with each other, real tight, until I caught her talking sweet to some dude named Katalo on the phone. He was the guy she called herself dating. She was telling him how she was going to bring him some money," Childress said as she drew in a long breath and let out each of her words like Morse code with a slow tap.

"I told Believa if she didn't get off that phone with that guy, I was going to knock her in her face so hard with my fist that she was going to think it was Thursday for the next two weeks!" Childress shouted, shaking her right fist with fury. "She dropped the call quick! Little did either of us know that Katalo was having us set up to get busted. We had just finished our last hit when we went to the bus station where he worked so she could tell him that she was breaking up with him, and that's when the San Antonio Police Department, SWAT, State Police, and U.S. Marshals showed up and busted both of us!" Childress had her eyes closed as she remembered all the events up until now.

"Katalo had cut a deal with the Feds, and we were going down for everything, the purse scam and the hot checks. I'll see him again real soon, cher," Childress expressed as her voice dropped frighteningly to a murmur.

"Do you feel you have been rehabilitated, Ms. Treemount?" Dr. Malveaux said as he sat motionless across from Childress.

Sitting with her back pressed to the couch and straight as a board, Childress peeled open her eyes and hissed, "Hell, no, I'm not rehabilitated, but you're going to say I have been rehabilitated."

Childress leaned forward in her seat and looked deep into Dr.

Malveaux's eyes and spoke, "Childress...is rehabilitated...Childress is rehabilitated...Childress ...is rehabilitated and is no longer a threat to anyone..." Childress continued to chant these words as she twirled the stray hairs in her hands that belonged to Dr. Malveaux. "...No longer a threat to anyone..."

Dr. Malveaux looked as if he were being strangled as Childress chanted on until Dr. Malveaux's eyes rolled into the back of his head. At that point, she shook him out of what looked to be a seizure.

"Dr. Malveaux? Dr. Malveaux? ...Dr. Malveaux?" Childress pretended to be shocked but was not surprised as her hex worked its evil magic.

"What was I saying?" Dr. Malveaux responded, looking disheveled.

"Uh, you were saying sir, that you are forwarding my recommendation for parole—did you forget that part?" Childress smiled innocently, with fluttering eyelashes.

"Rightly so, child, rightly so—and right away, I might add!" Dr. Malveaux interjected.

"Time's up!" a timid-looking jail guard called. "Let's go, Treemount!"

"Adieu to you, Dr. Malveaux," Childress said as she slithered her way out of Dr. Malveaux's office and out of the Huntsville State Penitentiary. The next day, Childress Treemount stepped outside of the prison gates. Klein was there waiting to retrieve his sibling and her few personal effects.

"Take me home, boy! I got business to attend to...starting with Katalo Nickelson and Believa Beaushanks," Childress said. They drove west to San Antonio to even the score with her targets.

5

It was 9:30 p.m. My head was swimming from all of the questions I had for Nacio and from drowning in the passion of his kiss. I ran my hand across my face and could smell traces of his scent all over me. His scent was a mixture of baby powder, and the ocean breeze. To be honest, I didn't know what a two-hundred-and-fifty-seven-year-old vampire was supposed to smell like.

This was all new to me, but I couldn't help but think that I could learn so much from him. I realized that he had seen so much in his lifetime and had more to offer than any dusty old books on a library shelf. I had let my mind wander and soon found myself sitting in the driveway at home. Chase's car was gone, so I knew I would have a few hours of peace before I had to get up for class. Grandma Olvignia was already standing in the window, with the blinds bent back. I also noticed the lower part of the blinds bent back as well, because when she looked out the window, so did our miniature German Schnauzer, Fritz. As soon as my feet hit the floor inside, the gauntlet of questions began.

"So what did he have to say?" Grandma Olvignia said, as she stood with her legs hyper-extended, and locked. Her hands were on her hips. She was in battle mode.

"Well, he told me about *me*, our family, and how he came to be," I said, chewing my lip and knowing that I couldn't hold back telling her anything. "I really enjoyed being with him, Grandma."

"What's his name?" Grandma said, standing with her shoulders a little more relaxed, but with legs still locked.

"He explained to me that his name is Nacio Galvazio De Puente. He explained that he was a slave and that he knows you too, Grandma. He explained that he came from the Canary Islands. He said that his family had been sold into slavery here in San Antonio and that all of his family was killed by...killed by..."

"Priestess Auldicia," Grandma hissed, back in battle mode again.

"Yes," I said. "He said that she had descendants, and that they are still roaming the earth. When he told me that, he explained that the children that raped me when I was little are some of her descendants," I said with little more than a whisper.

"They were a part of her bloodline?" Grandma questioned. "Did he say if he has any idea where they are?"

"No. He explained that he hasn't been able to determine where they are but said that it didn't mean that they might not be hiding in plain sight."

"I have to think about this, child. Go on to sleep, and I will talk with you tomorrow after you come back from seeing him," Grandma explained and then went off to her room.

There was no sense in me asking how she knew I would be seeing him tomorrow. She was Grandma, and anyone that stood before her was like an open book with size 16 Font to be read. I went off to bed just in time, because I heard Chase's key rattle the front door. I quickly jumped into bed and pretended to be asleep as his foots steps padded down the hallway. I could tell his footsteps stopped in front of my door to press his face to the door to radar whether I was awake and stirring in my room. No sound, he continued to his room and shut the door. I soon found myself drifting into a happy and peaceful slumber.

I had dreams of Nacio and me walking and talking during the afternoon before. He would smile, and I would instantly respond to his chivalrous gestures. He made me feel as if I was worthy of such treatment. This was something so new to me. He made me want to do my very best at anything. The whole vampire thing did take me for a loop, but I feel that I can deal with it. I find myself attracted to not just his physical body but the fact that he is literally older and wiser. I realized that I can learn so much from him, because he has lived those experiences so vividly, and that is not something that you can get from a book. I can't wait for the dawn of the next day to see him again as soon as possible.

The next day before class, I saw Elbithea sashaying down the hall. She was smiling at me from ear to ear as if I had some great big secret.

"Hey girl, what's up?" Elbithea said with a textbook, sneaky "Cheshire cat" grin. "Spill all the juicy details right now!"

"I literally met the man of my dreams! He is gorgeous in every way, and I can't wait to see him again today!" I said, barely able to contain myself. "He is such a gentleman: he carries my books and he kisses me so softly that I feel weightless in his arms."

"You sound so in love!" Elbithea chirped. "When are you seeing him again?"

"I'll see him as soon as class is over!" I said, grinning wildly.

"Alright then, girl, I'll see you later!" Elbithea said as she darted down the hall.

"Okay, I'll holler at you later!" I said as I turned the corner. Just when I was a short way from the door to my last class of the day, I felt that cool mist surround me once more, kiss my lips, and then blow away.

"Nacio," I said as I closed my eyes and enjoyed every minute of being in his presence again. No sooner did I speak his name than I opened my eyes, and my heart's desire was standing in front of me in all his glory.

"My love," he said. "I've missed you dearly." His smile was as brilliant as the sun.

"Hello, Nacio." That was all I could manage from my lips.

"As promised, I will be at your car when you finish," he said. By this time, others had started to notice this tall, handsome "man" standing there talking to me. I felt like the belle of the ball.

I went to class and, of course, had a difficult time concentrating. I took care to sit far away from Professor Porterfoy. I did not want to take a chance on being accidentally spit on by him, poor thing. Time flew in class, and like clockwork, as I approached my car, I could see Nacio's beautiful locks blowing softly in the wind. He was dressed casually, in black sneakers, black jeans, and a young-fitting short-sleeved shirt. His arms and chest are so toned that I would guess all of his shirts were his correct size but appeared tight and too small.

I walked towards him, and it appeared as if this were a scene right out of a dream sequence, totally in slow motion. I reached the car, went straight into his arms, and kissed him deeply.

"Are you ready to go?" he asked. "I have another special place I would like to spend the day at."

"Where are we going?" I asked, anxiously awaiting his response.

"Today, we will be going to the Japanese Tea Garden," he said. "There is a hilltop view I would like to show you."

"Let's go then!" I said. I started the car and drove there in what seemed to take only minutes. We turned down Mulberry Street and were soon entering the Brackenridge Park area. We parked the car, got out, and began a casual stroll through the gardens. It was a beautiful sight to see. The garden was full of tropical vegetation and flowers bursting with purple, orange, and yellow hues. The open garden was crowned with a 30 foot water fall. Blue water sparkled as it fell in a pond below. The flow emptied into multiple ponds that were filled with multicolored fish that called this beautiful paradise home.

"Do you like it?" Nacio asked, holding my hand and walking so close to me that anyone would have sworn we were joined at the hip.

"I love it," I said. "I've been here before and have often wished to walk through it with someone that I was in love with, and who was in love with me. Were you ever in love? I mean, have you ever married or loved someone special?" I stammered, feeling as if I were prying.

"I had someone special once," Nacio said. "Her name was Maline Engston. She was left for dead one night after she left the mayor's mansion. She had been robbed and beaten pretty badly. She was near death, and in order to save her, I changed her to a vampire."

"Was her transformation as long as yours?" I asked, eyes fixated on him and hanging on his every word.

"Yes, and just as painful," Nacio replied. "I took her back to my home, and she completed her transformation there. She had curly brown short hair that grew shoulder length and brown eyes that were soon a hazel color upon completion. She and I remained together over the next century traveling abroad and enjoying ourselves. She, too, survived the way I did, only on criminals that were offending against society. One night, we were in Salem, exploring the town. We had separated only for a brief interval to feed, and she was captured and beheaded during a horrific street massacre. The witch hunt trials were over several decades before, yet there were still people that believed that witches existed. Maline tried to overtake and feed on someone who appeared to be easy enough to approach, but the man had a silver knife. That is how Maline met her doom," he said with that familiar sorrow in his eyes.

"I grieved her loss over the next several decades, blaming myself for her death. After that, I wouldn't allow myself to love someone again. I felt that way until I found you. I vowed to watch over you at all costs and not let any more harm befall you," he said with what I could only recognize as desire and adoration in his eyes.

"You have been watching over me this long; so what exactly are you saying, Nacio?" I said, looking for clarity.

"I have been in love with you for quite awhile now, Solis. I hope you can allow me to be the one that you shower your love upon, and I promise you, I will not let you down," Nacio said with adoration in his eyes that could have melted the hearts of a thousand women.

"But why are you in love with me, Nacio?" I said. "You are so gorgeous. How can someone like me bring you the kind of joy and happiness that you have at your disposal when you want it?" I said, still not believing I am worthy enough to be loved and cherished.

"You are so wrong, my dear," Nacio said, standing to correct me about my self-worth. "You come from a bloodline of strong and determined women who have endured a lifetime of sorrow and despair, yet you all have risen above the things that would have normally destroyed some that were weak. Not you, Solis. You are a strong-willed woman, and I admire that. When ***you*** love someone, you love them totally and completely, body and soul, and that's what attracted me to you, and I completely surrender all that I am to you."

After Nacio spoke those words to me, I knew that I would never love another man the way I had just fallen in love with him that very moment. All that I had hoped for and longed for had been laid before me in an instant. It was as if time had stopped, and my search had ended with me finding someone who loved me more than I cared to love myself.

"I promise you I will love no other as long as I am in existence," Nacio said as he reached to pull me close and kissed me with desire that was hot enough to melt a candle down to its wick. The kiss seemed to go on forever as Nacio held me close. His embrace was so soothing, and he soon found his way underneath my shirt. I soon felt him pressed against my thigh with a growing erection that was as hard as a rock.

This exchange of passion was becoming more intense and I might say dangerous, because we were standing out in the open in the middle of the highest point of the garden. I didn't want this to end, but I soon pushed back from his grip.

"I apologize for my desire getting the better of me," Nacio said standing and smiling and looking very satisfied at the moment.

"This is getting to the point where I can't stop," I said, standing there inebriated with passion.

"I completely understand—I feel the same way," he said. "Come, I still have a place that I would like to take you. I so hope you are not afraid of high places."

"Of course I'm not!" I said. "I know how to enjoy an adventure when I get the opportunity to experience one."

"Alright," Nacio said. "Let's go!"

We soon walked back to the parked car, left Brackenridge Park and the Japanese Tea Garden. We entered the south 281 McAllister Freeway ramp and headed toward downtown. Traffic was light, and it made the travel time little to none. I soon found that we were exiting on Durango Boulevard and traveling west. We parked at the Hemisfair Plaza and the Institute of Texan Cultures. As we parked the car and got out, Nacio began telling me about the history of the Baptist Settlement, a section of the city where African Americans that lived in San Antonio had settled.

"As the city grew, there were some African Americans that settled in this small section of town. Now, the old homes have been demolished and there are condominium high-rises there and schools," he said, pointing to the area that clearly had been revitalized.

"Are you ready to go?" he asked, grinning what appeared to be now a sneaky grin.

"Sure, let me guess…we are going in the Tower of the Americas, aren't we?" I asked with a little bit of a sarcastic drawl at the end of the question.

"Yep, we sure are," he said. "Close your eyes!" he said, and away we went!

At that moment, Nacio teleported me to the top of the Tower of the Americas, which I boldly watched this time as I was rushed in a blur to approximately 750 feet above ground.

"Gracious!" I squealed as we whooshed to the top of the structure. Other buildings and monuments began to shrink from the speedy ascension to the top of the tower. The air on my bare skin was as light as feathers tickling me as it engulfed me on the way up to the top. I can now understand what it's like to fly. We landed on the platform that crowns the Tower of the Americas. The city looked like a kingdom below us. I was absolutely terrified but reveled in the safety Nacio's strong arms provided.

"I thought you weren't scared…," he smirked as he moved a few feet towards the edge of the revolving platform. I was frozen in place and felt if I moved I would break into a million little pieces.

"Well, I guess I am a little tiny bit afraid," I admitted. "I had no idea we would be standing on top of a city monument, especially one this high, so I think I am entitled to be a little vulnerable right now."

"It's alright, I won't let you go," Nacio smiled. "Do you like the view?"

"It is beautiful!" I said. "There is not a cloud in the sky."

We continued to look out over the city and admire its beauty. San Antonio is truly a beautiful place. Nacio pointed out that the Tower of the Americas was constructed in the 1960s and how, at that time, the city officials were so happy to see the structure erected here in Hemisfair Plaza. He explained that there were many people that lived in the old neighborhood just a mile from the monument, and that they were happy to have something near them that made them feel proud.

"Will you take me through the old neighborhood?" I asked him, wanting to feel solid ground under my feet once again.

"Are you looking to escape this height?" he asked, smirking as he neared me and nestled me under his arm. Before I could answer him, we were once again teleporting back to the base of the tower.

"Wow, I do admit I am glad to be back in control with the ground below my feet," I said as I steadied myself. "To be honest, I would like to take a tour of the little neighborhood not too far from the tower if you don't mind," I declared. "I would like to walk there if it's okay?"

"Wherever you want to go, my dear," he said. And with that, we took off on foot. One thing about Nacio: as long as he was willing to teleport us wherever the destination was, I could sure save on gas that way. Guess that is one benefit of being undead.

As we walked through the neighborhood, I began to notice how rundown some parts of it appeared. The houses appeared to be small one-story frame houses. Some had wraparound porches that led visitors to believe that the porches were the signature beauty of the intricately designed little starter homes. Now, the neighborhood looked as if it had fallen victim to whatever terrors had inhabited the neighborhood by the downtown library.

Some of the houses were abandoned and had the strange graffiti and pentagram-looking symbols on the sides of them.

"Nacio, these graffiti are the same ones that are on the houses by the library," I said, now beginning to recall all that I had seen over the past couple of weeks.

"It could be gangs fighting for turf," he said, looking

perplexed. "I know that there has been lots of gang violence in this neighborhood."

"Look at the side of this house, Nacio. This same circular symbol spray-painted in black is on several houses by the library. This dagger with the initials 'C. T.' written in the middle," I said. At that moment, the strangest feeling of apprehension washed over me.

"I haven't seen this symbol in a long while, Solis," Nacio explained. "This symbol is the mark of Priestess Auldicia or one of her descendants. This mark was bestowed upon her by the village women that fought her centuries ago and drove her out into the world. They did that to bring piece once again to the community," Nacio said as he began to clench his fist. "I was not able to sense the whereabouts of Childress and her brothers, but I would not be surprised in the least if they were the ones responsible for these markings."

"Nacio, I don't understand," I said. "I saw some of these markings scrawled on the side of buildings that were twenty stories high. How could Childress or her brothers get that far up the side of a building to tag it? That would require supernatural strength—or strength of a vampire, perhaps?"

"I understand where your questions are coming from, Solis, but remember what I explained to you earlier. Priestess Auldicia was a voodoo priestess with powers that she passed down through generations. It is highly likely that any voodoo magic and its history could have been inherited by her descendants. This would mean that Childress, who is the strongest of the four children, could have received the knowledge of how to cast spells for evil purposes. She could work all the magic against the family's enemies, or just commit evil for pleasure," Nacio explained.

Instantly, I started to feel sick. The ill feelings were planted seeds of anger and fear. The mention of the name Childress Treemount instantly made me want to punish Childress for all the wrong she had done and any she planned to do. The fear I felt came from being afraid of my own thoughts.

Entertaining thoughts of revenge was something I had never done before. For one, I guess I could never quite piece together all of the events that had occurred in my dream about that terrible evening I was raped by Childress and her savage brothers. Some nights after I awake from the dream, it is as if I can almost taste the dirt that flew into my mouth from being shoved on the ground by Klein. I remember how dirty and worthless I felt and how I wished that all the pain would stop. Now that I know who was responsible for me hating myself so much for all these years, all I could think about was punishment. Revenge tasted like an appetizer. My appetite for it was ravenous.

"Nacio, if Childress is anywhere near here, I want to confront her and make her pay for what she and her idiot siblings did to me!" I said, trembling now at how fierce my anger had become.

"What are you talking about? You are not going to confront Childress!" Nacio exclaimed. "You are out of your mind if you think that you would have any impact on making the Treemount clan have any remorse for the crime they committed against you! You would need to know about black magic and its consequences if used for wrongdoing and, especially, revenge!"

I guess this would be considered our first fight, because I immediately became more defensive and would not back down. "I can become like you! A vampire! So that I can protect myself and fight supernatural force against supernatural force," I said, determined to justify my point of view.

"Solis, I would love to taste your blood. It is all I can think of sometimes, but I will not turn you into a vampire for revenge—you must understand that. It would perpetuate and extend the curse that was already placed upon Priestess Auldicia. Evil begets evil, my love," Nacio said, determined to end the conversation.

"You said you would protect me, and this is one way that you can make sure that I am protected!" I said, raising my voice and trying to keep it from cracking.

"No, this is not an option," he said, shoulders becoming more rigid and tense. "Let's back up a minute. First, we need to locate where the family is exactly. We don't even know when these markings were put here. They could have been made years ago."

"You just said that there's been gang violence in the neighborhood; so that would lead me to think that they must be recent," I said.

"Let's go back and get your car," he said. "We can go to my house and do some research and try to track this family down."

"Oh, I think I might like that idea," I said, anticipating being alone with Nacio, away from prying eyes. Nacio teleported both him and me back to the parking lot, and we headed to the old King William area.

There in the middle of Cedar Street was a narrow alleyway that could have been easily mistaken as a narrow driveway. The alleyway was covered with overgrown vines that obstructed its existence, keeping it a secret from tourists and any other curious onlookers. Nacio instructed me to turn left into the alleyway, and drive. There was no way that this hidden road could exist in the middle of downtown San Antonio without the help of some extreme magic. The expression on my face must have yielded curiosity, because Nacio immediately responded.

"I have lived here for many decades under a protective glamour spell. It keeps my identity and well-being intact," Nacio explained. "I don't get many visitors."

"I am amazed," I said, still stunned. "You practice magic as well?"

"I do know something of the art. It serves for identity preservation purposes only," Nacio stated.

At the end of what seemed to be a two-mile ride down the alleyway stood a magnificent contemporary-style mansion. The mansion was faced with picture-style windows that were framed with green shutters and outside window plants. Nacio's home had a huge waterfall fountain that would welcome any potential visitors if he had any. Trees lined either side of the road leading up to the fountain in front of his home. The sight was unbelievably beautiful!

"Your home is breathtaking!" I said, trying to process the sight before my eyes. As we walked along the red-brick walkway up to the wraparound porch, the threshold of the shiny golden front door stood fifteen feet overhead, making the mansion look more like a castle. The precision of the brick that fortified Nacio's home truly gave the impression that the architect had been caring and skillful in his creation. A home fit for a king.

"I take it you approve of my home?" Nacio asked, assessing my reaction and loss for words.

"Yes, yes, of course!" I said. "I did not know what to expect."

"Let's go inside. I have something I want to share with you," he said. "After you," Nacio's ushering hand extended, motioning me to enter the exquisite home.

I placed my hand on the golden handle of the door and swung it open to paradise. The walls of Nacio's home were a creamy beige earth-tone color. Each wall was accented with white wainscoting mid wall and crown molding at the top of the wall just below the ceiling. The entire first floor was tiled with abstract beige tile that delicately brought out the color of the walls and instantly subdued and relaxed the mood of any potential visitor. Oh yes, his lair was a pleasant emotional confinement. I already wanted to detach from my usual surroundings and stay here forever.

Above me was the most beautiful image of Jesus shrouded in luminescent white robes. He was sitting in the middle of three wide-eyed children, staring back at him. Jesus was teaching a Sunday school lesson in the ceiling portrait. The artwork was so vivid with detail and color that, it looked as through you could sit right next to our savior and feel his mercy. Nacio allowed me a private moment with my emotions as I wiped away two tears that escaped my eyes.

"Did you paint this portrait?" I inquired as I stood motionless beneath the magnificent ceiling.

"No, honey, I did not."

"Were you religious at one point in your life? I didn't know that vampires accepted Jesus Christ," I replied. "I guess there is a lot that I'll have to put aside as myth and what applies to you."

"This is true," Nacio explained, holding his eyes on me. "I am still a Christian, Solis. Becoming what I am now has saddened me, because I do still love our savior very much. This painting was a gift and a reminder of how merciful our Lord is," he said. "There is someone I would like you to meet."

As I turned on my heels, I felt another presence, and before me was a fair-skinned man who stood an estimated four inches shorter than Nacio. He had striking gray-green eyes that were complemented by a green pullover. A full mane of short and curly sandy-blond hair crowned his head. His attire was completed by black jeans and soft black Italian loafers.

"Solis please meet my assistant and caretaker, Bose Puente," Nacio said, using his hand for introductions.

"Encantada," Bose spoke a sincere "*Pleased to meet you*" in the same familiar accent, as he gently kissed my hand.

"Mucho gusto," I replied in my most sincere voice. "My Spanish is a little rusty."

"Forgive me," Bose corrected himself. "Nacio and I often converse in Spanish and other languages."

"You have an interesting name, Bose," I complimented and inquired at the same time.

"I too am of mixed heritage. I'm Creole and Isleno, and my

family is made up of many skin complexions, nationalities, and languages. Bose paused and then said, "Our families originated from the Canary Island of La Palma. Branches of my family came from New Orleans when it was a young parish," he said, careful not to hint at his chronological age. "Would you like a tour of the rest of the home?"

"Why yes, I would," I said. It was as if the house were calling me to visit with it. The home had seven spacious suites. There were three suites on the first floor and four upstairs. Each suite was furnished with a California King bed in the middle of a huge wall that divided the sleeping area from the sitting area in each suite. Every suite had a different theme to it, ranging from a tropical paradise to a royal Egyptian court complete with a portrait of Queen Nefertiti. As a guest entered the room, Queen Nefertiti's eyes would assume command over their presence. It was if her eyes would tell all of the Egyptian history and secrets from centuries past.

Nacio's suite was at the end of the east hall. His suite was actually a loft, with entry from the first and second floors of the home. The first floor of his suite was a technological geek's play haven. There were flat screens on just about every square foot of one wall, a full executive's desk at another wall, and a full kitchen and bar fully stocked. The large windows provided most of the room's illumination, and the rest was completed by soft wattage.

The second floor of Nacio's suite was themed to island bliss. Several palm trees cornered the room, with a small water fall that gently ebbed and flowed to a soft rhythm. African artwork and statues accented the room presenting indulgent luxury, and reminders of the island home he once knew long ago before his capture. Nacio's bed comforter was quilted with black and gold satin. Dim track lights skillfully choreographed the room's ambiance as Smooth jazz, serenaded me as if I were at a vacation resort.

"Do you approve?" Nacio spoke. "I try to keep as many reminders of home as possible."

"So you sleep in a bed? So you do sleep?" I said, astonished.

"Well, if I want to feel somewhat human, I will lie down from time to time, but it is not something that I need," he said.

"This house is huge and you don't have visitors—why so much space?" I asked.

"Each suite reminds me of the different parts of the world that I have visited without having to go there," Nacio explained as he walked over and took me in his arms.

"Ahem," Bose cleared his throat, gently reminding us that he was in the room.

"Oh yes, Bose," Nacio reconnected. "I would like for you to do some research in the library. It appears that we might have come across some of Priestess Auldicia's family members here in San Antonio."

"Here?" Bose interjected. "After centuries of being dormant, her bloodline is finally traced here?"

"Yes, I know it is hard to believe," Nacio explained. "Please conduct an internet web search on gang activity in the area, any tribal unrest back home on the islands, and birth records from all slave trading from that time. We must have this information with all swiftness, my friend."

"Right away, Hefe," Bose concurred, and away he went.

"Will he be able to research all that information that quickly?" I asked.

"One of the most useful attributes that Bose possesses is the fact that he was a scholar in his prior life before he was turned into a vampire. He is more than capable of acquiring any information in the world, including classified top secrets."

"You make it sound like he could find out anything or find anyone. Can he?"

"I have faith in Bose. That is why I have trusted him as my caretaker the last several centuries," Nacio explained. "He has been with me throughout time."

"Speaking of time, it is getting late. I should go before Grandma Olvignia gives me the third degree. I am grown, but she still treats me like I just got my driver's license," I said fixing my lips in a twist.

"Yes, my dear, you should go," Nacio said. Just then, he reached for me and kissed me so deeply. Even though his skin is cool, his kiss is the match that lights my fire. He reached for my cell phone, punched in his number, and saved his contact information.

"Will you come to me tomorrow?" he asked with his eyes glistening like diamonds.

"Do you have to ask?" I said. "Fiesta is starting, and I would like to go to the Texas Taste Tease with you. Is this possible?"

"You mean on a real date?" he said. "So you're ready to introduce me to your friends?"

"I'm ready to show you off to the world. I have never felt this way before and actually had the feelings reciprocated by the other person. I've enjoyed being with you," I said. We walked back to my car.

"Until tomorrow then, sleep well and know that you occupy my thoughts every moment," Nacio whispered. He kissed me one last time. I started back down the long alleyway. The drive home was short. I was still intoxicated from his smell and his embrace.

When I arrived in the driveway, surprisingly, neither Grandma Olvignia nor Fritz was perched in the window blinds looking to see if I was home. That only meant she was asleep. I came in quietly and tipped down the hall to my room. I heard Chase in his room engaged in self-talk disagreeing with his inner self about which leisure suit looked better on him, lime green or powder blue. I took extra caution not to interrupt his dialogue or I would have been involved with his disagreement all night.

I reached my room and quietly changed for bed. I dimmed my light and looked steadily at my window, wondering if the soft wind blowing was Nacio watching over me. I could hear the leaves rustling from the trees in the backyard. I entertained my thoughts and desires of him. I knew without a doubt that by morning I would be deeply in love with him, with no turning back.

6

"Wonder why it waits to rain right when I get out of the clink?" Childress said. "I wanted it to be sunny and shining, don't you know?"

"Just be glad you out, girl," Klein said. "Go on inside there. Justice fixed you some gumbo. I know you're hungry."

"You know that's right," Childress said. "Get my bag, will you?"

"Alright," Klein said as he hauled the one bag filled with the possessions Childress had accumulated while serving time in the state penitentiary.

"Hey, Justice! Erland! Childress is here! Where are ya'll at?" Klein hollered through the house.

Childress walked up to the little four-bedroom shotgun house in the middle of a rundown neighborhood on the city's eastside. The house was located just around the corner from the notorious Drug Hill. Any illegal substance that could be sold or manufactured could be purchased by the youngest or oldest person just 25 feet away from the Treemounts front door. The screen of the front door looked as if it had been mauled by a wild animal. Splinters of wood represented the screen and were held together by a frayed wire mesh. A floorboard was missing from the front porch. When someone stepped on the porch, the missing floor board revealed a family of kittens that had taken up residence along with the Treemounts at the dilapidated property.

Right then, all of the Treemount brothers lined up side by side to greet their eldest sibling. All of them inherited the sandy reddish hair, each of them standing an estimated 6 feet 2 inches tall. All of the brothers had fair complexions with stunning jade-green eyes. All three young men were sexy—and deadly. Klein had taken over as the ringleader of the notorious Cut Throat Terrorists gang on the city's east side. Truth be told, law enforcement would never know that Klein Treemount was responsible for one hundred of the two hundred and twenty John Doe killings that were committed in the last two years. The rest were masterminded by Justice and Erland.

The Treemount men were any decent woman's worst nightmare. Klein is a convicted rapist and domestic violence perpetrator with a criminal record comparable to that of his sister's. He has fathered a dozen children that he established paternity on, yet has paid no child support to any of the mothers. Cocaine has been his drug of choice since the age of twelve. He has contracted a string of sexually transmitted diseases over the years and continues to live with syphilis.

Justice is a convicted arsonist and gun runner. He is responsible for several cat killings around the city. Many of the slaughtered animals were dismembered or skinned with the remains left in plain view. Justice is a poly-substance abuser, usually starting out with alcohol, and then ending up high as a kite from the multiple chemicals in his body.

Erland has been diagnosed with Bipolar Personality Disorder, and with Intermittent Explosive Disorder. He is prescribed a cocktail of medications to maintain his emotional equilibrium on a daily basis. With their mother in ill health, his mood swings and explosive anger episodes have become more frequent and more dangerous to those within his reach. Erland often likes to take Xtasy. When he comes down off his high, Klein and Justice never know what to expect. They just make sure to allow him access to food and make sure all knives, guns, forks, and anything that can be a weapon is put away.

"Glad to see you, Sis!" Justice and Erland harmonized as they greeted their sister. "We missed you!"

"Yeah, I missed you too!" Childress grinned. "Fix me something to eat!"

"I'm on it!" Justice barked. "It's made just how you like it with mussels, squid, scallops, oysters, fish, crawfish heads, shrimps, one turtle shell, a baby alligator tail, a side of gravy, and one beignet just for you."

"Whew lucky me!" Childress hollered back. "It sure feels good to be home."

Just then, Klein's expression changed to a more somber presentation as he told his sister about their mother's failing health.

"Mama's not doing too well, Childress," Klein began. "The doctor said that the Alzheimer's is in its last stage, and she has completely forgotten all of us, and even how to eat. He's giving her only a few more days to live at the most."

"Fools, why didn't you tell me Mama was dying?" Childress shouted. "Ya'll are so ignorant and basic. That should have been the first thing out of your mouths when you picked me up!"

"Well, we knew how you were going to react," Justice said in a drawn-out slur, coming down from the tail end of a hangover.

"Take me to her now!"

The Treemounts jumped into Erland's 1964 Chevy Impala. Erland's car was loaded with heated springs and hydraulic lifts that made it bounce when he turned on his amplifier and subwoofer. The rims and tires were stolen straight from a train yard shipment last week. Erland and Justice stole the car parts and left graffiti behind with C.T. marked on the freight car. Childress was becoming aggravated because Erland would not drive any faster due to his car's enhancements.

"Why are you driving so slowly?" Childress barked. "You told me my mama was going to die soon, and you drive like you are already in her funeral procession. Hurry up, boy!"

"Look, this is my ride, my gas, and my…," Erland was saying, just before Childress drew back her right fist and sent it sailing smoothly across the surface of his right jaw, bruising him instantly and sending the car onto a curb. Erland howled in pain but quickly recovered from the swerve and slammed on the brakes.

"Say something else smart, and see don't I come around on the other side and knock your face back the other way," Childress said, her face in a scowl and her eyebrows now joined together in the middle of her forehead.

"Why did you hit me girl? You'd better quit playing," Erland mumbled as the throbbing from the pain on his face soon began to pound in time with his heartbeat.

"Move boy! I'm driving!" Childress said, getting out of the car and shouting at Erland. Hesitantly, Erland got out of the car and moved to the passenger side of the vehicle. Klein and Justice sat quietly throughout the whole incident, knowing not to intervene in any way or else they too would have to endure the same unpleasantness as their youngest sibling. Both brothers sat and waited for the situation to resolve itself.

Childress was driving as fast as she could to reach the downtown Metro Hospital, where her mother was in ICU. Frances Treemount had been transferred to this medical care facility some time back. When Childress turned down the street where the hospital was, she parked the car in the middle of the street, hopped out, and ran towards the hospital. She looked back in the direction of the car and yelled at Erland.

"Park the car, fools, and come inside!" Childress said as she ran into the hospital and up to the information desk, straight to the information desk attendant.

"Uh yeah, uh, my mother, Frances Treemount is on the IQ floor—can you tell me what floor that is?" Childress inquired.

The Information Attendant first rolled her eyes with irritation, looked at Childress cross-eyed, and then said, "You mean the ICU floor?" Why did this clueless Information Attendant do this? This clueless woman was about to get the scare of her life. Before the woman could straighten her posture from her irritated response to the question that was asked, Childress was in the woman's personal space. Sharing only an inch of air that provided distance between the fierce words that Childress spoke and the woman's vulnerable right ear, Childress hissed this treacherous warning:

"The next time some damn body comes up to this desk and asks you a question, the only thing you are supposed to say is *'May I help you?'*" The humidity from Childress's hot breath on the woman's ear was like an evil yellow film that could be felt and seen.

"Do you understand?" Childress continued.

"Yes, yes, I do," the attendant said, turning to look into the fiercely colored jade-green eyes Childress possessed. At that moment, the woman's jaw dropped while being held captive in Childress's gaze. It was as if the woman was looking at every frightful thing she has ever known in her life. The woman's face twisted in utter terror without a sound escaping from her gaping mouth. Childress leaned in again and began her inquiry once more.

"What floor is my mama, Frances Treemount, on?

"She's on the eighth floor," the trembling attendant whispered. The words barely escaped the woman's mouth. Just then, Childress leaned back from the attendant, and the woman jumped from her chair, leaving behind an unsightly accident in her seat.

"Let's go!" Childress barked out to her siblings, and off they went on the elevator up to the intensive care unit. As soon as the elevator opened on the intensive care floor, it was as if the medical staff could instantly sense the sinister presence of the Treemount clan.

The swing-shift staff was on duty, and all the nurses were female except one. One would have thought that the lottery had been won, because Klein was on the prowl. His sexual sickness was immediately heightened, and his arousal hit him like a bat to a baseball. Klein drew in a long and deeply exaggerated breath as if to smell floating pheromones in the air as the nurses marched up and down the hallway assessing patients.

A very attractive dark-brown-skinned nurse, with straight shoulder-length black hair, passed in front of Klein on the way down the hall. He interrupted her pace and inquired about Frances Treemount.

"Oooh! La la, cherie! How you doing, baby?" Klein crooned as he licked his lips. "Darling, I was wondering if you could escort me to the room of one Ms. Frances Treemount? I can't find it without the much-needed guidance from you. Ya'll think you could help me? You look like you're the one in charge of this here place, and you certainly look good enough to eat, cher!" Klein continued with a lecherous smile splashed across his devastatingly handsome face.

The nurse was mesmerized. Before she could respond, Klein's wandering hand reached out and made contact with her shoulder, sending shivers down her spine. She closed her eyes, and looked as if she were about to faint.

"My name is Candy Myers," she finally responded. She then continued with a very faint, "Yes, I sure can take you to Ms. Treemount."

"Ummmhmmm!" Klein hummed. "I sure enjoy myself some Candy as often as possible," he said, again running his tongue across his teeth and lips referring to more than just a friendly dialogue between acquaintances. The thoughts he was entertaining about Nurse Candy were sharply interrupted by a snatch of the ear by Childress.

"Can't you put your peter on pause for five minutes? We are

here to see about our dying mother, not a slow screw on the floor—you understand? Now get yourself together, and let's go see about Mama."

"Look girl, you'd better stop hitting me like that or else you are..." Klein tried to finish but instead tasted the salty right palm of Childress as she delivered a slap across his face like a window swipe. The sound of the slap on his face echoed up and down the hall so loudly, you could have heard a fork drop from the dietary cart of dinner trays being delivered. The medical staff froze, and no one moved. With his eyes bulging, dazed and confused, Klein bucked his eldest sibling no more.

"What are you getting ready say, Klein? I dare you! Say something else, and you will be lying in this hospital next door to Mama! Play stupid if want to!" Childress squealed, now on the defensive and ready to strike again. "Now let's go and see Mama! Where is she...*Nurse Caaandy*!" Childress exclaimed, chewing on Nurse Candy's name.

Unnerved and shaking, Candy led the unruly clan of Treemounts to their expiring mother. Klein was the first to enter room 805 with his two bumbling male siblings and Childress who was still hot and mad.

There in the middle of the room, with her eyes shut, lay a very still and very peaceful looking Frances Treemount. Her skin was fairer in color than that of her children. Her hair had grown to long, curly, sandy-blond reddish locks. Frances looked like an older version of Childress. She was strikingly beautiful and had lived her life exactly how she wanted. She never took anything less than respect from anyone nor would she be watched or controlled by anyone. She would immediately punish her enemies if they crossed her and taught her children to do the same thing.

Now, Frances was on a respirator that made harsh gurgling sounds as she drew in and exhaled her breath. Her life was monitored with leads to notify the charge nurse of any change in pulse or blood pressure. Her heart was beating shallowly as if each beat was the one next to the very last one.

Childress was the first to go to her mother's bedside, and her brothers followed suit. Childress extended a hand to her mother's sandy mane and stroked it soothingly. She took a small pair of scissors from her pouch and cut a healthy lock of her mother's hair. She began whispering what would be the last words spoken to her mother while she was still alive.

"Mama, I'm home. If I have ever hurt you or made you cry, please forgive me. I love you so much, and I only wanted to make you proud of me," Childress continued as hot tears leaked down her face. "Some people said that you were not a good mother, but I am so proud that you were my mama. I will remember all that you have taught me. You taught me to hold my head high, no matter what people would say about me. You taught me to crush our enemies, no matter who they were, and no matter which one of us they tried to harm, and crush the life right out of them," Childress said as she began to grip the bed sheets near her mother's arm.

"Mama, I promise to keep all that you have taught me sacred, continue our family bloodline, and curse those who stand in our way!" Childress shouted, stood up, and began to study the leads that ran out from the wall and onto her mother. She slowly and steadily reached for the power switch on the respirator and turned the power to the machine off.

Immediately, Frances Treemount's hazel-white eyes flicked open and stared straight up into the ceiling. Her heart monitor flat lined and hummed on a steady tone as the life of Frances Treemount came to an end intentionally at the hand of her eldest child.

"What the hell are you doing, Childress!" Erland cried out. "She was our mama too! You should have let her go on her own!"

"She was already gone, boy! Mama wouldn't have wanted to suffer! You all know that; so don't give me any of that damn mess!" Childress shouted, clenching her fists. "Let's go!"

All three left the room and started up the hall as several staff, and drooling Nurse Candy went flying past them, into room 805 to resuscitate their mother, but were unsuccessful. Frances Treemount had expired.

Childress went up to the nurses' station and slammed a piece of paper down on the counter in front of a male nurse. The piece of paper had the number to Auchan's Funeral Home and Sunset Services written on it.

"Call Auchan's—they'll come and pick her up. You have my permission to have her transported; you don't need to call me for nothing else, got it?" Childress sniped.

"Yes, ma'am," the timid male nurse said, looking every bit of twelve years old himself.

"Go get the car, fools—and hurry up!" Childress said, standing curbside next to the hospital's emergency area carport.

"Take me to Camelot! It is time to pay our little wandering friend Believa Beaushanks a visit."

"Mama just died, Childress. Can't that wait?" Justice said, wiping tears from his eyes.

"Mama taught us to deal head-on with our enemies. She crossed me, and now she is an enemy to all of us. So deal with it!"

"But, Childress, don't you think…," Justice started and was cut off by his sister.

"Justice, you are starting to piss me off!" Childress hung on her words as she snapped at Justice.

"You usually don't have much to say, and when you do, it's not something that makes me mad; but, tonight, you are close to the edge."

"Chill out, Childress! He didn't mean any harm," Erland said with his face eggplant-purple, swollen, and sore. "But I tell you what, if you reach for me again, I'm gone whoop your ass!" He said, throwing his arm over his face.

Having done that, Childress couldn't help but let out a sizzling snicker that was contagious, and Klein and Justice chimed in too as their youngest sibling jested with their sister.

"Let's go stomp, this wench. I hope Katalo is there too. I have a few choice words for his ass too," Childress said.

They drove to northeast San Antonio into the Camelot subdivision. They approached a fairly large ranch-style house in the middle of a cul-de-sac. The lights were on, and a little black Volkswagen Beetle was in the driveway.

"Yeah, that hoe is home. Let me out right here. Ya'll go to the corner and park the car and come back," Childress instructed.

All the Treemount men took their orders and met their sister back in Believa's driveway. They were ready to strike.

"Klein, take the back door. Justice, you and Erland take either side of the door. I'm going in first," Childress stated. Each of the men positioned themselves and readied for the brawl on the queue from Childress.

Childress worked her way up to the front and rang the doorbell. "Who is it?" a half lit up Katalo responded. Childress continued to ring the doorbell several times at once, until he finally opened door. Before the inebriated Katalo knew what had overtaken him, Childress kicked the door in, sending him flying backward so hard that he imprinted in the sheetrock in the wall behind the door.

Just then, Klein came crashing in through the back door, shattering glass and sending it flying through the air, and it embedded in Katalo's right cheek and temple. Blood trickled down the side of his face as he slid down the wall to the floor.

"Well, well, what have we here? Bet you didn't think you'd see me again, did you, asshole?" Childress said. As she nursery-rhymed her words, she reached down and sliced Katalo across his face with her razor-sharp nails.

"Since you snitched on us, I have a little surprise for you."

"What the hell do you want? You better get the hell out of here, Childress. I'll rat your ass out again!" Katalo said.

"Where is Believa? And try not to lie to me."

"Screw you, hoe!" Katalo shouted back.

"Wrong answer," Childress hissed and smacked her tongue. "Tsk, tsk, tsk—wrong move."

Just then, Childress reached in her pouch and pulled out a perfume-sized canister. She whispered the words "crawl and scratch." Childress opened the canister and threw the contents of it onto Katalo's sweat-beaded skin. Within seconds, the surface of Katalo's skin was covered in black-striped maggots that were squirming and crawling, making his skin the new host for their living environment.

"Oh yeah Katalo. How does it feel to squirm like the maggot you are? Now you are in good company!" Childress sniped. Katalo screamed in agony as the flesh-dwelling parasites burrowed into his skin. He scratched in response, and soon mayhem took over, and he panicked. Katalo began to scratch chunks of his flesh off his body. After five minutes, Katalo looked as if he'd been attacked with a fork. Tissue and blood lay all over the carpet.

All too happy with her handiwork, Childress turned on the balls of her feet and looked at Justice and Erland who had now entered the house.

"Find the keys and the title to that cute little Beetle outside. I'll take that, because your damn car is too slow for me. I got places to go and things to do!"

Without a second to spare, her car thief brothers got to work.

Justice scoured the house until he found the title to the car, made out to Katalo Nickelson and Believa Beaushanks. Erland found the keys on the kitchen counter.

"I'm taking this car as retribution for money you stole from me, and for ratting me out. Looks like you'll be busy, itching and scratching for the rest of the night," Childress smirked. "Try to keep your mouth closed—if not, you'll have visitors in there too."

"Screw you, Childress!" Those were the last words Childress heard Katalo Nickelson speak as she and her motley crew walked out the front door. Childress found her way in the driveway and opened the door to the black Beetle that she now called herself the rightful owner to. As she cranked up and backed out, she heard the last screams Katalo made as he scratched himself into oblivion.

Three days had passed since Frances Treemount died. Auchan's Funeral Home had her body and was preparing her for the funeral. Auchan's is the only funeral home in San Antonio that is prepared to have a true New Orleans style funeral as Frances had requested long before she died. Klein had contacted as many of her family members as possible. Some family members still had not been located since they were displaced by Hurricane Katrina.

The ones that did come for the funeral service had to stay in hotels, because Justice and Erland had lots of stolen merchandise in the home and didn't want to spike any suspicions or answer to anyone. Female family members were not necessarily safe in Klein's presence either. The Treemounts were feared by many of the extended family and were often left alone because of the treachery that their mother had instilled in them. Many family members were afraid not to come, because many felt that Childress would curse them. With her being the head of Frances's estate, many extended family members felt that there would be no end to the evil that Childress would indulge in. The rest of the family had true cause to worry.

"Childress, Mama left you a letter here," Klein said as he handed it to her. "She wrote it one day while we were visiting with her in the hospital. This was before she was too far gone to remember anything."

Childress was in her room getting ready for the funeral. She took the envelope from Klein. "Alright, you can get out now."

Childress looked at the envelope with her name written on it in her mother's handwriting. She felt a tear well up in her eye and then flow down her face. The envelope smelled like her mother's scent. She opened the envelope and read these words…

…My dearest Childress, my oldest baby, you have my ways and my image…by the time you read this letter, I will have passed on into the next life, and you will be the new queen mother of our voodoo religion and culture. Take and keep control of your life. Let no man or woman hold you down. Make your enemies dust under your feet; watch out for your brothers. Trust no one. For centuries, our bloodline has been carried through the women in our family. Our great ancestor, Priestess Auldicia, has left protection for us on earth that no man would harm us, no woman would scorn us.

All the knowledge of spells and charms I have left to you and you will find them in the attic of this house. Study them well. See you on the other side someday, my child…

Love always, Frances Treemount
Your mother

After reading the letter, Childress wept softly. The letter fell from her hands onto the bed. She touched it, and a fluorescent light shown from the letter on the opposite wall. Childress fell onto the bed and began to convulse wildly. Her eyes rolled to the back of her head, and she began to mumble the name *Priestess Auldicia, Priestess Auldicia, Priestess Auldicia*. This continued for the next hour, until there was a knock on her door.

"Childress, you ready?" Erland called. "It's time for the service."

"I'll be out in a minute." Childress walked over to the mirror and staggered at the reflection that now stared back at her. The sandy-blonde curly mane that once crowned her head was now woven with *Just After Midnight*-colored black streaks. The midnight-black streaks mixed in with the sandy-blonde reddish hue made her hair look as if it were infested with coiled snakes. Shocked, but accepting of the change before her, Childress looked down to find that she was dressed in a black satin dress. She was accessorized with a choker that was gold and looked to circle her neck four times. In the middle of the choker sat a three-inch onyx stone.

Childress reached for the doorknob, and to her surprise, the door slowly opened without her even making contact with the knob. She stood in the threshold of the door and looked straight ahead down the hall of the house. At the end of the hall, the other three Treemounts looked in awe at their sister as she walked slowly towards the front door and what was to become her new destiny.

All of the extended family members were gathered on the front porch. Childress walked slowly out of the house and down the sidewalk. As she did so, a path parted to allow her to reach the edge of the yard. To the left, she could see her mother's hearse. Childress requested to be taken straight to the cemetery after a very brief ceremony at the funeral home.

As soon as the cars pulled up at the cemetery, a brass section was fully assembled and ready to do the second line, a traditional line dance done in many celebrations by native New Orleanians, often done at jazz funerals.

Childress led the procession in the first line. She was truly a sight to see. Emanating her mother's image and kissed by the magic held in her mother's good-bye letter, Childress appeared more sinister than ever. Her lips were stretched wide in a smile that had some of her family members feeling as if she were mocking her mother's death by not crying. Her hair was blowing in the wind, making the black streaks look like serpents dancing in the air as they fought for a place to crown her head. Childress began to holler and shout as she led the first line. Traditionally, her behavior would have been more appropriate if she had come through on the second line; but again, no one questioned Childress and how she ran things.

The Treemount men were all tailored in black suits and patent leather shoes. They waited until the first line was started, then jumped into the second line and partied their way to the graveside with the brass section as the rest of their family looked on in unspoken shock.

Bump, bump, bump, bump, tada, tada, bump, bump, bump, bump! The bass drum delivered the beat as Frances Treemount was laid to rest in her final resting place. The procession stopped, and right when it did, Childress bellowed out an eerie screeching laugh that some could attest could be heard for miles. All eyes were on Childress; and all were hoping to make it home without feeling her wrath.

On the way home from the graveside, Childress did not utter a word. Klein wanted to inquire about the new look but knew better than to speak at all, especially after looking at the just-now-subsiding bruising on Erland's face.

After being home for awhile after the service, Childress ventured up into the attic. She was becoming weary and frustrated as she paced up and down in the attic in search of the family's history that her mother had left to her.

"I wished you would have given me a hint, mama," Childress said in total anguish now, kicking old newspapers and boxes aside.

"She said *...make your enemies dust under your feet...*"

Childress lifted her right foot and stepped back, revealing a floorboard that was loose. She bent down to remove the floorboard, and sure enough, there was a book that was extremely old with a worn spine. She opened it to reveal parchment paper that had once been scrolled but was now housed in this book. In a box underneath the book were old chicken bones, a shark-tooth necklace, candles, and a pentagram. Instantly, Childress could feel the power and enchantment that she had experienced earlier before the funeral service. This time, she felt her veins pulsating, extending up and down her arms. She quickly collected her newfound belongings and hurried to her room.

This time, when she passed the mirror, her image was accented by her veins being blue and close to the surface of her skin. The transformation to Queen Mother has begun.

7

I was instantly awoken by the shrill sound of the telephone ringing next to my head. I looked at the caller ID. It was Affinity, full of questions no doubt. I had been spending all my time with Nacio, and that left little room for anything or anyone else. I guess I better go ahead and get my tongue-lashing from her. It was going to happen sooner or later.

"Hello."

"What's up, girl? Where have you been? You know it's just like you to put me down when you get a man on the side. I know that must be the case, because it happens every time you find someone new," Affinity chirped through the phone.

"So who is he? What is his name? Where did he come from, and what are you doing with him? Are we going to the Texas Taste Tease today?"

The Texas Taste Tease is an event that is part of Fiesta in San Antonio. Fiesta is also known as "La Semana Alegre," the week of happiness, in which parades and other events celebrate Mexican culture and history. The Texas Taste Tease is celebrated by the African Americans in San Antonio, bringing both Mexican American and African American cultures together in a fun-filled event with Cajun, Creole, and Mexican food events held at the city's Japanese Tea Garden.

As I said, she gave me a tongue-lashing. It was entirely too early in the morning for the verbal assault. Affinity lit into me with so many rapidly fired questions that I needed a reporter's notepad to jot them down.

"Well, remember when we were out that night at the NCO? Oh yeah, you couldn't remember, because you were too wasted!" I jabbed back and then laughed.

"Yeah go ahead and laugh!" Affinity sneered.

"Anyway, I met him then. His name is Nacio. He's really tall with olive-colored skin. Oh yeah, his hair is really long, black, and wavy. He has his own business, and he likes me," I said to catch myself and steer the conversation carefully. There was absolutely no way that I was going to let Affinity in on the fact that I was in love with a vampire who was centuries old, and he claimed to be totally obsessed with me.

"Well, knowing you, he probably looks like a prince from a fairytale," Affinity said.

"No doubt, he is easy to look at and drool over," I hummed, rolling over and sitting up in my bed.

"So are we going to the Tease?"

I knew I had to answer this question in a way that did not put a wrinkle in our friendship and not make Affinity feel like she was being totally ditched. I had to come up with a quick plan. I couldn't take Affinity to Nacio's home. I decided to call him, and then we could pick up Affinity later.

"Yeah, yeah, we're going! Let me call you in a few minutes," I said.

"Alright, I'm going to go and pull my outfit together. What time will you be through to pick me up?" Affinity said.

"Around 4:30," I said.

"Alright, that sounds cool."

I next reached for my cell phone and scrolled through my contact list. Strangely enough, I found Nacio's number. It was not filed with the Ns for Nacio but under the Ls, and entered as *Love of my life*. Immediately, my heart beat quickly three times in a row, skipped one beat, and then resumed its regular cadence. I pressed Send on my phone, and Nacio picked up on the first ring.

"Good morning, my love. I trust you slept well?" His voice said, melting me into a morning liquid mess.

"Hi" was all I could manage.

"You want to ask me about going to the Texas Taste Tease?" he inquired, aware of my every thought.

"Yes, I did…I mean, I was…I mean," I stammered, trying to pull myself together.

"I can come to your home. I think it might be okay to meet Grandma today. What do you think?"

"Uh sure, if you're ready."

"I can be there at 4 o'clock. I've been missing you. I'll see you soon," he said.

"Bye," I said, hanging up.

Each time I heard his voice or felt his touch, I would lose total composure from within. I am just now starting to grasp the fact that I just might be worthy enough to be happy. I fell back onto my bed and was smiling inside and out until my bedroom door flew open and Chase stuck his early morning face in my door, which looked like a zombie from hell.

"Lou, Lou. What're you doing, Lou, Lou? Are you going to the Tease?"

Uhhhggghh. Dealing with Chase early in the morning is like trying to get away from a swarm of bees. If you swatted at them, they would call for reinforcements, and that would surely ruin your day.

"What do you want, Chase? Shut my door! You are supposed to

knock, fool!" I shouted in protest.

So then he backs his entire face out from the threshold of the bedroom door and stands at the door and knocks.

"Lou, Lou, Lou, Lou. What're you doing, Lou, Lou? Let me have five dollars, Lou, Lou!"

Uhhhgggh! As I said, it ruins your day.

In an attempt at relief, I slid a crisp $5 dollar bill under the door. I knew it was retrieved, because there was a crescendo from the closing of a door, and then silence.

I eventually got dressed and went into the kitchen to find something to eat. Remarkably, I saw the shadow of Grandpa Leonine. He had his face plastered to the television screen. It was Saturday, and the Western movie channel had a John Wayne marathon going all day. I knew I wouldn't see anymore than his shadow all day. Grandma Olvignia would feed him all of his meals in that same spot that he lay in across their bed. He loved Westerns, and that would occupy him all day.

"Hey, Grandpa!" I said. "Are you feeling alright?"

"Hey, baby!" Grandpa Leo said. "I'm doing fine, and you?"

"I'm good," I called out. I turned around and there stood Grandma Olvignia grinning, and standing as still as a cat.

"What time is he coming?" Grandma said, already anticipating meeting Nacio.

"He'll be here at 4 o'clock."

"Alright, I'm going be ready. Some things I need to ask him; some I won't have to ask—I'll just know."

It was spooky the way Grandma just knew things. I hope I get that trait if it's for me to have.

As soon as 4 o'clock rolled around, the doorbell rang. Fritz barked and took off towards the front door. He was chasing his tail and barking loudly. He then ran to the window blinds to his lower watch spot in the window to see visitors as they approached the house.

I went to the door, hoping that I looked okay. Blue jean shorts, mule tennis shoes, halter top, hair in a high ponytail, and Mardi Gras makeup—all suitable for the Texas Taste Tease.

I opened the door, and there he stood. Nacio was dressed in a crème-colored silk and linen short set that loosely draped his frame but still allowed for his rippling chest to peep through nonetheless. Leather crème-colored, multi-woven sandals graced his feet. A leather necklace with a small conch seashell and matching bracelet were the only accessories he wore with his clothing. His heavy black mane curtained his shoulders as he turned to greet me.

"Hello, Solis."

"Come in," I smiled.

Before I could turn around, Grandma Olvignia was standing behind me in the den, assessing Nacio as he entered our home.

"Welcome, lone stranger," Grandma said. "You've traveled from afar."

"Greetings, Mistress," Nacio said. "It is my pleasure to be in your presence, and I am happy to be in your home," Nacio said bowing his head.

"Please come and sit. Let us speak in peace."

Okay, at that moment, I was totally lost. It was as if Nacio and Grandma had known each other, or something of the sort. They spoke in a manner that totally excluded me, and I sat in amazement.

"I see you have taken an interest in my grandbaby. She is delicate and vulnerable," she said. "What will you have from her?"

"Uh, hello, I am in the room!" I said, trying to determine the connection the two of them had.

"I have taught her some of the history, but I feel that it is okay if you finish what I have started," Grandma said, still assessing Nacio. Fritz even appeared more at ease and had calmed down from his barking spell.

"With your blessing, Mistress, I will give her the knowledge of our parallel family histories."

"Well, uh, we should go now, Grandma," I said, feeling a little embarrassed at the fact that I was clueless as to what bizarre communications Nacio and Grandma had between each other.

"Well, go in peace. Something is blowing through here again. This time, it's bringing some bad spirits. Please be careful, my friend, and protect my grandbaby," she said.

"I will, Mistress. I will," he said.

As we headed out the door, I looked back at Grandma and whispered, "I'll talk to you later."

"I'm looking forward to it, child. I'm looking forward to it."

I was about to head to my old Mustang and had to do a double-take at the absolutely breathtaking gunmetal grey Lexus LS 460 that sat parked in back of my old clunker. The license plate read Puente 1.

"I hope this particular car is okay for the occasion and to pick up your friend," Nacio said as he gently kissed my hand and opened the door on the passenger's side. Just before he sat me in the car, there was a bouquet of yellow roses on the seat with a letter attached to them.

...I am now with you love of my life, yours forever...
Nacio.

"You never cease to amaze me," I said. I reached over to kiss him, but he caught my lips in mid air.

"You are the one who is amazing," he said, turning the key in the retractable ignition switch. For a second, I started to ask if the car was even running, because I heard absolutely nothing from the engine.

The navigation screen directed us straight to Affinity's front door. When we pulled up, she was already standing outside, and she lost it when she saw me get out of the car.

"What in the world, Solis? Where did you get this…?" Affinity tried to finish, but I knew right away what stifled her words. Before Affinity could take another breath, Nacio stepped out of the car, and she froze. Nacio walked right up to where she and I were standing.

"Hello, I'm Nacio. It's good to meet you, Affinity."

"Ummm, hi," Affinity stammered, totally knocked windless after getting her eyeful of Nacio's presence.

"Uh well, we should go. Are you ready to roll out?" I said.

"Ready! Let's hit 'em where it hurts!"

Nacio opened the car door for Affinity, and then he placed me back in the front seat. Off we went.

When we arrived at the Texas Taste Tease, the park was already packed. The entry gate had a line that snaked all the way down to Mulberry Street. Nacio gently held my hand while we were in line. Affinity sniggled and made heart symbols teasing me as we crept our way up to the entrance. Once inside the park, the ambiance was electric, and the event was truly a freak show.

Some of the partygoers were either scantily clad or flamboyantly over-accessorized. Cliques of any preference were available to fall into as we strolled casually along the pathway of food booths on either side of us. A group of females that looked to be in their early twenties wore bikini tops with short shorts that covered their smiling thong underwear that peeped out from their behinds. The volume of their conversation and beer spilling gave clues that they might have been on their way to getting fully wasted within the next hour.

Exotica, a well-known female impersonator, stood with two other female impersonators a few feet from the boisterous young women. Exotica had her lips and nose turned up in distaste as she looked over at one of the young women as she stumbled and fell into a puddle of beer she had spilled. I had known Exotica from being in my friend Jordica's wedding a few years back. She had done the makeup for the wedding party.

One thing about Exotica, she couldn't be beat when it came to making any female look like she could be on the cover of a magazine. She owned a theater troupe and musical review. She was dramatically made up with her eyebrows arched nearly as high as her hairline. The eyelashes that she wore danced on her eyelids as the wind blew them back and forth. Her hair platinum blonde hair stood at least a foot off her scalp in a disciplined, hair-sprayed bouffant. She wore a sequined green ball gown that dragged on the ground everywhere she went. The starlet accessorized her ensemble with a deep purple boa with huge peacock feathers, and her lips were kissed a ruby red color. I had to go and greet the diva properly.

"Hey, Exotica honey!" We passed air kisses between the two of us, careful not to disturb her makeup.

"Hey, Solis, baby—how you doing?" she said, smiling then scowling as she turned in the direction of the now drunken, thong-clad harlots a few feet away.

"UmmmmUmmmUmmmm," Exotica mumbled. "Girl, look at these hoes. If they can't act like ladies, they could at least act like proper drunk hoes and quietly get drunk. But no, they have to fall in the beer they spilled, and then turn their nose up at me like I made them fall. They had better leave me be or I will come out of these eyelashes and wig and really put them on the ground. You hear me?" Exotica lectured.

"I hear you, Diva."

"It never fails…there's always one in the crowd that…," Exotica batted her eyelashes as she saw Nacio, and then flashed them back at me.

"Exotica, this is my man, Nacio," I said, beaming from ear to ear. Nacio smiled at me and desire filled my eyes.

"Hello, Exotica. I'm charmed to meet you," he said as he reached to respectfully shake her hand.

"Ooohhh, hello Nacio," Exotica crooned. "Let's see, nacio—that's Spanish for 'born,' right?"

"Correct, Madame, it is," he said smiling.

"Well, I must say, Solis, honey, you have finally been 'born' and have done something right for a change," Exotica grinned and raised her extreme eyebrows up and down in approval of Nacio and me.

"Yes, I have, Exotica, and see you soon!" I said as we passed air kisses between us once more, and I left her to her companions.

"She is quite a character," Nacio said. "She seems sincere."

"A character—she truly is," I said. "Where's Affinity?"

"Next crowd over," Nacio said, nodding ahead of us in the direction of three Chippendale-looking guys that were dressed in just below the knee denim shorts and gladiator sandals. All of them were wearing wife beater T-shirts in purple, green, and yellow. Each guy was of a different ethnicity—Anglo, African American, and Latino. They were much too appetizing for an attention-starved Affinity to pass up. Nacio and I discreetly paused near Affinity and her company to listen in as she worked social magic.

"Yeah, I live around here. You?" she said, speaking sweetly to the caramel-colored Latino guy with the short brown curly hair. Affinity was standing with her weight on her left leg, head tilted in the same direction, and her arms folded across her chest. This was her "I'm approachable and I think you are delicious" stance.

The guy was smiling and talking so low that I couldn't make out what he was saying, so I asked Nacio, knowing his sensitive hearing would inform me of what was said.

"What's the guy saying?"

"That she's sexy, and he likes her eyes," Nacio said, smirking.

"Well, let's give it a couple of hours; she will have found out his date of birth, social security number, driver's license number, blood type, HIV status, and credit score by the time we leave," I said, knowing how my friend operates.

"She's that good, huh?" Nacio laughed.

"Just watch—when it's time for us to leave, you'll have a full report," I said.

It was as if everyone you could possibly know was at the Texas Taste Tease. If you wanted to catch up with someone you hadn't seen in a long time, you would surely see them here today.

Laughter that sounded like little munchkins came from an "all too happy to be there" blonde with blue eyes. I would have recognized that laugh from anywhere. It was Kennedy Berlanger from school. She too appeared to have downed a few beers or wine coolers to celebrate the day's events. She was walking through the crowd with her neck loaded with Mardi Gras beads, laughing and blowing bubbles from a bottle given to her at the gate. Right behind her from school were Elbithea, Dinah Burns, Amalisa Leonard, Haze Morris, Jina Grant, Elva Baines, and Welburn Bennett. Welburn was the only guy from school that hung with the crew. He was more of a chaperone for the girls.

Welburn was known for his wardrobe and how clean he kept his shoes. It was nothing for him to show up in any crowd, with no less than $1,000 dollars worth of clothing and jewelry on his back. The crew he ran with often teased him for being so fresh and so clean for any occasion, even amongst the dust and wind out here today at the Tease.

"Hey there, Solis," a voice called.

It was my Uncle Clive at his gumbo booth. He was there behind the counter with my Uncle Ronald. Both of my father's brothers were pulling in the monies from the food sales. Nacio and I went over. I hugged them both. My aunts Raelynn and Rose were standing there laughing and helping out.

"Ya'll want a bowl of gumbo?" Uncle Clive said. "Ronald, give the girl and friend some gumbo."

"Uncle, this is Nacio."

"What's up man?" Nacio said, shaking my Uncle Clive's hand and then my Uncle Ronald's hand. My aunts each hugged Nacio.

The day just couldn't get any better, and I couldn't be happier. The man of my dreams was escorting me around at an event, and he was making his debut as mine. I guess fairytales can come true if you give them a chance to. I wanted mine to come true very much.

"No, you are not riding with me with all those gold chains wrapped around your neck looking like an 'out of a record deal' rapper!" Childress admonished. "You had better lift some of those off your neck, Klein, or you will get left here at this house!"

"You don't know what you are talking about, Childress. This is the look, and I'm going to catch me some females tonight," Klein said, purposely intoxicating his mind with images of female private parts just to get his motor running. He will surely be a menace to any female that chances being alone with him tonight. Whoever the unlucky soul might be, may she return home safely, but it certainly couldn't be guaranteed with Klein once again on the prowl.

"Just look at you," Klein fired back. "What's up with the nasty black streaks in your hair? I've wanted to ask you that since the funeral service, because you look crazy!"

"I look crazy, huh?" Childress said. "Well, keep looking!"

Childress slammed her foot down on the accelerator of the black Beetle she and her henchmen brothers had stolen, and left Klein standing curbside in front of their home. His mouth was agape from disbelief that Childress would leave him with no way to get to the Tease. Justice and Erland had left before daybreak that morning to get a good parking spot and tickets as soon as they went on sale.

Stuck like Chuck, Klein had to catch the bus to get to the Tease. As he finally realized how stupid the nine gold herringbone chains looked around his neck, he conceded and removed two of them. Now, he looked like a rapper that needed a producer. He took the laces out of his high-top shoes, tightened the belt over his buttocks that had his blue jean shorts hanging on for life and exposed his plaid striped gold boxers, and he unbuttoned his shirt. Klein walked to the corner and was on the bus in minutes on his way to the Tease. He cursed Childress throughout the entire time he was on the bus. Passengers sat far away from the mumbling and self-talking he did as he rode in complete agitation.

"I'm gonna whoop her ass on-site—watch," Klein mumbled during the 45-minute bus ride. "Leaving me like that, hell! Don't know who she thinks she is."

"Young man, you alright back there?" The bus driver called out to Klein, clearly concerned about his vocal agitation.

"Just drive the damn bus! And hurry up too!" It was a long ride.

After weaving in and out of traffic and nearly causing two major accidents on 281 McAllister Freeway, Childress finally exited on Mulberry Street. The little black Beetle swung in front of two cars just before it turned into the Texas Taste Tease parking lot. Childress stole a parking space from another patron that courteously had her turn signal on to get the space. As soon as she was able to turn, Childress made a sharp left turn into the space barely missing the foreleg and foot of a young female getting out of the car just next to hers.

"Watch it, bitch! You almost hit me!" the mocha-skinned young woman screeched. Before the young woman could close her car door, Childress wrapped a handful of the woman's waist-length brown hair around her arm. She then yanked the young woman off her four-inch heels she was standing in, sending the woman toppling to the asphalt. The young woman landed on her elbows, leaving them skinned and bloodied, rendering her helpless on the ground. Childress fixed her lips with a grin from succeeding in her terroristic behavior.

"Say something else to me like that, and I promise to mop the floor up out here with your ass! Do you hear me?" Childress warned, stepping over the young woman as she lay sprawled in the middle of the parking lot with bloody, frayed elbows.

Childress was so tickled at what she had done, she sashayed her way up to the entry gate in her version of a runway walk that models do in a fashion show. She was dangerous and she didn't care who knew it. This was her debut back home since she had been released from prison, and she knew she had to look appealing.

She wore shorts that were no bigger than a body washcloth that allowed her cheeks to reveal themselves from the bottom. She giggled to herself, because she recalled her mother called the shorts "face towel shorts" for their small size. Her hot shorts were accompanied by a purple sequined top with no bra for support. A green boa made of chicken feathers and a gold Mardi Gras mask accessorized her apparel. With her natural hair color blondish red, mixed with the midnight-black streaks, her mane looked like a radioactive waste dump.

She had made sure to shave her legs, bikini area, and underarms. Childress had mixed a special body lotion with coconut oil, honeysuckle, and gardenia root to attract as many admirers as possible. She had finally made it to the entry gate and instantly became the object of desire of a-none-too bright security guard at the gate.

"Hey there, cher!" Childress said, making her bowlegs shift her hips from left to right as the guard gave her a glance. His eyes were fixated on her hips. She returned the gesture by captivating him with her jade-green peepers.

"Be careful. You are going to hurt someone with those," the guard spoke as he nodded his head in direction of Childress's bouncing hips.

"Come find me later, cher. I'll have something for you," she said, licking her lips and going straight through the gates without paying admission, taking in with her a roll of concessions tickets for beverages and food. The guard watched her cheeks smile at him as she entered the park. He was left entertaining a thought of having an opportunity to exchange intimate body fluids later, before the night was over.

At that moment, Justice and Erland were keeping a low profile as they entered the gate and fell in line with their sister's footsteps. The youngest Treemounts had just used a slim jim to burglarize two cars in the parking lot down the street. Justice and Erland were gang members, and they had many enemies throughout the city. Both were keeping a lookout for rival gang members in case a brawl was to go down. The two of them had left before dawn to sneak into the park and plant three handguns and two hunting knives. They did this knowing that they would be searched with a metal detector prior to entry into the park, and they needed weapons. In the past, Childress would slice her enemies with a knife. Now, with the spells and enchantments, she can will punishment against her enemies any way she sees fit.

"Where the hell ya'll been?" Childress squealed, intently picking at the accumulated lint and dirt under fingernails. Just then, a discombobulated Klein came through the gates, still cursing from being left at the house by Childress after his snide remarks about her hair.

"You better be glad I finally got here, girl! Don't know who you think you are driving off like that!" Klein squawked but made no effort on the promise he made to himself to whoop Childress on-site. For he knew if he had made any attempt, his punishment would be severe.

"Bet you won't get smart next time," Childress said shooting her middle finger at Klein. With her lengthy fingernail, her finger looked more like a small tree branch. With this gesture, the new Queen Mother commanded her court through the crowded park to mingle.

"Let's make a move!"

Childress and her brothers continued perusing the event when suddenly Childress noticed a petite dark-skinned female with low-riding skintight jeans standing wrapped arm in arm with a male slightly taller than she. Beyond a shadow of a doubt, it was Believa Beaushanks. She had obviously either had not heard about what happened to Katalo or she flat didn't give a damn, because she was in a lip-lock with someone else.

"Stay here, and watch me!" Childress commanded of her goony brothers. Childress over exaggerated her seductive walk, as she made her way over to Believa and her company. Childress took both of her hands and put them between the faces of the lovers and shoved their faces apart with such force that each of them crashed to the ground. He landed in dirt, and Believa landed in fire ants. As Believa swiped at the pests that had begun to sting her with fury, Childress commenced a beating on her face that sounded like fists hitting raw meat.

"Do you really think that I would let you go free while I went to prison? That you could screw that maggot Katalo and take my money and not be punished?" Childress continued to tap out her speech as her fists pounded Believa's face. The swelling was instant, and the pain was deep as Believa knew not to make a sound in the middle of the park.

No one in the crowd said a word, mainly from drunkenness. Also, many knew Childress and didn't want to take a chance on the repercussions of her wrath if she discovered who notified the authorities. After the last punch was delivered to Believa's face, Childress spit on her and kicked more ant-filled dirt on her. Believa was left with multiple contusions and a highly likely subdural hematoma from the intense beating. Childress turned and looked at Believa one last time.

"Now you and that maggot have been taken care of!"

"Do you like it?" Nacio asked, feeding me a crawfish head.

"Yuck! It's too sweet!" I said.

"Well, I know what not to have Bose cook for you," he said slyly.

After a gross Texas Taste Tease test experience, I happen to notice that the band had just finished assembling their instruments. The bass drum kicked off a Zydeco beat, and the "oh's and ah's" from the crowd signified it was time to shuffle to the dance floor. Just ahead of us, I heard Affinity's acknowledgment of the music.

"Hey, Solis, let's go start the Zydeco shuffle," she said, still coherent and sober. I knew I had better do so, because I might not catch her like this again before the end of the night.

"Go ahead and enjoy yourself, sweetheart," Nacio said. "I'll get you two ladies something to drink."

"Thank you, sweetie," I said, kissing his lips. "Let's go, Affinity."

We hit the dance floor and started the shuffle. The bass drum boomed, and the accordion was the maestro. The floor was packed as a sea of Mardi Gras masked partygoers swayed back and forth. Affinity and I danced the next four songs straight. Nacio found his way through the crowd with the drinks. Just as he handed Affinity and me our drinks, he became trancelike. His eyes became dilated and fixed. He completely spaced out.

"Sweetheart, what is it?" I inquired, becoming afraid and wondering what had caused Nacio's sedate behavior. There was no response from him. People continued to dance and enjoy the festivities while my fear escalated.

"Nacio, honey, what is it?"

No sooner had I finished my question than I was pushed by a wild-looking scantily clad harlot with a gold Mardi Gras mask on. She pushed me so hard with her butt I went flying into Nacio who seemed to have snapped out of his trance. Without any further thought, the female turned around and started insulting me as if I had been the one to push her.

"Can't you excuse yourself, you clumsy hoe?" she said.

"Hey, you were the one to push me, tramp!" I sniped back. I couldn't quite identify her voice, but I shuddered at its familiarity. I began to sweat from the sound of the drawl as each of her words echoed. It hit me in that moment. As she peeled her Mardi Gras mask off her face, I realized that standing before me was one of the demons in my nightmare…Childress Treemount.

"Oh, so you're a bold bitch, huh?" Childress said just as she drew back her fist and swung at me. For the first time, Nacio's face was unrecognizable to me. His fangs were showing, and his eyes and fingernails were black. He hissed a warning to Childress.

"Watch yourself, Childress! This time, you are the one going to get hurt!"

The wind had begun to blow wildly and black clouds blanketed the sky. Her green eyes had begun to glow, and Childress spit out her own warning.

"This is just the beginning!"

In a bolted flash, Nacio jumped in front of me and moved me out of the way. Childress landed a punch on someone that was a rival to the Cut Throat Terrorists. The guy receiving the punch was from the Inner Circle Cannibals, known as Flick. He was infamous for flicking out a butterfly knife and carving his initials in his rivals. When he saw it was Childress that had hit him, he pulled his knife to begin his handiwork.

Standing in the distance, Justice saw the commotion and ran to get one of the handguns that he had hid in a small burrow at the base of a tree not too far from where he stood. Once he got his piece, he fired into the crowd where Flick stood. The bullet pierced Flick in his back, shredding a major artery, fatally wounding him. Complete mayhem had broken out in the crowd as Justice, Erland, and Klein began to randomly shoot at rival gang members in the crowd. Fire was returned as people ran for cover.

Nacio had safely placed me in an area away from the stray bullets. I begged him to go back for Affinity.

"Affinity—you have to go back for Affinity!" I pleaded. "I can't leave her—please find her!"

"I will! Stay put, Solis!" In the blink of an eye, he was gone.

Terror had seized the evening. The mellow ambiance of the Texas Taste Tease had been replaced and taken over by a stampede filled with bloodcurdling screams. The entrance was filled with people that were being trampled as gunfire continued to ring out through the air. One male had fallen victim to the terror-stricken crowd as he lay just to the side of the gate. His leg was hyper-extended from his hip joint, with his knee bent, his calf rotating inward, giving him the appearance of a just-broken pretzel as he agonizingly attempted to crawl further out of harm's way.

San Antonio Police Department was being assisted by SWAT to safely direct the remaining crowd out of the park and to get emergency medical technicians on the scene. I was becoming impatient waiting for Nacio and worried about my friend's safety. I was standing in a cave hollow on the side of a boulder not far from the entry gate. Some of the not so critically wounded Inner Circle Cannibal gang members were running for the hills of the park. Trails of blood stained the dirt and made an awful brown paste that smeared the asphalt as the stampede continued into the parking lot. A traffic jam from hell formed, causing a blockade and more potential danger for those trying to escape.

Back inside of gates at the park, Nacio quickly spotted two gang members firing at the Treemounts. He allowed the two rival gangs to continue to battle it out. In a far corner near the edge of the dance floor, Affinity was lying still. Her neck was noosed with the green boa Childress had accessorized herself with. The asphyxiation from the noosed boa had caused Affinity's eyes to bulge and the delicate eye blood vessels to burst.

Affinity was near death and in a coma-like state; Nacio was carrying Affinity's limp body to me.

"I found her this way," he said. "I need to track where they are." His eyes were still black and his face was looking completely transformed with fangs showing. I screamed as I saw my dear friend clinging to life.

"You need to leave before you are discovered," I warned. "You can't take a chance on being discovered or implicated in the trouble here today."

"I don't want to leave you, but I will begin tracking the Treemounts," he said. "I will follow up with you soon."

Knowing things were very bad at that moment and being terrified, I said goodbye to Nacio.

"Please be careful."

"I will. I will see you soon," he said as he teleported away.

An EMT approached me not a moment too soon after Nacio vanished. A path was being cleared so the EMT could begin working on Affinity and load her into the ambulance. By this time, SWAT had the place on lockdown, and SAPD had the roads cleared for the ambulances to triage victims to all the nearest hospitals. The death toll was not complete and speculation was climbing.

Among the dead being carried out was my friend Exotica. She had taken a bullet to her left temple, completely disfiguring her face that had been so beautifully made up earlier in the day. She was only physically recognizable from the lovely ball gown that she had worn for the event. Now, Exotica's once very animated personality was absent as her body lay bloody and still from death's tallied inventory. Crinkling sounds of a plastic body bag and its zipper accompanied her into the shadowy dark of the coroner's van. Two other female impersonators that were with Exotica that day stood to the side of the van screaming and crying as their beloved friend was driven away.

Other gang members were also killed in the random gunfire, along with a few elderly patrons. Luckily, I glanced up and saw my aunts and uncles giving statements to the authorities. They were amongst the vendors that were far enough away to escape when the first gunshots rang out in the air. Unfortunately, Kennedy Berlanger was not so lucky. She was one of several stabbing victims in the park. Evidently, the Cut Throat Terrorists were not the only thugs to bring knives into the vicinity. One of my other friends from school stood with a police officer giving her statement about Kennedy's death.

Channel 12 News was now covering the shooting at the Texas Taste Tease, and I was sure that Grandma Olvignia was worried sick. With this much carnage being reported on television, it was sure to raise the blood pressure of any parent to confirm the whereabouts of their children. The door to the ambulance slammed, and I rode in the back with Affinity. The EMT continued to work on stabilizing her.

My heart was beginning to break as memories of us in high school flooded my mind, and burning tears washed down my face. We had shared and laughed through so many days in our youth that it just didn't seem possible that it could all be over in matter of a few seconds. What had started out as a day that would we would have looked back upon and laughed turned out to be a horrible nightmare to be remembered for years to come.

Darkening the facts even more is that my old nemesis, Childress Treemount, and her insane brothers are responsible for today's events. The only reason I could come up with that Affinity might have been harmed is that Childress saw Affinity and me together during the day. After all the years since she had her brother Klein rape me and the other two watch it happen, she was still a cold, insecure, heartless bitch. Childress Treemount! I can't believe she's really back in my life again.

The speeding ambulance driver made it feel as if the ambulance turned under the emergency room pavilion on two wheels. We came to a screeching halt, and the door to the ambulance was flung open. Affinity was rushed inside, and I was grabbed by the admitting clerk for contact information. My mind was garbled with sights and sounds of the day's events. Answering the clerk's questions and providing contact information was proving to be a task. Mental pictures of Nacio jumping in front of me, and the awful green glow from Childress's eyes preoccupied my mind. I was able to give the clerk Affinity's mother's phone number. The nurse was notifying Ms. Johnson, Affinity's mother, of her hospital admission.

My mind continued to dwell on all that had happened. I had spent years in therapy trying to convince myself to overcome the terroristic behavior I experienced growing up in the midst of Childress and her insane brothers. I was kicked, pushed, threatened, cut, and punched by all of them, escalating into the rape itself. How I hated going to school and coming home. Living every day in fear and not knowing the outcome caused anxiety to become a permanent part of my life. I never could understand how or why they hated me so much. I had never hurt a soul as I was growing up, yet I was despised so greatly. Surely, there had to be a reason that I was the target of the Treemounts hateful acts of violence.

Today proved that nothing had changed in all the years we lived our separate lives. The Treemounts still thrived on evil and fear. It appears that they have taken on a new meaning in terror, by making their acts of violence fatal. As I allowed my thoughts to race though my mind, I was interrupted by a sympathetic touch to my shoulder. It was the attending triage doctor on duty for the evening.

"Ms. Burkes?" he said, confirming my identity.

"Yes?"

"I'm very sorry to inform you. Ms. Affinity Johnson expired. She was pronounced dead on arrival a few moments ago. We have just notified her family, and someone is coming. I'm very sorry for your loss."

Mental fatigue crashed in on me as the room began to rapidly spin out of control.

"Aaaaffffinnnitttty!"

My own screams carried me further and further into a state of darkness, and all went black.

8

Nacio had teleported to the other side of the park and stood in the wooded field. He'd picked up the scent to where the trail of the four murderous Treemount fugitives had made off on foot. They had made their way to a parking lot at a museum not too far from the event park. Erland once again took out the slim jim and popped the lock on the door of an old black Jeep Cherokee. Justice provided the swift electrical rewiring to start the ignition, and the Treemounts made their getaway.

"I popped that bastard Flick right in the back! *Bam*!" Justice hollered as he drove like a bat out of hell, trying to get himself and his siblings to their eastside hideaway they called home.

"I threw that big hunting knife in the crowd and I know it knocked the hell out of somebody!" Erland chimed in.

"Hell, I took out at least three of those punk-ass Cannibals myself," Klein woofed.

Childress was quiet, too quiet. She stared blankly ahead into space. Klein waved his hand in front of his sister's face trying for a reaction.

"What's up, Childress? Who was that wench you were about to connect that right hook on?" Just then, Childress turned to her brother and began her explanation.

"You remember when we were little and we were playing at that empty house in the neighborhood? Well, that fat little black bitch that you screwed was there tonight. That's who that was!"

"No shit! Really! Did she know who you were?" Klein squealed in disbelief.

"At first, I don't think she did, but after I took off my mask, that tramp knew exactly who I was," Childress confirmed. "Seeing her actually made me laugh! All she ever did was whine and cry, and that's why I was always knocking her around."

"Oh yeah, that was my first taste of honey!" Klein blurted out. "She's somebody I could do again."

"Right now, I want to hit those Inner Circle fools and finish them off!" Erland said.

As the murderous thieves made their way home, they hadn't noticed the misty fog bank that they had been riding in since they had stolen the Jeep. Nacio had formed a moving curtain of fog that followed them all the way home. He hung over the vehicle and listened in on all of the treachery that was being plotted. This gave him the opportunity to determine what Childress was up to.

The brothers continued to plot their next hit to take over the rest of the eastside and shut down the Inner Circle Cannibals. Childress quickly retreated to her room. She pulled out her book of spells her mother had bequeathed to her. Her fingers followed along the lines of the very ancient parchment in the book. She read her family history, which was traced all the way back to Africa. The ancient literature went into specific detail about one extremely powerful voodoo priestess named Auldicia. She practiced black voodoo magic. Priestess Auldicia was very beguiling, often making men succumb to her lustful enchantments. After each intimate encounter with a man, whether the men participated willingly or not, Priestess Auldicia would curse the men and offer them as sacrifices.

Each sacrificial ceremony was done to keep her powers on earth.

Childress learned that her ancestor was damned by a lust demon that enslaved her soul for all eternity. Within the curse was a lust for human blood, making her a vampire. As long as Priestess Auldicia sacrificed victims, her reign would continue. Should she ever renege on her part of the evil contract, she would become the sacrifice and her existence would end.

The education Childress received at that moment was invaluable. After processing what she had just read, Childress noticed that deep within the pages of the book were two sealed little plastic bags with little red flakes in them. The flakes smelled like blood. On one bag, the word Priestess Auldicia was scrawled, and on the other, the word Frances. In an instant, Childress knew that within her hands, she held blood from both her ancestor and her mother. Her one desire at the moment was invincibility. She knew should she become the undead and hold reign as the Queen Mother, invincibility would be accomplished.

Strong wind gusted outside her window, blowing leaves and tree branches against the window, putting Childress on the defensive. She sensed she was being watched as she recalled the strange man whom Solis was with at the Tease. Remembering his catlike reflexes, his strength, and—yes—his fangs, Childress concluded he was a vampire. But who was he and where had he come from? She struggled with these questions as the sense of being watched continued to linger. Childress went over to look out her window. Once more, her eyes beamed the eerie green glow. As she stood looking out into the blowing wind, Childress became amused and bellowed out a wicked laugh. She hissed, "Make yourself known to me."

To her surprise, the only visible thing she saw was mist. Childress considered the sinister precipitation as some sort of magic. She sensed it was the vampire that she had encountered at the park. As the wind continued to blow, the mist disappeared. She retreated from her window just in time for Klein to holler that the news was on.

"Hey, ya'll come check this out! The Texas Taste Tease is on the news."

The newscaster described the highly anticipated Texas Taste Tease Fiesta event as a war zone...

"...The annual Texas Taste Tease started out with its usual festive fanfare, and then all went devastatingly wrong for the partygoers as gang violence erupted as shots rang out among the 85, 000 people in attendance leaving 75 people dead, and another 25 critically wounded. Several people have gone missing, their whereabouts unknown. There was a 1964 Chevy Impala at the scene of the crime, believed to have been one of the alleged suspects' vehicles. The vehicle has now been impounded as SAPD continues its investigation."

As the story continued, Justice noticed that his youngest sibling was weeping quietly in the dark.

"Are you crying over those punks we smoked?"

"I ain't crying," Erland squealed, sniffing and snotting as he used the back of his hand to wipe away his tear-streaked face. "I just miss my car that's all. Quit looking at me!" he shouted. "Take your eyes off me!"

Klein and Justice started in with the jeers as their brother's emotional equilibrium continued to teeter on the manic side. Normally, Erland would have cursed them out; but over the last few days, he had not adhered to the strict antidepressant and mood stabilizer cocktail he was prescribed, possibly putting the family in imminent danger. Erland's manic mood continued to escalate. Soon he was shouting at all of them, throwing air punches at the furniture. Childress soon became irritated.

"Erland! When's the last time you took your medicine?"

"I don't know," Erland shrugged his shoulders. "I guess before Mama passed away."

"Fool! You'd better go in there and eat you a few of those mood pills before you get yourself put in a body cast in here tonight because you are acting stupid!" Childress barked out her command. "You two other fools shut the hell up!"

Klein and Justice snickered one last time before they realized what it might cost them. They took their sister's advice, and each went to his room and slammed the door shut. It had truly been a wild night.

Nacio had done his reconnaissance by spying on Childress. He now knew what she was up to, and he had to decide how to handle the situation. Determining that the neophyte Queen Mother would soon find out who she is and where she came from, he knew he had to act fast. Nacio knew it wouldn't be long before Childress would be spiraling toward her destiny and continuing the reign of evil as her ancestor had done.

After all the years of emotional agony, Nacio was reminded of the loss of his family to the wicked ways of Priestess Auldicia. How his heart broke over and over for centuries longing for his family connection. It wasn't until he and Solis fell in love that his heart had mended and allowed him to love again. Now he will have to battle evil magic once more. Hopefully, he will be the victor and eradicate the bloodline that flowed through Childress and her siblings.

Without making eye contact with Childress, Nacio allowed himself to vanish away from the Treemount lair and return to his own fortress. He needed to be with Solis now, because he felt her sorrow for the loss of her dear friend, Affinity. Nacio also needed to touch base with Bose for a strategy to battle the Treemounts. It had been awhile since he had been in the midst of so much sorrow.

Through their telepathic connection, he felt just how empty and nonexistent she felt after the unexpected visit from death that had come to claim her friend. Revenge was starting to cultivate a deep trench through her heart. The current of hatred that flowed through her was strong enough to drown out everything else. Nacio realized he too felt himself swim in the same current of resentment for the Treemounts as she did. They had to be stopped.

As soon as he made it home, Nacio summoned Bose. He instructed his caretaker to call for a wrecker to have his car towed to the Puente Masonry where it could be retrieved. Again, no one visited the Puente Estate. Nacio began to update Bose on the happenings of the evening before.

"Priestess Auldicia's descendants have shown themselves. Many innocent people are dead, and they must be stopped. Solis's friend was killed by the one called Childress."

"I saw the news and had an awful sense that it was more than just the usual gang thugs warring over turf," Bose stated, shuffling though a very organized stack of paperwork. "I have gathered the information you asked for, Hefe," Bose said.

"What have you discovered, my friend?"

"Evil Black Voodoo was the source of Priestess Auldicia's power. Centuries ago, she was driven out of the nearby village by several families prior to capture into slavery. Priestess Auldicia had come between many couples that were married or ones that were betrothed to each other," Bose continued. "Her power of seduction was too strong for many in the village. She was intimate with several men, giving birth to several children and spreading her evil."

"Eventually, the women of the village, some being Solis's bloodline, drove Priestess Auldicia out of their midst, forcing her to raise her children in solitude. No man would marry Priestess Auldicia, mainly because none would survive after falling victim to her seduction.

While copulating with her, a man's body would automatically start to wither away his mind, making him zombie like. His body would then be prepared for the sacrifice to the lust demon, Vulklus," Bose explained. "It is written that she felt she had outsmarted the demon by continuing to deliver sacrifices, but the demon eventually wanted her body as payment rendered for her power on earth, ending her existence."

"The descendants of her bloodline have a strong origin in New Orleans and throughout the region between here and there. Many have scattered here in Texas due to Hurricane Katrina. Many are as vicious as their ancestor and continue life as convicted criminals and murderers. Should the descendants be destroyed, Priestess Auldicia would have no way of returning to this world. As long as her blood flows through others, her evil will continue on earth through them and through the practice of Evil Black Voodoo magic."

"Then destroy them, I shall!"

"Hefe, you will need forces of your own. This magic that was passed on for generations has not diminished, only strengthened," Bose reported. "If the evil contents of knowledge of Priestess Auldicia's power have fallen in the hands of one of the descendants, you will need magic forces of your own to defeat them."

"We will destroy them one by one! From the weakest to the strongest! We will start with the outer branches of the Treemount family tree and then annihilate them down to the roots," Nacio whispered.

"I have the location of all the family members that are still living," Bose said, handing the information to Nacio.

Nacio listened intently, but he also began to have an uncontrollable thirst. Bose noticed instantly.

"Hefe, you must feed! Go now! This will be waiting when you get back."

"I promised Solis that I would not hurt anyone and that we had not done so in many years; but so much has happened, and yet so much has to be done still," Nacio explained. "I love her, Bose. I will not be without her. I will not allow her to be harmed. I made that vow so long ago, and I intend to honor my vow! The Treemounts must be destroyed, starting tonight!" he said. "... from the outer branches to the roots."

"Then we must begin, Hefe!" Bose exclaimed. "Time is of the essence. This will be no easy task. There are many family members, and some might be as innocent as the many innocent lives claimed tonight. Not all of the extended Treemount family is evil. Some ran from their roots, due to experiencing the treachery that Childress has put upon them."

"As I said, I will start with what you have presented to me here, and go from there! I will return soon," Nacio stated as he vanished out the door. Once outside, Nacio began to walk faster and faster until his form evaporated into the warm humidity of the night. He began moving with the wind and was soon traveling across the sky. Thoughts of Solis filled his mind as revenge coursed through his veins. Soon Nacio was beginning his descent at the home of one of the Treemount family members. He transformed back into a human state. Excitement was fueling Nacio as he entertained thoughts of the actual hunt and the anticipation of a fresh feed. He hadn't done so in centuries, trying to make good on the vow that he only fed on humans if they were evil or a true threat to the innocent, as in the case of the Treemount clan.

Dukane Treemount was living in ransacked trailer hovel 20 miles outside of the city limits. The all-too-small trailer was decorated with empty beer cans and broken wine bottles. The beer cans and wine bottles also served as wind chimes if a breeze wandered through the yard. Cigarette butts tiled a path up to the front door. A skunk neighbored nearby as his scent lingered from just having visited the front porch of the home. Wood splinters sharply pointed up from a crumbled stair banister and sunken floorboard.

Calmly Nacio began to stalk his prey. He peered into the picture window of the trailer to find an inebriated Dukane mumbling to himself. Dukane was sprawled across a grime-slicked couch that sat in a sea of trash in the middle of the living room. Shadows from the television set danced across his face as he slipped in and out of consciousness. Dukane appeared to have weighed all of 475 pounds. A soft middle girth, which gave his chest the appearance of bosoms, shifted from side to side as he tossed and turned on the couch.

He grunted as he gave himself one heaved push to turn over on his side, revealing hips that could have been mistaken for a woman's in the dark. It was obvious now how the hole was made on the porch. Dukane was a cruel soul. He worked with elderly patients in a convalescent home and had several past complaints about his treatment of residents that have long since been forgotten by their loved ones. Dukane once stole a set of dentures from a resident to claim the gold that was formed in the moldings. Many residents were assessed with unexplained injuries and stolen personal effects. He was one of Frances Treemounts nephews, and he was rotten to the core. It wouldn't be long before he too would join the prison ranks like his vile first cousin. So it begins.

Nacio knocked on the door. A drunken and irritated Dukane cursed at the unannounced visitor knocking at the door.

"Who the hell is it?"

No answer. *Knock, Knock, Knock.*

"I said, who in the hell is it?"

No answer still. *Knock, Knock, Knock.*

Now attempting to hoist all 475 pounds in a heated rush, Dukane rolled off the couch, falling onto an open can of bean dip, cutting his leg, and releasing the smell of fresh plasma. Nacio, allowed his fangs to creep down from the hidden hoods inside his gums to their rightful place for feeding…anticipation.

After stumbling and finding his way to the door, Dukane swore once more as he flung the half-unhinged door open. He stepped out on the porch, careful not to go spiraling down into the hole that had gleaming cat eyes staring back at him.

"Dammit, who the hell is out here? I have a gun, and you better…," Dukane tried to finish, but Nacio shrouded him with his body in one single bound from the right, knocking Dukane off balance, and through the gaping hole below, imprisoning him as Nacio lunged for his right arm that was the shape and size of a king-sized pillow sham. He hungered no more.

Nacio's thirst was quenched, but there was no containing the wild and painful emotions he felt. Getting to Solis at this very moment was his only concern. Invisibly moving through the night air, Nacio made his way to the downtown Metro Hospital. Following his emotions and his strong connection to her made him able to find her exact location in the hospital. Remaining invisible, Nacio was able to climb up the south wall of the east wing to the sixth floor. Outside of the hospital window, he saw her slumbering comfortably. She was nestled under white blankets lying in the hospital bed. He telepathically opened the window to the room and reappeared in human form.

Longing to touch her, he eagerly rushed to her side and gently kissed her lips, her cheek, her nose, and her chin. In doing so, he imprinted the smell of her hair and skin in his mind. Gazing at her as she lay still and peaceful, he leaned in closely to inhale the air she was exhaling. She began to stir, and he continued to stroke her face. She slowly blinked her eyes. Her sight was hazy from the sedatives that she had been given. Solis pressed her face to Nacio's hand as he continued to touch her soothingly, reassuring her everything was alright, for now.

"Hi, baby," Nacio whispered. "I couldn't wait until the morning to see you. I just wanted to be near you. I'm here now, and I will be here when you open your eyes again in the morning."

"She's gone. Affinity is dead, and I just wished...," I tried to finish.

"Sssshhhh, sweetheart, don't worry about all that now. I'm here," he said. Just rest for now, and we will talk in the morning. I promise... okay?"

I nodded and soon found myself drifting back into an anesthetic-like dream state. I could feel his presence throughout the rest of the night. This was our first time spending time together so late; and look at the horrible circumstances that led us to being here. As I slept, I dreamt of all that had happened the night before...

...gunshots rang out, people running and screaming, blurry visions, smeared images, Childress staring at me with glowing green eyes and snakes nesting in her hair; her fingernails the length of actual rusty nails, Klein grinning evilly as he licked his tongue across his lips, Exotica losing her face, Affinity wearing the awful green boa Childress had draped around her neck, the green boa turning into a boa constrictor squeezing Affinity to death, Kennedy blowing bubbles and then drawing in her last breath with her face fixed in horror as she toppled forward with a machete knife sticking out of her back, Klein again licking his lips, lying on top of me and laughing, Childress laughing, Justice laughing, Erland laughing... the same sequence over and over; all night.

Sunshine greeted me in the early morning light as I lay in the hospital bed. I heard my name being called softly and tried to answer as best I could. The voice was a familiar one that demanded an answer.

"Solis, Solis, baby, wake up," Grandma Olvignia and Grandpa Leo stood at my bedside. Grandma softly patted my hand.

"Hi Grandma and Grandpa," I said, still groggy from the medicine wearing off. I looked in the corner and saw Nacio smiling at me. "Oh, what a beautiful world" was all I could think!

"Good morning."

"Hi," I said, returning the smile.

"How are you feeling, baby? The doctor said that you fainted yesterday, because your blood sugar was too low," Grandma continued. "You have to eat, Solis. You could have been a whole lot sicker."

Grandma held me in her arms and hugged me. I immediately began to weep softly.

"She's gone, Grandma—my friend is dead!" I sobbed. "They killed my friend!"

"I know, baby, I know! She is with the Lord now. He's going to take care of everything, sweetheart," Grandma said. Grandpa paced the small area with his arms folded across his back. This agitated behavior was a sign he wanted to wrap his lips around a cigarette to calm his nerves.

"You'll be getting out later today," Grandma said. "When you are ready, we will go and see Ms. Johnson. She wants to see you later; but for now, just rest, child."

"Yes, ma'am," I said, still looking at Nacio who was now approaching my bedside.

"I will see to it that she gets home Mistress."

"Thank you, friend," Grandma said. "That would be very helpful right now. We will see you when you get home, Solis. I want to stop and get some groceries for you, baby." She and Grandpa left. Nacio and I were alone once more.

"You were a bit listless last night as you fought for sleep."

"I dreamt of Childress and her hateful eyes," I said in a firm voice.

"I need to speak to my Grandma. She knows something that she is not telling me. I need to know these things now."

"Bose gave me lots of history on Priestess Auldicia and her bloodline to Childress," Nacio stated. "This is getting dangerous. I must ask that you stay out of it, Solis. I will handle the Treemounts myself. I have already begun to rid us of their evil."

"Nacio, if you know anything about me like you claim to, you would know there is no way I am staying out of this!" I shouted. "Several of my friends are dead at the hands of hateful trash. Childress was right...this is just the beginning!"

9

I was admonished by the doctor prior to being released from the hospital. Other than the few brief words from the doctor, the discharge went smoothly. Nacio had Bose pull the car around to the admission and discharge ramp at the hospital to drive me home. A long black 2009 Cadillac DTS stretch limousine sat curbside with Bose holding the door open. Nacio gently placed me in the car as if I were a frail piece of glass. He hadn't left my side since appearing in my hospital room in the wee hours of the morning. I don't believe anything could have made him leave me at that moment. The ride home was long. As I sat in silence, I realized I was gathering strength to face my deceased friend's mother. Nacio held me close as we rode.

"I have to talk to Grandma today, Nacio," I said, determined to get to the bottom of what's happened in the last twenty-four hours. "I want the Treemounts to pay for what they have done. They have to pay!"

"I agree that you need to talk to your grandma, but I do not agree with your being involved with anything having to do with going after them," Nacio explained. "You have no idea what you're up against."

"Then tell me what I am up against!" I said, irritated that I was being protected like a naïve adolescent.

"I'm not going to argue with you, Solis," he said. "Let's get you home, and we can figure this out." We rode home the rest of the way in silence. I know Nacio could feel the turbulent emotional storm that was raging within me. He would pull me closer to him as if to console me whenever my thoughts of Affinity would run through my mind. When he demonstrates his affection like this, I can't help but fall deeper and deeper in love with him.

When the long limousine pulled into the cul-de-sac, a feeling of relief washed over me signaling that I was now in my safety zone. Grandma and Grandpa were home. Nacio helped me out of the car and walked with me up to the porch. We made it to the front door and went in inside. Chase was standing at the door.

"Come on in, Lou Lou. Are you alright?"

"Yeah, I'm alright." I said. "I just want to lie down." Just then, Nacio kissed my forehead and hand.

"I want to come with you to see Affinity's mother," he said, looking at me lovingly.

"No, I'm okay. This is something I need to do on my own; thank you though," I said.

"Will I see you later?"

"Yes, you know you will after I leave her house; I will come by the mansion," I said, hating to leave him.

"Alright, I'll see you later," he said, planting a kiss on my lips. Nacio then turned, went back to the waiting limousine, and headed out of the cul-de-sac. Chase stood and asked if I was alright.

"Are you hurt, Lou Lou?"

"No, just tired. I'm going to my room."

"Alright, I won't bother you. I love you," my thirty-three-year-old uncle said. One thing's for sure, my uncle Chase got on my nerves, but he was also a sweetheart. I know deep down inside that he really cared about my safety. He knew how close Affinity and I had been and how upset I was at the moment. Chase left me alone for the rest of the day and was quiet as a mouse.

I lay across my bed wishing for a key that would turn my mind off. I wanted silence, and I wanted to be pain free. I knew those things were just not possible. There was no key to turn off my mind or undo the past. Friends are hard to come by. Things have always been that way for me. To lose the only friend I had was awful. Actually, I guess that was one thing in my life that I had on a regular basis: have people in my life die. Having to mourn the loss of one of the few people that are truly "Solis fans" seems to happen to me every few years. I will not blame God for this loss. Oh no, he is not the one to blame. The hellions responsible have taken someone's life so often that they wake up looking to do the same thing each day. I won't stand for loss anymore. I can't, because I am no longer the same weak person I was. I am going to bury Affinity, and I am going to start my life anew. That new beginning starts with the end of Childress Treemount.

"Come on in, baby," Vyanne Johnson said, looking like an older version of Affinity. The eyes that stared back at me like Affinity's were swollen and tender from the river of tears that flowed from them. Ms. Johnson usually had every hair on her head in place, but now it looked like broom straw, stiff and angling in all directions. It was late afternoon, and it appeared as if she had just gotten out of bed from what had been a sleepless night. Several somber family members lined the walls of Ms. Johnson's living room. All of the family members displayed that anxiety and distress that comes from losing a most-valued possession. Each stood, shaking their head, wringing their hands, pacing, crying, wailing, cursing, and asking God, "Why?"

"I wanted you to come by and pick out a dress for the wake tomorrow night," Ms. Johnson said, trying to keep herself composed as she spoke to me.

"Yes, ma'am," I said as she and I held each other for a moment. "I got here as soon as I could."

"I knew you could pick something out, because you two were so close, and I just wanted to make sure you were okay, and that I wasn't going to lose you too!" Ms. Johnson took one more breath before she exhaled the most heart-piercing cry I hope never to hear in my life as a parent. With that exhaling breath went Ms. Johnson's strength to stand upright, and she fell to the floor. She literally became a puddle of misery and sorrow. As I struggled to get her to the couch, Affinity's uncles, Cody and Jacque, came and helped Ms. Johnson to her room. I was trying to keep from following suit and falling to the floor to drown in tears.

"I'll pick the dress and take it to the funeral home," I told the two brothers.

"Thank you so much," Cody said, and he helped his brother take his sister to her room, where she continued to mourn in private.

I wiped hot tears from my face and quickly went down the hall to Affinity's room. I paused and drew in a deep breath, and then slowly opened the door. A huge poster-sized picture of Affinity and me at last year's Texas Taste Tease greeted me as I felt my knees buckle.

There were all kinds of pictures of us together. Many of the pictures of us were shot during our senior year in high school. One picture in particular was of Affinity in her famous "I'm approachable" pose for the camera. Look at her, my friend. She was funny and silly and could stop any guy right in his tracks—just to get an eyeful of her. Affinity's hair was a short, stacked bob style that was full of body and swung left to right as she turned her head. She stood 5 feet tall and was athletically built and shapely.

Her teeth were straight and shiny, and her smile often looked as if she knew something you didn't. That smile was what usually planted the seed in a guy's head that "you had better talk to her or else you might be left out." I was missing my friend terribly, and I knew that it would take a long while before I would be able to let go. One thing was for sure, I would never let go of the memory of my friend. She was the one that would always listen to what I had to say, and she never judged me. She kept secrets and made sure that we protected each other. I ran to her closet and found a beautiful purple dress that she loved to wear to church. That was her favorite color, and it was cheerful. I grabbed it and some under things for her and ran out of the room.

Ms. Johnson's crying had slowed down to just soft weeping now. Affinity's uncle Cody saw me in the hallway.

"They have her body at Laurence Funeral Home," he said as he began to walk me out the door. "I'm worried about Vyanne. She has a heart condition, you know, and I don't know how she is going to hold up for the service."

"I understand," I said, wiping my now-saturated face. "I will take the dress and things there. Don't worry about anything."

"Alright, baby, thank you so much. That sure will help out," he said, hugging me.

I left the house and got into my car. Before cranking up to drive off, I gripped the steering wheel and let out a primal scream. It was a scream that should have been high pitched enough to shatter glass. As I banged my fists on the steering wheel, I cried until I had no more tears to shed. I regained composure and drove home. I needed to talk to Grandma.

When I returned, my grandma was sitting in the living room with a beer sitting on the table. Her legs were crossed at her ankles, and her hands were folded in her lap. She had soft jazz playing in the background. She was ready to talk.

"I know what Nacio is," she said, reaching for her sweating, ice cold beer. "He looks good for his age, don't you think so?" Grandma was being a bit facetious.

"Come and sit down, child," she said. "There is much to be done, and I'm not sure how long it will take us to get it done, or for you to learn it."

"Learn what, Grandma?"

"Learn what you are truly dealing with here!" she shouted. "Affinity's death was no accident. Do you really think that you just happened to meet Nacio by chance? This was all destined to happen long ago, before you and before me. Nacio has been watching over you for years. He is your soul mate, and whether you are together for a long time or a short while, you are going to be with him."

"I'm scared, Grandma Olvignia," I said. "I don't know what to do."

"Yes, you do, you just don't know that you know. You come from a long line of women—women that had strength in their bodies and knowledge that runs through our blood that makes us capable to endure anything. I, too, am from the bloodline of ancestors that practiced magic. The magic that I was taught was not used for evil, but to fight against it. Our ancestors were slaves, as you know. We summoned magic to protect us under the hands of the slave master. The magic that we used and prayed for couldn't set us free from bondage until years later, yet we still endured, sacrificing for future generations.

"When Priestess Auldicia plagued our village, one of my grandmothers several generations back fought her off. Priestess Auldicia has sought revenge for my grandmother's defiance, and this still stands true today. You have often asked why the Treemounts hate you so much—well, there you have it. They were born to hate us and any other people that dared to defy them because of their ancestor's lust for vengeance."

"Grandma, this is so stupid," I said. "That happened several hundred years ago; why can't they just let it go? I never did anything to that psychotic Childress or her crazy brothers, and yet they still want to punish us?"

"A curse is a curse, child. It doesn't matter if it was spoken one day ago or one hundred years ago. It is still a binding tie that holds, no matter what. I was taught how to fight evil magic and win. You must learn to do the same if you want to have any type of a life. All that you need to know shall be given to you. You will start to develop your own foresight, and you must rely on it and trust it," Grandma explained.

"Do you know what was written long ago as well?" Grandma asked, sending her left eye brow up close to her hairline.

"What?" I asked.

"That you would be next in line to carry on the knowledge to protect our bloodline from the wicked curse that Priestess Auldicia placed on our family. You will know how to deal with the evil her descendants indulge in," Grandma whispered. "Long after I am gone, child, you will be the one who will take your rightful place as 'Mistress.' This term is used because we are not evil people. The term 'Priestess' refers to the evil black magic that Priestess Auldicia practiced."

I sat quietly now trying to take in everything Grandma Olvignia had just said to me. I then took a chance and asked her how Nacio was connected to our past.

"He was a young man that was a protector of his village. He was honorable and well respected within his community," Grandma explained. "Many women found him to be a suitable mate, but I guess at the time, he still had not found someone he loved. Priestess Auldicia soon let her lustful eyes fall on him, and she turned him into...a vampire."

My mouth dropped when Grandma said the "V" word out loud. She looked at me, and a sneaky grin splashed across her face.

"I'm Grandma," she said. "Surely you don't think I will have someone come in my house and not know who it is, do you?" she questioned. "I knew exactly who he was when you brought him here."

"But how is he my soul mate, Grandma?" I asked, hoping for him to be the one that would give me what I felt was absent from my life. For me, it meant no more searching and wishing for someone who wouldn't hurt me or for the most part, leave me. Grandma just smiled and beckoned for me to come and sit next to her.

"I know he is your soul mate because, although it has been a long time since your mother passed away, this was her wish too. She wished that you would stop using your body as a doormat with these men and believe in yourself, honey, because you are worthy of being happy. Never forget that," Grandma whispered as a tear slipped down her face.

She reached for a cup that had steam rising from the top of it.

"Tonight as you sleep, you will begin exploring your roots and your past. You will drink this root, I've mixed for you," Grandma said as she handed me the cup with the strange clear bubbling liquid in it.

"You are going to begin by learning to trust your foresight. You will do so by recalling your dreams in order and telling me about them tomorrow," Grandma said as she took a sip of her own toddy. "Dreams are hard to remember when we wake, but you will soon be able to see past your dreams and your thoughts. You will continue to do this every night until your mind trains itself to seek more knowledge from others."

"Grandma, I don't know…it sounds like...," I started and then was tongue-lashed by Grandma.

"Don't doubt it, child! Didn't I just say not to doubt it? When you live in doubt, Solis, you put yourself and others in danger—don't do it!" she exclaimed. "Now drink!"

I nearly knocked over the cup as Grandma roared her command, and I wolfed down the warm, bubbling clear liquid. I don't know what I expected, but I didn't feel any effects from the drink. I looked at Grandma puzzled.

"Was something supposed to happen?" I asked while Grandma continued to look and sip.

"You will soon feel your mind unlocking. Trust it," she said.

After I finished the tasteless drink, I stood up and took the cup back to the kitchen. I wanted to get back to being within reaching distance of Nacio as soon as possible. I gave Grandma a quick kiss.

"Thank you, Grandma, I love you."

"I love you too. Sometimes it brings tears to my eyes to look at you. You look so much like your mother," she said, and it put a little sunshine into my aching heart at the moment. Grandma knew what it was like to lose a child. She knew all too well.

There was a long line outside of Laurence Funeral Home that trailed all the way inside the building. They were all waiting to view Affinity's body. There were city officials that came to pay their respects to her family. Police officers and city council members all fell in line to view my friend. I guess the city felt responsible for the massacre at the Tease. Immediately, my family and I went to the front of the line and went in. Ms. Johnson and the rest of Affinity's family were inside, ready to go in the chapel and view her body. Ms. Johnson had her brothers flanked on either side of her as we slowly approached the chapel where Affinity was.

Bishop Dukes Doug of the Green Wreath Missionary Baptist Church would be officiating at the funeral service tomorrow. He was dressed in a white and blue plaid–patterned, three-quarter-length pantsuit. White square-toed patent leather shoes graced his pigeon-toed feet as his short bowed legs carried him up to Ms. Johnson. Two other ministers from the church followed closely behind him.

"Uh, Sister Vyanne, I believe we're ready," Bishop Doug said as he stood in his white shoes with his feet turned in making the shape of the letter "V." Ms. Johnson appeared heavily sedated for the wake this evening. I wished there was something that could quell the pain she needed to escape. Bishop Doug began to pray outside of the chapel and all of the Johnson family and visitors went in behind the bishop. There at the end of the isle was a paradise of flowers of every color that made the chapel look as if a small meadow had been placed inside this little room. My best friend lay in the middle of that flower meadow looking as if she were fast asleep. She was so beautiful.

Ms. Johnson began to wail as if she were being dismembered. She quickly reached down to touch her eldest child, kiss her face, and call her name. As she looked at her daughter, it was as if you could see pictures of their life together in the emotions on Ms. Johnson's face. She continued to touch Affinity's face as she sang the ABC Song and Happy Birthday to her daughter's peaceful face. As Ms. Johnson sang and spoke softly to her daughter, her baby, every man and every woman that had space to breathe in the chapel sat and wept along with Ms. Johnson.

"Mommy loves you, baby, Mommy loves you!" Ms. Johnson cried as her loyal brothers took her arms and led her out of the room. Onlookers continued to come in and pay their respects to my friend. There were so many. Old high school friends found their way over to me, bearing hugs and kisses along with condolences. As I pulled away from a hug, I noticed a veiled woman that had come in. She was dressed in black from her head to her toes. She oscillated around the room until she made her way up to the altar where Affinity lay. I watched her as she stood for a moment. No one else seemed to notice the woman as she visited with the deceased, but I found it strange that she hadn't shared condolences with the family.

I tried to move closer to the woman that now stood at the altar looking down at my friend. Another high school classmate caught me mid stride on my way to find out who the woman was. My way was blocked by Bline Caldwell, the quarterback during our senior year.

"Hey, Solis, how are you doing? Long time, no see," he said as his massive shoulders towered like columns over me.

"I'm doing okay, Bline how about you?" I said, craning my neck to look around the wall-sized man. The woman was now gone. No one seemed to have noticed her in the first place to even realize she was gone. As I walked back up to see Affinity, my eyes caught sight of something so vile and disrespectful that I wanted to curse out loud. There, lying across Affinity's chest, was a green boa feather... Childress had just left the building.

I turned around on the heels of my feet to scan the crowd for the uninvited intruder that had desecrated Affinity's memory. Her ill gesture of leaving the boa feather behind was an insult, a mockery. It was how Childress found humor in what she had done, and demonstrated the unyielding audacity she possessed to humiliate those around her.

I raced out of the funeral home chapel hoping to confront my longtime nemesis, but she was nowhere to be found. This was typical cowardice from a bully that had long taken up terrifying victims on a regular basis. I was overcome with rage. It trickled through my veins like hot needles, down my arm, and to my fists that were now curled.

I went back inside and noticed someone that looked vaguely familiar to me. I couldn't quite place her face; she seemed like someone I knew—but wait! I think she was one of the people that was at the Texas Taste Tease the day Affinity was killed. I didn't know her name, but I took this opportunity to meet her. She was a petite, brown-skinned female with a short haircut. I walked towards her and noticed that she was crying. Her face had some bruising, and some cuts that were healing.

"Hello, I'm Solis Burkes," I said. "Did you know my friend, Affinity Johnson?"

"Uh no, my name is Believa Beaushanks," she said. "I'm here to see my boyfriend's body—Katalo Nickelson. His funeral service is tomorrow."

"I'm sorry for your loss," I said. "Was he at the Texas Taste Tease also?"

"No, they found his body in a field behind his house," she said. "He looked like he had been attacked by a wild animal."

"Affinity was killed at the Tease," I said, still hoping to see Childress amongst the mourners that moved through the crowded funeral home. I was curious to see who Believa's deceased boyfriend was.

"Do you mind if I visit with Katalo?" I asked. "I want to see if I know who he was."

"No, you can go ahead. I need to leave anyway," She said as she left. "Nice meeting you."

"Nice meeting you too," I said as I began to go into the chapel that was opposite the one Affinity was in. There were no mourners in Katalo's chapel. I walked up to the bare altar. Evidently, Katalo was not held in as high a regard as Affinity. There were no flowers present, no bouquets, nor wreaths of condolence for his loss of life. I was instantly nauseated at what lay before me in the wooden crate-style casket.

The surviving Believa was correct. Katalo Nickelson looked as if an animal had gotten ahold of him. Vertical zigzag stitches for multiple facial incisions mapped his face. The stitching continued into his scalp, which was covered by a dry, twisted toupee that sat crooked over to the left side of his face. Katalo's eyebrows were drawn on his forehead. Both of the charcoaled eyebrows were smudged, making his face a frightful expression of terror. As I looked at the young man in the casket, I wondered what could have possibly taken his life so violently. Before I switched my train of thought, the answer was revealed so clearly. Beneath his jacket pocket lay another green boa feather.

The next day, the funeral service went on as planned. I spoke during the service and did fairly well. It was difficult to stand there at the podium and give the remarks on Affinity. This just wasn't something you were supposed to do at this stage in our lives. Ms. Johnson held up as well as could be expected. During the service, I looked all through the crowd for any sign of Childress and her rotten crew. I didn't see any of them, and the funeral concluded without any happenings. I could feel something was going to go down between Childress and myself. Grandma Olvignia was right. The change that would take place within me had begun. I could recall my dreams vividly. Relying on my natural instinct was becoming second nature. It wouldn't be long before other things would come true as she had said they would.

I was looking forward to seeing Nacio. Kissing him was something that I was looking forward to doing. We had become so close to each other. It felt good knowing that he was often just a thought away.

10

I returned home and slipped out of my clothes into some jeans and a T-shirt, and then quickly headed to Nacio's house. I picked up my phone and called him. He answered on the first ring.

"Hello, my love," he said happily as if he were smiling. "I can't wait to see you. I sent Bose to the store to prepare a special meal for you."

"I am starved, and I can't wait to see you either," I said. "What is Bose cooking for me?"

"It's a surprise," he said. "You are going to love it without a doubt."

"I'm on my way," I said, hanging up the phone.

I drove as quickly as I could without getting a speeding ticket. In no time, I was turning down Cedar Street into the long alleyway that would take me straight to my beloved's arms. I felt so exhilarated the closer I came to the front door. Once again, right before my eyes, appeared the beautiful waterfall. I felt like I was home.

I jumped out of the car and ran up to the front door. As soon as my feet hit the pavement, the door swung open, and there stood Nacio. He was shirtless with only white linen pants to cover his muscular legs. He was divinely gorgeous. His hair was draped across his back, covering his old scars. He extended his arms, and into them I went.

"I missed you so much," he said as he began to kiss my face.

"I hate being away from you," I said, catching every kiss he threw at me. I had never seen such an immaculate physique. This was the first time I had ever seen him half dressed. I will make sure to definitely recall this moment as a dream shot when I close my eyes to sleep tonight. A slight, downy trail of black hair led from his doorbell-shaped belly button below into his pants. I could only imagine what wonders lay beneath his waist.

"Bose has been busy cooking something for you all day. I do hope you are hungry," he said, smiling.

"Whatever it is, I promise to eat it...as long as it's cooked...and as long as it's not Brussels spouts...as long as it's not...," I tried to finish.

"I thought you said you were hungry," he laughed.

"No crawfish?" I questioned teasingly.

"No crawfish," he said, kissing my forehead once more. He took me by the hand and led me to a very hypnotic smell that wafted from the kitchen. It beckoned for me to surrender to it the closer I got to the kitchen. The kitchen was another beautifully crafted Olympic-sized room. Every appliance was digital, and the room looked more like a space center than a kitchen. There, in the middle of the kitchen, was a cooking bar that was bistro style. There was a counter to eat at with comfortable oversized barstools. I fell in love with this room as well. I would be lying if I said that I was not thinking about licking caramel and chocolate off of Nacio's firm pectoral muscles on top of this bistro counter. What's even more embarrassing was the fact that he was grinning at me right then, because he knew exactly what I wanted to do!

"Hey Bose!" I said, smiling at Nacio's loyal servant.

"Mistress," he said, reaching to hug me.

"What is that I smell?"

"I made you some shrimp Creole, jambalaya, beignets, sausage, and of course, homemade oatmeal and raisin cookies with lots of vanilla and raisins in them."

"Gracious! That's enough for a whole football team," I said. "I'm going do my best to eat as much as I can."

"Well, if you can't finish it, you can certainly take it home to your family," Bose said, all too proud of his culinary creations.

I looked over at Nacio, and he stared back approvingly. Bose began to fix and serve to me a well-balanced plate. For him and Nacio, there were two tall fluted Champagne glasses filled to the brim with what I knew could only be blood and plasma.

We all sat at the bistro counter while I ate quietly. The food was absolutely scrumptious.

"I take it since you are silent the food is appealing to you?" Bose said as he raised his left eyebrow in question.

"Yes indeed," I said, chasing after a grain of rice that disobediently tried to get away from my mouth by falling off my fork. "You are a true chef, Bose! Your dinner is sinfully delicious!"

"Thank you, Mistress," he said as he began to clean up the area with such speed. I had to blink twice. Bose had superhuman speed as well. He continued to tidy up the kitchen as I washed down the last bite of food with a delicious blackberry wine. Nacio's seductive eyes never left me. They were summoning for me to come over to them. I easily gave in. I knew he wanted to be alone with me.

I stepped down from the bistro and walked past Nacio, allowing my fingers to stroll over the arches of his shoulders. I then went towards the staircase. I walked up the stairs, admiring the portraits that hung on the wall. Most of all, I admired my favorite ceiling portrait of Jesus and the children.

Making it to the top of the grand staircase was a delight in itself. As soon as my foot hit the top of the last stair, Nacio was behind me. His cool hand was clearing my hair away from my shoulders. He kissed the nape of my bare neck. The tips of his fangs grazed my skin. He wanted to bite me, and I would not stop him if he had. He knew that and loosened his embrace and walked ahead of me. I couldn't help but continue after him as he entered the master bedroom.

The French patio door to the second floor of the bedroom was open leading to the manicured garden outside and below. Spring flowers of every color called this beautiful paradise home, and they were a feast for hungry eyes. My ears were once again serenaded by smooth jazz as Nacio lay on his bed. His eyes were summoning me to take my rightful place next to him. Once I walked over to the bed, I slowly crawled up next to him, assessing every inch of his tall frame. I soon forgot my inhibitions and began to caress and kiss him lovingly. After all that had been said and done, I needed to be close to him more than ever. Being with him helped me take my mind off Affinity's death. It felt so good to be near him. As we lay with each other, I wanted to know what he had been doing since I was released from the hospital.

"What did you find out about Childress?" I asked.

"They live not too far from here," Nacio explained. "Bose has discovered that Childress and her brothers have inherited the curse of evil that dwells within them from Priestess Auldicia. This is the energy that drives their evil nature," Nacio explained. "Childress grows stronger each day, and she soon will be as powerful as her deceased ancestor."

"Can't the curse be broken somehow?" I questioned.

"It's not that simple. You see, as long as any descendant of Priestess Auldicia remains alive, the curse perpetuates itself," he said. "The only way to stop it is to kill off all of the Treemounts. This means every drop of blood—every single drop of blood in existence."

"Can that be done?" I wondered.

"Yes, but it will not be a quick process," Nacio stated. "My love, I must tell you something."

"What is it? You are scaring me," I said, now sitting up and at attention.

"I made a vow to you long ago when you were a child that I would protect you at all costs, and I meant that. I also explained to you that I had not hurt anyone in several hundred years. Now that has changed. I have already begun to eradicate the Treemounts. As long as they know you exist, they are going to target you, Solis, and those around you that you love," he explained. "That is not acceptable, and I will not allow it."

"Wait, what do you mean?" I asked. "You've already begun to get rid of the Treemounts?"

"After the Tease, I started my work. Bose gave me the names and addresses of the extended family members. I have started on them first, mainly because they would be less likely to be missed," Nacio explained. "Those family members that are on the list to be erased are just as evil as Priestess Auldicia herself. This must be done, because I will not have you at the hands of those mongrels ever again! In the past, I would feed on those who were criminals; this is no different."

"I don't know what to say," I said, shocked. "You would kill for me to keep me safe?"

"Just say you're mine," he said. "Yes, I would do anything for you."

"How is Childress getting stronger?" I asked. "She still seems to be the same childish tramp she's always been."

"She's learned black voodoo magic, and her powers are growing each day. I don't want you involved in this in anyway, Solis, and I mean that," he said, stroking my face.

"Nacio, you can't expect me to sit and do nothing. I now understand what my grandmother was talking about. She's explained that I am to become the new 'Mistress,' and she wants me to be aware of all the knowledge that she possesses to fight the Treemounts," I said, stubborn and headstrong. "You see, I meant what I said as well. The Treemounts must pay!"

"Solis, I don't want you to put yourself in danger by trying to do anything to them," he said. "You can't even begin to imagine what they are capable of!"

"My friend is dead!" I shouted. "What could I possibly not understand about that? Childress is so disrespectful that she came to Affinity's wake and put a feather across Affinity's chest right in front of her mother and family. What kind of trash does something like that? The Treemounts are that kind of trash."

"I can see you have your mind made up," he said. "I guess there is nothing left to say on this matter."

"No, I guess not. Well, look—it's getting late. I'd better get home," I said. "Tell Bose thank you for the wonderful food for me, would you?" I was feeling edgy. Nacio always disagreed with me on how I wanted to handle the Treemounts. I guess this was another fight that we'd had. I hated fighting with him. I had just one more question for him before I left.

"I don't want you to get hurt either; so why is it okay for you to do what you did, and not for me?" Nacio took one look at me with his left eyebrow raised and let me know exactly why.

"Because, baby, I'm a vampire."

With that smart-ass statement, I left. He knew I was pissed. If I didn't know better, I would have thought he was picking a fight with me just to get me to leave. I wanted him to bite me; he wouldn't. I wanted to make love—he did too, but he wouldn't; and just a few moments ago, things were fine; then we fought. I drove home frustrated. He knew every emotion that went through me as I drove.

Nacio was alone once again. He hated having to initiate an

argument, but he had work to do tonight. He took one look at the list for the next Treemount that had to be annihilated. Nacio went to his patio doors and began to evaporate into night mist.

Montclair Treemount was a hermaphrodite. He had spent the majority of life identifying with the male gender, but during menstruation, natural estrogen spurts would allow him to visit with his femininity. Montclair was nowhere nearly as attractive as the rest of his Treemount clan.

All of his features were more pronounced than the rest of the family's. The bridge of his nose was long and turned up on the end. A recessed hairline made Montclair's forehead look as if it were breathing when you looked at him. Thin lips and huge teeth gave his smile the appearance of a crookedly carved jack-o-lantern. Knowing Montclair's secret would almost make someone pity him until you discovered that he was purposely sexually active with men and women and conveniently refusing to disclose that he was HIV positive. The one thing he had in common with the rest of his clan was the fact that he, too, was a deadly force to be reckoned with.

Several men and women that have crossed intimate paths with Montclair have discovered that they now are hosts for the deadly HIV virus. Many past partners of Montclair have already passed away from the lack of precaution taken during intimacy. Montclair continues his silence, and in doing so, he continues his killing spree throughout the community.

Nacio arrived at Montclair's condominium. Still in mist form, Nacio traveled down through the air-conditioning duct. Montclair had just arrived home. He was standing in the bathroom looking at his body from head to toe, admiring what his mother called a "double blessing," because he could make a man and a woman extremely happy with his genitalia. He began to sing as he turned on the shower water. The water is piping hot, and the bathroom soon began to steam up, including the mirror. Nacio began to feel that sensation again, anticipation. The thrill of the hunt steadied him as he stalked his victim.

Montclair showered quickly, as the water had become uncomfortably hot. He stepped out of the shower, and visibility is zero in the bathroom. Montclair reached for a towel to dry off and noticed how extremely cold the air had become in the bathroom.

"Why is it so damned cold in here all of a sudden?"

Instantly, Nacio enveloped Montclair in a misty cloud, making it difficult for him to breathe. He is finding more and more pleasure in fulfilling the need to feed. The urgency was driving Nacio to continue his hunt. This was the second of the Treemounts to be exterminated as the pests they are. He had to work quickly, just as he did in the old days when it came to getting rid of any trace of the victims. Nacio meticulously completed his tasks, making it look as if Montclair had simply vanished without a trace.

Nacio prepared himself for his next target. He shape-shifted once more into the deadly mist that lingered through the night air—on to the next unsuspecting Treemount victim.

Judd Treemount has always been a domestic-violence perpetrator against women. He served time for aggravated assault of a female victim who happened to be his girlfriend at the time. He held her hostage after the near-deadly beating, refusing to allow her to seek medical care. In doing so, she acquired an infection in her broken bone in her shoulder. The infection spread to her back. By the time she was able to get medical attention, she was stooped over in the form of a hunchback. She was never the same again.

Judd Treemount was a bouncer at one of the strip clubs on the northeast side of the city. He stood 6 feet 6 inches tall and looked every bit like a lineman on a football roster. Bulging muscles and an extremely thick, cylinder-shaped neck indicated possible steroid use. Veins lined his forearms like rivers branching off into the ocean. Muscles rippled on his back underneath his youth-sized shirt, making his appearance more threatening.

It was the change of shift, and he had propositioned one of the dancers earlier in the evening. He had long suffered with erectile dysfunction, which could have contributed to his insecurities and the maltreatment of females. Once a female discovered his "little secret," Judd's temper would become explosive, unleashing his rage on any female that discovered his insecurity.

Leaving the club through the back exit, Judd waited anxiously for Isadora, the lead exotic dancer and headliner at Club Taboo. Isadora had just left the stage and was coming out of the club and saw Judd standing there. Isadora approached Judd who was standing with his back against the wall, licking his pasty lips. Isadora was a large-framed, medium-brown-skinned woman. She stood 5 feet 8 inches tall and was athletically built with bob-style curly brown hair. To Judd, she looked like a bronze goddess.

"What's up, Judd?" she said as she rested her weight on her left leg. "You got what I need."

Isadora had developed a crush on Judd, completely unaware of the danger that awaited any unsuspecting female that found him attractive.

"Yeah, I got what you've come for," he said, leaning in to kiss her. Touching her emotionally aroused him, but he was unable to achieve any physical response from his manhood. He grabbed her hands and placed them on him for assistance, but still to no avail was there any response from his body. Instead of pleasure, anger followed, and Judd became explosive.

"Touch me, tramp!" he shouted. "You know you want it!"

Isadora stepped back to retreat from him, but Judd grabbed her right arm and twisted it up between her shoulder blades, dislocating and fracturing the beautiful woman's arm.

"Help me! Somebody—help me, please!" Isadora cried, lying on the ground in back of the filthy club amongst glass and trash.

Judd soon took off and left the nearly unconscious woman in her agony. He went to his car and opened the door. He started the ignition and left the parking lot, cursing under his breath. Judd kept looking in his rearview mirror as he drove, watching the lights of Club Taboo fade to black in the night. He lit a cigarette and drew in a long puff. He then nervously checked his rearview mirror once more. This time, he almost swallowed the entire cigarette as Nacio spoke to him from the passenger's seat.

"So, you like to punch women in the face for fun, huh?"

Judd slammed on the brakes, and the Charger he was driving made a black screech line in the road. He jumped out of the car, leaving the engine running and door wide open.

"Where the hell did you come from, bastard!" Judd hollered as he stumbled backward nearly falling in a pothole.

Nacio was nowhere in sight, and Judd stood there out of breath and terrified. He looked around his perimeter and could not find the voice that had spoken to him. There one foot behind him, Nacio questioned him again.

"You …still ...have...not ...answered…my ...question," Nacio enunciated his words as his fangs lowered and revealed themselves to a now weeping Judd. "Do you like punching women for fun?"

"Screw you, man! You are about to get your ass beat!" Judd said as he lunged at Nacio. Judd threw and connected a right hook that was aimed at Nacio's face but was interrupted by the palm of Nacio's hand. Judd's fist slammed into the palm of Nacio's hand, causing his knuckles and fingers to crack and crumble like crushed ice. Judd howled in misery. Nacio returned force.

"Tell me how it feels to have your teeth removed by an unlicensed dentist," Nacio said as he swung a punch at Judd that could have been fatal. Instead of killing him, Nacio struck Judd in the face. The blow sounded like a baseball bat to a ball as the sound of shattering tooth enamel echoed off buildings standing in the distance. Judd hit the ground, continuing his weeping and cursing at Nacio.

"You just wait 'til I get up!" Judd mumbled.

Nacio picked him up and gave him a kick in the butt like a football, and Judd came crashing down on his tailbone fifty feet away. This time, Nacio could smell the fresh plasma as it oozed from Judd's mouth. Judd continued to wail as he rolled over on his side and began to crawl back to his car.

It took a while, but once he made it back to his car, he instantly flooded his mind with false hope of being safe. In excruciating pain, Judd put the car in drive and began up the road and onto the freeway ramp. He had gotten the car up to cruising speed, and then looked over and saw a materializing Nacio sitting in the passenger's seat. Nacio lunged for Judd's neck as Judd slammed his foot on the accelerator, losing control of the steering wheel, sending the car over the freeway overpass into a 250-foot drop and into a ditch below. On impact, the car exploded with orange flames shooting into the night air.

Nacio stood 200 yards away and watched the blaze as Judd Treemount was burned beyond recognition, leaving no evidence. The Treemounts were beginning to vanish without a trace. Soon, none of them would remain, leaving the world to be at peace and of goodwill to all men. Or so he hoped.

When he arrived home, Bose was in the study still diligently working on his assignment and finding the locations of all the Treemounts.

"Hefe, you look all too refreshed. Have you continued your task?" Bose asked with his eyes looking like Sapphire stones.

"I have, my friend. I believe I will need some assistance from you as we get closer and closer to Childress. Her extended family will soon be alerted to the disappearances of those family members, and they will begin to take precautions," Nacio said.

"As you wish, Hefe," Bose said. "Eventually, we will need our own clan. I have contacted Armando Caraway. He explained that he will be available as needed."

"Ah yes, my compadre, Armando," Nacio said. "It has been too long since we last visited with each other. Please let him know that our home is open and to bring his family when the time comes. He will be able to assist us in the thoroughness of the mission and to make certain of any alternatives that need to be considered while dealing with the descendants of Priestess Auldicia."

"Yes, Hefe," Bose said obediently. "It will be nice to have visitors within the walls of this house. I did so wish for you to have a family so that all of the space here would not go to waste."

"You sound like Mama, Bose," Nacio said as he stood recalling the sound of his mother's voice. "That was literally a lifetime ago, Bose. Those thoughts of my previous life do sadden me at times."

"Perhaps those dreams of you having a family could come true?" Bose said with both eyebrows hiked up on his forehead.

"How could this be possible?" Nacio inquired.

"According to what you have told me, Solis has the bloodline of the Mistress; therefore, giving her the capability to bring forth the things her heart desires most," Bose said. This gives you the possibility for the things you both wish for the most. Having children could be a possibility for the two of you. If she loves you half as much as you love her, this is more than a possibility, Hefe."

Nacio smiled as he withdrew to his room. The thought of consummating his relationship with Solis intoxicated him with arousal. He reached for his phone and dialed her number. A sleepy Solis answered on the first ring.

"Hello?" she whispered.

"My love… please forgive me for our quarrel."

"It's been forgotten, honey—I miss you," she said. "I'll be over first thing in the morning."

"I'll be waiting."

11

Childress turned over and slapped the alarm clock on the floor as it blared loudly. She had been home for a while now and had not made any effort whatsoever to report to her parole officer, Mr. Parker Shemsham. The Texas Parole Board was all too familiar with the Treemounts. Rather than having several parole officers visiting the four criminal siblings, they were assigned to the same officer. She figured she would get a visit any day now from Mr. Shemsham and possibly a constable to arrest her for not reporting sooner.

Reaching for her robe and house slippers, Childress rolled out of bed and walked past the mirror. She noticed that her hair had grown at least an inch in the last week. The black streaks that nested in her honey-wheat-colored hair looked like shiny water moccasin snakes slithering about her scalp. But she didn't give a damn, because in her mind, she was a goddess.

She went and washed up, and then joined her three stooge siblings in the kitchen. It was a usual morning episode in the Treemount home. Klein had poured himself a huge mixing bowl of cereal; Justice had burned a pot of grits, creating a cloud of smoke in the air; and Erland was sitting in the corner as if he had been punished and was in time-out. His eyes were red, which led Childress to believe that one of the others had been teasing him and made him cry. Erland had probably been high the night before, making his central nervous system and emotional control sensitive to ridicule.

"Now what's wrong with you?" Childress said, already irritated with the smell from the burned grits and stupid smirk on Klein's face. "Every morning, there is always some shit happening in this kitchen! Stop acting crazy and throw that damned pot out of here!"

"Aw man, here she comes always telling other people what to do!" Justice shouted, as he had what looked to be a cat's paw dangling from the end of a golden key chain. "Look at my lucky charm, Childress!" Justice said, holding the shriveled animal foot up in front of her. "You want one?"

"Did you kill one of those cats and cut off its foot?" Childress inquired with disgust. "You are going to have all kinds of disease in this house, and the day that happens, you will be sleeping outside. You'd better quit killing those cats, Justice. You hear me?"

"Shut up, Childress—you're always talking trash!" Justice said as he turned to walk down the hall. Before he could reach his room, Childress took a plate and Frisbeed it across the kitchen to hit Justice directly in the center of his head. Justice screeched in pain as he grabbed his head. His eyes turned fire red as he turned to face his eldest sibling with fury.

"What else you got to say, hmm?" Childress said as she licked her lips, parting a greedy grin on her face.

Silence overtook Justice as he ran back into the kitchen and grabbed a perforated freezer knife and pulled it on Childress. Justice was fed up, and now he wanted to take a stab at his sister regardless of the consequences.

"Come on, tramp! Come get me! Come on!" Justice egged at Childress, knowing what was to come was going to be far worse than the flying plate to the back of the head. Since Justice had scorched the pot of grits, he was making another successful attempt at breakfast by putting more boiling water on the stove. Childress reached for the pot handle and sent scalding water sailing across the kitchen towards Justice. He ducked his painful fate by inches as he dropped to the floor to take cover.

Just then, a car door was heard slamming shut, and then foot steps were heard on the raggedy front porch. Someone had come to the Treemount home. The broken doorbell rang off key.

"Bling-dong, bling-dong, bling-dong."

"I can just bet who the hell that is, just in time to save your ass from stitches!" Childress said. "Get the damn door, fool!"

"Shut up, girl!" Justice said as he continued to rub the now-bleeding part of his head that had a lump rapidly swelling under his scalp.

Justice hesitantly opened the door to find Parole Officer Parker Shemsham whom Childress had suspected would visit. Mr. Shemsham was dressed in green slacks that were too short in length, giving them the appearance of male-style Capri pants. His pants were pulled high and choked off at the waist with an elastic belt.

Mr. Shemsham was draped in a red-and-green sport coat with sleeves that were cheated two inches in length. A brown derby sat on top of his head, broken down low over his left eye demonstrating the style called the East Coast Breakdown. Yes, Shemsham was a joke. He stood no taller than a light switch on a wall but had a big mouth and an even bigger ego. He walked right into the Treemount lions' den.

"Good morning to you all!" Mr. Shemsham said, nervously shifting his weight from leg to leg as a well-gnawed toothpick hung carelessly from the corner of his mouth. The criminal siblings all froze as their assigned parole officer perused their home, slyly assessing for any contraband. Justice still held the knife that he was going to fricassee Childress with in his hands. All of the Treemounts stood dumbfounded as Mr. Shemsham continued.

"Well, well, well, what have we here?" he said, reaching for the freezer knife Justice held. "Were you going to slice some freezer meat—or slice your sister to put her in the freezer?"

"Uh, no sir!" Justice said. "I was showing Childress how to use this particular knife for cutting brisket. We wanted to barbeque this weekend, right Childress?"

"Brisket and sausage," Childress chimed in, rolling her eyes and making faces as she turned to go and sit on the couch.

"Either way, looks like I'm just in time to save you from each other," Shemsham said.

"We don't need saving; we need to be left alone from the likes of you," Childress hissed as her shoulders tensed up while she sat still on the couch.

"What was that, Ms. Treemount? I couldn't hear you. What did you say?" Shemsham repeated as the toothpick rolled back and forth from corner to corner in his mouth. "Let's see, uh, you should have reported to me when you first got out, yet this is the first time I've seen that lovely mug of yours since you've been a free woman."

"Look, man, my mama died, and I had to do what I had to do! So don't come in here talking about why I haven't reported!" Childress snapped. Shemsham quickly retreated and extended his condolences to the siblings.

"Oh, please forgive me, Ms. Treemount. On behalf of The Texas Department of Criminal Justice, please accept my heartfelt condolences," Shemsham said. "You still could have called in, Childress."

"Yeah, whatever," Childress sarcastically replied.

"Mr. Klein, Mr. Justice, and Mr. Erland, your last report visit was three months ago when I came here. The problem is, you boys were supposed to do some office visits and give urine samples for drug testing, and you haven't. Any of you want to explain that?" Shemsham asked.

Erland and his catatonic self finally rejoined the conscious folks in the room and gave his spin on the question asked.

"We all had the Vivian bird flu, and it twisted our backs and we couldn't walk, and that's what happened," Erland said with his nose still running from his emotional crying spell earlier. Shemsham twisted his face in confusion.

"You mean the Avian flu, Erland?" Shemsham asked. "Or were you talking about scoliosis?"

"Bird flu," Erland said.

"Well now, let's see, that would mean that you all would have been hospitalized if it were that severe, possibly quarantined. You'll have to come up with one better than that."

The television was on, and the regularly scheduled program cut away and was interrupted by breaking news.

"...Channel 12 breaking news, Vanaya Austin reporting. A car was discovered a few moments ago here in the ditch behind me. It appears that the car jumped the guardrail and dropped 250 feet into the ditch below. It is speculation that the car burst into flames, burning the driver inside. The County Coroner's office is on the scene. It is too soon to have the body identified. More details at 5 o'clock..."

Childress looked at the news report and didn't think anything of it. She then turned back and looked at Shemsham and was so wishing that he would leave on his own without her having to hex him.

"Mr. Shemsham, I think we're done here today. We'll report—just leave."

"I have a couple more questions," Shemsham interjected. "You all know anything about what happened at the Texas Taste Tease the other week? The local police seem to think it was just random gang violence, but I feel there is much more to the story than that."

"Naw, we don't know anything about that," Childress lied. "In fact, we were spending time in the country at our cousin Dukane's house."

"Really?" Shemsham asked. "Was that before or after he went missing?"

"Missing?" All the Treemounts chimed in.

"What are you talking about—Dukane is missing?" Klein asked as his mouth hung open.

"Yes, that is what I said—missing. It seems cousin Dukane has not been seen by his lot owner for quite some time, and he is behind in his rent. The lot owner wants to press charges on him, but when he went to check his trailer, there was blood on his front porch. The lot owner said that it wasn't like Dukane not to be at home. He knew that was one thing that big booger did was come home to eat. When he saw the blood, he called the police. So I ask again, were you with him before or after he went missing?"

"We saw him before the Texas Taste Tease, and then we left town and rode through New Orleans," Justice said, lying through his teeth with every breath he took as he stood before Shemsham.

"Oh yeah? Well, where's the car you took? I don't see Erland's classic sitting in the driveway," Shemsham said. "I like Beetle's though—when did you get that one in the driveway?"

Knowing that they never retrieved Erland's car after the massacre at the Tease, the Treemounts had to make up a well-fabricated alibi. Not knowing how long they could keep up the lie, Erland created a self-induced panic attack by sneezing several times in a row. That was his queue to Childress to redirect the conversation. Justice joined the mayhem by running over to his youngest sibling as Erland continued to dramatize his psychosomatic symptoms.

"Erland—man, you alright?" Justice said as Erland went into a convulsive state. Childress jumped off the couch and ran into the kitchen to retrieve a spoon for her brother's tongue, and also to escalate the situation with Shemsham.

"Hold him down, and be careful with him," Childress shouted. "Mr. Shemsham, he's having a seizure. He'll be alright, and I promise we'll report next month. Right now, I have to attend to my brother, bye!" Childress took Shemsham's arm and escorted the height-challenged man out the door, and then slammed the door in his face.

All too happy and relieved for Shemsham to have left their presence, the Treemounts began to digest what they had just learned. Klein had begun to pace like a restless tiger.

"When the hell did Dukane come up missing?" Klein asked. "Nobody called us and said anything. I wonder if those Inner Circle Cannibal punks took him out."

"If they did, I'm ready for some retaliation!" Justice said as he stroked the shriveled cat's foot. "Childress, did anyone from Mama's side of the family call you?"

"You know damn well this phone hasn't rung. You also know they don't call us. We find stuff out just how we did today—screw 'em."

Erland stood up, proud of himself for his over dramatization of a seizure and getting rid of Shemsham. He mopped up the puddle of water Childress had thrown and put in his two cents.

"I think I'm in to hit those fools too," Erland said.

Childress was eerily quiet. Deep in thought, she sat still as her brothers carried on about their strategy against their rival gangs. Childress couldn't quite seem to pinpoint the strange disappearance of her rotund cousin Dukane. He didn't get around much. Work, the grocery store, and the liquor store were his only destinations. So where was he?

"Childress, did you hear me?" Klein said, raising his voice to get his sister's attention. "What are you thinking about?

"I'm trying to figure out if that bitch Solis had anything to do with Dukane being missing."

"How the hell does Solis have anything to do with Dukane?" Klein inquired. "Did she used to mess with him?"

"I don't know who the hell Dukane sleeps with, and I don't care!" Childress shouted, sending her brother into a corner in retreat. "What I do know is the fact that Solis was with a very nice-looking man. That man just happens to be a vampire!"

"What? A vampire?" Justice questioned. "Girl, those black streaks in your hair have rooted in your brain, and your mind is jumbled up."

"A vampire—or did you say 'umpire'? Childress, where did you get that from?" Erland added his spin to the confusion. "I thought umpires played baseball."

"Erland, you need to leave that dope alone, fool," Childress hissed. "You are really dumb! In fact, say something else stupid…I promise you will go to bed and not wake up until tomorrow!"

"Seriously, Childress, you think that dude is a vampire?" Klein continued. "I thought vampires couldn't come out in the daytime?"

"Well, this one can, and I want him!" Childress smiled slyly. "If he and I could be together, we could rule the family as immortal beings, and our family generations would continue."

"How so?" Klein asked. "How are you going to get close to him?"

"I can do whatever I want!" Childress interjected. "I went to Solis's friend's funeral—surely, I can get him to give in to me once he sees all this," Childress hissed as she rubbed her hands over her hips.

"So what are you saying?" Justice asked. "You think that dude snatched Dukane? If he did, he had a lot of snatching to do, because cousin Dukane was more than a handful to deal with. Another thing, they haven't found his body yet."

"Yeah, Childress, we have to be sure before we make any waves," Klein said. Just then, the doorbell rang again. Erland jumped up and looked out the blinds and saw that it was one of his homies from their gang who was known on the streets as Got To Do. This gangster was named because of his motto. Before he pulled the trigger on his victims, he would tell them just before they died, "I got to do this." Those were the last words any victim would hear before they met their violent end.

Erland opened the door, and his gang buddy walked in. He had on pants that were five times bigger than he was. The pants swept the ground every step he took, showing off the streaked seat of his white boxer underwear. Got To Do was wearing shaggy-looking, three-month old cornrows and a full platinum grill in his mouth.

"What's up, man?" Got To Do said as he extended his arm for a fist bump with Erland. "You got some stuff for me?"

"Yeah, man, hold on," Erland said as he slipped down the hallway to his room and retrieved a brown paper bag, which the rest of the Treemounts could only assume was either a weapon or illegal substances. Money quickly exchanged hands, and then it was back to conversation as usual.

"We're going to hit those fools from Inner Circle Cannibals tomorrow—so be there, man," Justice said, stroking his hand across his chin.

"I'll be there, man. Alright, I'm out. I'll holler at ya'll later," Got To Do said.

"Alright, man," Klein said as the rest of the Treemounts waved to their leaving visitor. All eyes turned back to Childress, awaiting instructions on the brewing situation at hand.

"What's up with this girl, Solis? You never could stand her," Justice said.

"I just can't stand her," Childress said. "She and her family always thought they were better than everyone else. I just want to get rid of her now that I know she's still around and anyway…"

"Hush up a minute! Listen to this report," Justice said as he turned up the volume on the television for another breaking story.

...this just in...The Vallejo Gardens Condominiums property manager called police when an odor was discovered coming from inside of the condo. Neighbors notified the property manager of their concerns and said that they hadn't seen their neighbor in a while. When police arrived, there were bloodstains leading to outside the door, and some were left trailing from the bathroom, but the resident wasn't found...the Property Manager has not released the name of the resident until next of kin can be notified.

...Police are baffled as to what started the massacre at the Texas Taste Tease during Fiesta week. ...Witnesses say that it was gang related, but as yet, no arrests have been made...

...Several churches throughout the city have had their parishes robbed of petty cash and the monuments outside on the church grounds destroyed... many of the monuments were sprayed with graffiti, leading the gang task force to investigate...more details at 5 o'clock...

"Montclair lives in Vallejo Gardens, right?" Justice said. "Klein, call Aunt Bibi and see if she's talked to Montclair."

"Hell naw, I ain't calling Aunt Bibianna," Klein said. "She is crazy as hell, and her eyes are cockeyed. When you're talking to her, you don't know which eye to stand in front of to know if she is looking at you or not. You call her!"

"Give me the phone, fool!" Justice shouted as he snatched the handset from its base. Justice carefully dialed his aunt's phone number. When she answered the phone, his suspicions were confirmed. Aunt Bibianna was wailing and screeching in the phone that she didn't know where Montclair was and that she was afraid for her.

"I know she owed some people some money—oh goodness, I hope they haven't taken my daughter," Bibianna cried. She had always considered Montclair to be a female, even though Montclair had cut all of his hair off and wore men's clothing. She remained in denial about Montclair's choice of gender and his lifestyle. Aunt Bibianna was never too emotionally stable. Now that Montclair was missing, it was devastating. This will be the thing that will send her over the edge and into a nervous breakdown.

"Montclair was such a pretty girl, and she's my baby! I hope my baby's okay!" Bibianna continued. Justice couldn't take any more, because although he was concerned for his cousin, he also wanted to laugh at how stupid his Aunt Bibi sounded on the phone.

"Here, Childress, you talk to her!" Justice whispered as he covered the phone and Aunt Bibianna continued. Justice started to giggle. He passed the phone to Childress.

"Aunt Bibi, this is Childress. When did you last see Montclair and what did he… I mean, what did **she** say?" Childress said covering up her verbal slip.

"She said that she was going to work and that she would call me once she got home. I haven't heard from her since then. That was a month ago." Aunt Bibi said, obviously disoriented.

"Aunt Bibi, you haven't heard from him in a month?" Childress asked.

"Who the hell is 'him'?" Aunt Bibi interjected. "I'm talking 'bout my daughter—I don't know who you're talking about." Aunt Bibi started humming and then started singing.

"Wade in the waterrrr, Wade in the waterrrr, children!" Childress became irritated and took her frustrations out on her aunt.

"Aunt Bibi, you are dumb as hell!" Childress shouted as she slammed the phone down as hard as she could. *Blam*!!!

12

With the events being revealed through the media, the mood in the Treemount home became tense as they became more apprehensive. Anxiety set in on Justice, and he began to bite his already gnawed-to-nub fingernails. Erland began to coast into catatonia again, and Klein cursed. Childress rocked back and forth to calm herself.

"We need to find out what's going on—and then make a move," Klein said. "We need to go and get the car out of the pound."

"Yeah, Childress, we need to make a move, and I want my car back!" Erland rejoined the conversation.

"Look my nerves are bad! Ya'll are going to have to shut up so I can think!" Childress barked as she started rubbing her forehead. She quickly formulated a plan to keep her goony siblings busy for the next couple of hours. She needed some "Childress time" to get her thoughts together for the next strike against her sworn enemy.

"Alright, this is what you need to go do," Childress said, glaring at her brothers. "Take this sniveling fool to get his car, please, before I have to hurt him," she said, pointing at Erland. "I want you all to find out where Solis lives. Meet me back here tonight. We'll go out to Santa Ana's I need myself a drink—too much is going on right now, and I just want to go out and chill."

"We're going to go look for those Inner Circle Cannibal punks and cut them down," Erland said. "Then we're going to lay low for a while until everything blows over."

"Yeah, we are going to take over the whole eastside and the northeast side of town," Justice said.

Klein was about to give his take on the situation at hand when his cell phone rang. From the irritated tone he took with the caller, the siblings were led to believe that it was one of his latest female admirers. He must have promised her something, and then didn't follow through with it.

"Look tramp, I said I'd be through there tonight, don't aggravate me!" Klein hollered in the phone. "I don't give a damn if he doesn't have diapers—hell tie a rag on his little ass and set him down on the couch for all I care!" Klein argued. "If you keep calling me, I'm going to come over there and knock you in your…Hello! Hello!"

Childress, Justice, and Erland all burst out in laughter at their brother's soap opera personal life. They had no idea how many nieces or nephews that they were aunt and uncles to due to Klein's carelessness during intimacy.

After being given their instructions, the Brothers Treemount began to mobilize. Each of them had concern about what was going to happen next. It was obvious that someone was out to get even with them. It was their obligation to each other to find out who was out to get them, turn the tables on them, and strike first.

"What are you going to do for the rest of the day, Childress?" Klein said, prying and fishing for answers.

"What did I just say? Stay out of my business. Don't you have some woman to go and impregnate? Or a child that needs to be named? Leave me the hell alone!" Childress shouted.

"You must be getting your mentalstration right now, because you are grouchy!" Klein mumbled as he retreated down the hall.

"You are so basic, you can't even say it. It's pronounced

'menstruation,' fool!" she growled. "Now leave, dammit!"

"Hey, Childress, give me the keys to the Beetle," Justice said as he stood patiently waiting for his sister to hand him the keys.

"Are you high?" Childress inquired. "You must be if you think you're driving my car and leaving me here."

"Well hell, we stole it!" Justice fired back. "How are we going to get the Chevy back then?"

"Sshh, sshh! You hear that?" Childress whispered. "You just missed the bus. Oh well, guess you better wait 'til the next one comes. You have exactly ten minutes until the next one pulls off from the curb."

Rather than take a chance and argue with Childress and lose, the brothers decided it was in their best interest to take a stroll to the corner for the bus. Once she was alone, Childress decided to take a hot bath. Before she could start running the bathwater, the doorbell rang again. She cursed under her breath, thinking it was her three goons coming back from missing the bus again. She opened the door, and there stood a very tall and muscular police detective. He had come to the Treemount home in an unmarked vehicle, possibly just missing her brothers by mere seconds.

"Hello, ma'am, are you Childress Roarquel Treemount?" the delicious detective asked.

"Who the hell wants to know, cher?" Childress shifted her hips from side to side, swooning to the attention she was now receiving from the detective.

"I'm Detective Mathis Bouvier. I need to ask you a few questions about your missing cousin Dukane Treemount. May I come in?"

"Sure, cher. Come on in and make this your home," Childress whispered as she found herself attracted to the masculine man. She realized that it had been awhile since she had been in the presence of a man that she was truly physically interested in. This hunky beefcake that stood before her made her lick her lips with desire. He stood in her living room in a white long-sleeved, athletic cut, button-down shirt with a black tie. He wore tight black jeans and black lizard roper boots. Honey-colored eyes stared at her with a well-groomed goatee, a bald head, brown skin, and bowlegs. He looked too sexy!

"When was the last time you saw Mr. Dukane Treemount?"

Childress knew she had to lie on the spot. She also knew that she had to keep the lie together so that they would not be implicated in the Texas Taste Tease mess.

"I last saw him a few days ago. My brothers and I were passing through his neighborhood and decided to stop and visit for a second." Childress focused her eyes on Detective Bouvier's crotch. She began to entertain naughty images in her mind that actually made her gasp for breath as he continued his line of questioning.

"Ma'am could you be more specific, please?" he asked.

"Only if you call me Childress," she said.

"Alright, Childress, can you be more specific, please?" Detective Bouvier said, smiling as he began shifting his weight from leg to leg. He felt his manhood begin to inch towards the zipper of his jeans. It pressed outward on the denim, making an obvious imprint as Childress had willed. For Detective Bouvier, the longing to touch Childress was unbearable. He asked to sit down, but before he could make it to the couch, Detective Bouvier brushed past Childress and moaned.

Knowing the effect of the spell she was casting on him was making him consent to her advances, Childress planted her hand on the hardened mound that rested underneath Detective Bouvier's jeans. Childress grabbed Detective Bouvier's belt buckle and teasingly took her time unfastening the belt. She knew that she was literally working her magic to enchant him, and he did not object to any of her advances. Speaking a chant that made him moan in ecstasy, Childress soon felt the good Detective's mouth on hers.

"Touch me and caress me," she whispered in his ear as she nibbled his earlobe. This caused urgency within the detective, and he couldn't come out of his shirt fast enough. He needed to feel his skin pressed against hers. Warm and wet, his lips eagerly searched for the next touch of her tongue.

"Please don't make me do this," he begged as her hand stroke on his manhood quickened, sending shudders up his spine as he looked in her eyes.

Childress pulled away from Detective Bouvier. She began walking down the hallway to her room, leaving him wanting more. He soon followed suit and found her bathrobe lying in the hallway in front of her door. Detective Bouvier stepped into her room, and lust sealed his fate into emotional enslavement. He would now be cursed to do her evil bidding forever.

A few hours later, Childress woke up next to her beefy masculine conquest. They had been lying in a pool of sweat that came from satisfying their physical needs. She looked over at his sleeping profile and instantly began to despise him. She despised all law enforcement agents. Careful not to disturb him, she slithered from her bed and went into her closet to retrieve the book of spells her mother had left to her. The secret compartment in the book held some chicken bones, which she removed and put in her hands. Childress was ready to put forth her plan to strike at her enemy.

Quietly, she crept down the hall to the bathroom. Childress prepared to further her spell and have someone to assist her in her evil plan to kill Solis off. She needed to have some essence from Detective Bouvier for her spell to be complete. Standing in front of the bathroom mirror, she opened her mouth, licked her tongue across her teeth, and found two pieces of his pubic hair lodged in between her front teeth. She carefully flossed them out without breaking them and dropped them into a small medicine cup on the sink. She then took some toilet paper, and wiped herself clean. Then she dropped the toilet paper in the medicine cup as well.

"...Mine, mine, mine...you are mine...you do as I say...you steal for me...you lie for me...you kill for me..." Childress whispered closing the chant. When she finished, she immediately wanted to bathe and wash him out of her. The bathwater was scalding hot, and Childress soaked in it, making her skin look strawberry red. She finished her bath and returned to her room. Detective Bouvier was still asleep on his back, sprawled all over the bed.

Childress walked over to the enchanted man lying in her bed. She drew back her hand and slapped his face with such force to awaken him that it broke the surface of his skin. The startled detective jumped from his rude awakening.

"Ouch, baby, that hurts!" he said. "Did I do something wrong?"

"Yeah, you're still here!" Childress shouted.

"Where else am I supposed to be? I can't be without you, Childress," a love-struck Detective Bouvier pleaded.

"I need you to find out information on a tramp named Solis Burkes. I want to know everything about her, and I need to know it now! So get busy!" she snapped.

"I will, baby, I will—I promise," he said, reaching to kiss and caress her. Instead of receiving his affections, Childress took her hand and pushed his face back away from hers.

"Hurry up and get dressed—I told you I need this now!"

"Once I get the information, baby, what do you want me to do with it? Do you want me to run her in for questioning or do you want her locked up?" a curious Detective Bouvier inquired.

"No. Let me handle it. You just get this back to me by tomorrow, and don't have me waiting!"

"Tomorrow?" Detective Bouvier said. "I'm hard for you tonight. I want to come back tonight," the lustful detective whispered.

"Don't bring your ass back here until tomorrow, or you'll regret it," Childress warned. "Now hurry up!"

The confused detective gathered his clothing and dressed himself. He began to weep as Childress commenced a verbal assault on his pride that left him emotionally distraught. He gathered his wits about him, and then started walking out of the room towards the front door. Just before leaving, he turned to Childress once more to attempt to recapture the lingering passion that saturated his mind. Instead of reciprocating his affections, Childress pushed the detective out the door. She slammed the raggedy screen door, leaving him standing on the porch like a cat that had just been put out for the night.

Childress laughed as she heard Detective Bouvier sniffle while walking to his vehicle. Her lust spell was working, and he was at her mercy. She knew that by tomorrow morning, she would have all the information needed to make Solis go away forever.

The Brothers Treemount got Erland's car out of the city pound smoothly without trouble. They cruised their turf and everything seemed to be alright. They then proceeded to go over to the north side to rouse some of the weaker members of the Inner Circle Cannibals. Since Flick was gunned down by the Treemounts at the Tease, the brothers felt as if they had truly accomplished something. Knowing that they were going to continue the turf war that had started, the brothers found an office building that was the after-hours turf of the Inner Circle Cannibals and crossed out Flick's name.

"Give me the spray paint can, Klein," Justice said. Justice began crossing out Flick's name and Inner Circle's name, and replaced everything with the Cut Throat Terrorists insignia. Their work was done there, and now they had to wait for the fallout to continue.

"Let's roll," Erland said as Justice jumped back in the car. The car peeled out, leaving rubber streaks on the asphalt. Trouble was brewing and the Treemounts were calling it out. They wanted to take over the whole city, and this was their way of making sure to immobilize the weaker gang.

When the brothers returned home, they found Childress ready to go out for a night on the town. Her hair was swept up in a clip, and then cascaded down into a loose ponytail. She was dressed in black ripped, see-through hot pants. She wore a halter-top and four-inch heels. The heels made her swanky runway walk unbalanced as her bowlegs tried to steady her and keep her from falling.

"Did ya'll find out where Solis lives?" Childress asked, knowing that her three goony brothers would not have followed through on getting the information that she had asked for. All three of them stood before her looking guilty and lost. None of them spoke up to answer her question.

"I had told Erland to go and find out where that girl lives, but he wouldn't do it," Justice quickly lied. It still didn't save them from a verbal tongue-lashing from Childress.

"Like I said, all of you are so basic and ignorant, it makes my head hurt!" she said. "I knew you wouldn't be able to do it, because you would have been so caught up in doing your own dirt! Hurry up and get dressed, I'm ready to go!"

"We went by Aunt Lela's house. The car that landed in that ditch was Judd's car. He was burnt to a crisp. Aunt Lela was called by the police, and she had to identify what was left of him. They told her it was best that he just be cremated," Klein said. "Some tramp he was with the night he got off work said that he took off after he broke her arm. She told police he was mad after she wouldn't screw him."

"Yeah, Aunt Lela said that the memorial service would be sometime next week," Justice said.

Childress continued to listen. She was beginning to figure out that someone was trying to kill off the Treemounts. The question that was unanswered was whether it was gang related or if it was Solis getting back at her. Right now, she did not want to think about any of it.

Each of the brothers quickly showered and dressed to go out and terrorize the town. The first stop was at Santa Ana's nightclub. This fell right in with the plan that the brothers had to meet up with the rest of their gang. Childress was hoping to bump into Solis again, with her sexy new companion. She was hoping to finish the punch to Solis's face that had been interrupted by her vampire companion. Childress wanted to have the vampire as her own. She took pleasure in knowing that she could hurt Solis by taking away her man.

All the Treemounts were dressed. Klein looked like a mismatched poor pimp, with solid-colored sherbet-orange pants and a mauve-colored sports coat. His feet were graced with black eel-skin boots. Justice decided to take a chance on getting kicked out of the club with oversized blue jean pants and an oversized blue jean jacket. Erland took the fashion cake with black leather pants, black alligator boots with two-inch heals on them, and a green satin shirt. All of the brothers had their necks weighted down with multiple gold chains that clanked like wind chimes with each step they took. In their confused minds, they were the most handsome men on earth. They liked breaking the hearts of innocent women. With their minds full of vanity and each with a pocket full of illegally obtained money, the Treemounts hit the streets.

When they arrived at the neighborhood nightclub, the place was already packed. The dance floor was crowded. The deejay chopped and screwed one song after another. Strobe lights hypnotized those that were buzzing from the overpriced, watered-down drinks. The females sat to one side of the dimly lit club, and the males stood against the wall like animals stalking their prey.

Like a scene out of a movie, a crowded path parted as Childress stood in the threshold of the club entrance with her henchmen brothers flanking her. The Treemounts walked through the club like royalty, but also because no one wanted to have them as enemies. The music continued to roar on as Childress found a table to claim. She had become thirsty and wanted some drinks.

"Go get me something to drink, and hurry up!" She shouted at her brothers. All three jumped up and went to the nearest bar. Childress was left unattended, and males swarmed like vultures trying to get her attention to dance. One bold soul, who obviously didn't know her reputation, took a chance and asked her to dance. He was a fairly handsome-looking brown-skinned man. He looked weak and controllable; this made him easy prey for Childress. In fact, he looked so easy she knew she would not have to cast any spell on him to get him to do her bidding. He asked her to dance, and Childress rejected his invitation right away.

"Hello, Ms. Lady. My name is Chase. You look so lovely sitting here in this chair. Would like to dance with me?"

"Hell naw, and don't come back here either! You look too weak to handle a woman like me. Move along, please!" Childress said rolling her eyes in disgust.

"You don't even know me. If you'd like to get to know me, here's my name and number. You call me when you want to satisfy your curiosity about a real man," Chase said. He left his name and number on a napkin as he licked his pride wounds and continued to circle the club.

Just then, the brothers made it back to the table with drinks. They had just sat down when the deejay mixed in the song "Cold Touched." Childress grabbed her drink and downed it in one gulp. That song was her cue to hit the dance floor. She got up, and the crowd parted once more and allowed her to take over the whole floor.

As the bass drive thumped and clapped up against the beat of the drum, Childress started her dance slowly at first. She stretched her arms over her head, which teasingly showed off her midriff and pierced belly button. Her full hips swayed and rocked to the beat as she did a highly erotic belly dance. The men in the club went crazy! They literally howled like wolves as Childress bent over and raised her hips up and down like a hydraulic car jack. Her ripped hot pants showed large portions of her toned thighs as she continued to lure men to the edge of the dance floor.

"Break!" the song said as it took the beat to the bridge of the music. Childress then lay down on the lit-up dance floor and did pelvic thrusts up to the ceiling. By that time, men were hurting themselves to get to the edge of the dance floor and see the spectacle. All the women in the club had their noses turned up in disgust at the free wild and sexy sideshow Childress was performing. When it was over, Childress sashayed past a table of three very annoyed women.

"Who does that bitch think she is?" one of the women muttered. Before the woman could blink her eyes once more, Childress had taken a pitcher of beer from another table and cracked it against the side of the woman's head. The impact caused glass to cut the woman's face and beer to splash on the other two, ruining their dresses.

"Speak up hoe, so I can cut your lips off!" Childress sniped. No one in the club moved as the music continued to play.

13

I was sitting in my room about to call Nacio when I heard Chase coming in. I could hear the soft padding of his feet coming down the hallway. He stopped in front of my door and knocked softly.

"Lou Lou, you awake?" Chase said.

"Yeah," I said as Chase stood in my doorway.

"What are you doing, Lou Lou?"

"I was just sitting here. What's up with you?" I said, wanting to call Nacio.

"The club was crunk tonight. It was crowded. They weren't shooting at all, so it was a good night," he said. "I met this chick and she was the nicest looking girl in the club. She was beautiful!"

"Well, that's good, Chase. Is she nice?"

"Well, she's beautiful. She could be a movie star," he said with his eyes as big as fifty cent pieces.

"Well, I hope she's nice, Chase. Some of the women you bring here are awful, and they look sneaky."

"You don't know what you're talking about, girl," he said, becoming irritated at the truth. "I'm going to bed."

"Goodnight," I said. Chase wasn't exactly the brightest star in the sky, and he was worse at choosing women to date. He was nearly thirty-four years old, and he was still living at home. I just hoped that he would be able to find someone that cared for him. He was a talented musician. He played the xylophone and the bongos. Even with his talent, he still hadn't been blessed with that one special person. Nevertheless, it didn't stop him from trying. He, too, went through a streak of bad relationships.

I was becoming sleepy. My dreams were becoming more vivid. I could recall each of them in sequence. My foresight was becoming stronger as Grandma Olvignia had said it would. This was a good thing, because I was still harboring a deep resentment for the Treemount family, and I wanted them stopped. Although I hadn't gone into a deep conversation with Nacio, I knew that he was the one responsible for the missing Treemounts that had recently vanished. My eyelids were becoming heavier until drowsiness crept in on me and I lost the battle to keep them open.

I felt as if I were floating gently. A dream sequence began. In the dream, I found myself in the kitchen sitting at the table. I looked up and, low and behold, there stood my mother. It had been nearly two decades since she had past away. She looked a little bit older than she had when she died. Her skin was still fair and golden and her hair dark brown. She and I were of the same shape and build. Her soul looked at peace.

The luminescence from her angelic face let me know she had been in God's presence. She looked blessed. There was no sickness or sadness on her face. She stood before me with a high wattage smile that made me feel so loved at that moment. She kept standing there smiling at me. I knew this had to be a dream, but I wanted it to be real. I could smell her and could feel her entire presence. Even after all these years, I still recognized her voice. I had so many things that I wanted to ask her. There were so many questions I had that were unanswered at the time of her death. I didn't know where to begin. I guess she felt my stirred curiosity and she spoke to me. Her lips did not move. She greeted me telepathically with the loving nickname I had not heard in the many years of her absence.

"Hello, Little Hammer," she said as she never stopped smiling nor did she take her eyes off me.

"Hi, Mama" was all I could say. There were so many things I needed to know. "Are you here even when my eyes can't see you?"

"Yes," she answered as I continued to stand in awe of this beautiful angel that I knew as my mother.

"I miss you, Mama," I said as she continued.

"I love you," she answered. "Have faith. Never doubt yourself. You've been through a lot. God has his hand on you. Look inside yourself for the strength he has blessed you with. Always remember: you are worthy. Always remember I am with you. Take the gifts you've been blessed with and do what you have to do. You are never alone. You will succeed over your enemy. I know what's happened to you, and it made you who you are. Don't blame yourself for anything. You will succeed...You will succeed, child," she said as she embraced me and kissed my cheek. "I will see you again someday. I love you with all my heart, Hammer."

My mother's kiss had given me a new confidence as any mother's love for her child would. I could feel the warm stream of tears wash down my face as I slept. My mother's love for me reminded me of all I had accomplished, and all I was going to achieve. I knew my mother was with me, and there was nothing that Childress Treemount could do to stop that. Grandma Olvignia had made certain to give to me what was needed to conquer our enemy. Over the last few nights, the knowledge of spells and alchemy were being unlocked within my mind. Soon I would have the strength to mark Childress for annihilation.

When I woke up the next morning, I felt a newfound strength that made me want to embrace the day. I looked at myself in the mirror; I noticed that my skin was radiant, and my spirit felt redeemed. I no longer felt the guilt that I had lived with for so long. My reflection showed me a woman that was worthy to be loved, and someone who was strong. The woman in the mirror was no longer in emotional bondage. I wanted to talk to Nacio and let him know that it was time to take the rest of the Treemounts down. I dialed his number. He answered on the first ring as usual.

"Hello, sweetheart," he said.

"Hi, baby, I'm headed your way in just a bit," I said. "We need to finish what Childress started."

"I'll see you when you get here."

I quickly showered and dressed. Chase was still asleep, and I did not want to bother him. I was headed to the kitchen and found Grandma already sipping on her cup of coffee. She had a look on her face as if she had been keeping a secret. This wasn't an unusual look for Grandma.

"How was your visit with your mother last night?" she started. Again, rather than question her as to how she knew I dreamed of my mother, I just answered her. "You have your mother's blessing on your face. She's with you and will be with you until the end, and so will I."

"Grandma, don't talk like that," I said, becoming apprehensive. "I need you, and I don't want to hear that from you. Not now!" I said. "I need you to be with me, here."

Grandma just looked at me. I guess she felt sorry for me, but she just sat in silence. She and I had been working on using my mind as a muscle to pick up and move objects.

"Let's begin, Solis. Send me the coffee crème in the refrigerator," Grandma said. I didn't think anything of it. I went into the kitchen and was about to open the fridge but was shaken by the boom in Grandma Olvignia's voice.

"Don't touch it! Use your mind!"

I was nervous, but I knew I had no choice but to honor her wishes. I focused on the handle of the refrigerator. Nothing happened. I continued to concentrate on the handle, but still nothing. Grandma became angry, and soon went off on me.

"Stop doubting yourself! You have a tramp out there that is trying to kill you, and you can't defend yourself as long as you are in doubt!" she shouted. "This wicked witch of a woman has killed your friend, and you are still feeling sorry for yourself!"

When Grandma said that, it struck a raw nerve! All it took was one second for my mind to pull the handle on the refrigerator, nearly yanking it off its hinges. The door swung open and slammed the side of the refrigerator, flapping back and forth. Grandma was all too happy at the strength of my ability.

"Yes sir! Thank you! Thank you!" She rejoiced. "That's what I'm talking about! You are a strong one, Solis, but you should not have to be taunted to have control over your abilities," she said. "Practice meditating and moving objects every day to build and strengthen your control."

I was shocked at what I had just accomplished. It only boosted my confidence, and I knew that I would be able to defend myself. I was ready to leave, but before I did, I hugged Grandma. Just as I walked out the door, I heard her say these words.

"Solis, it's time—this battle will be long."

"I'm getting ready. I'll be late getting back tonight, Grandma."

14

I couldn't believe the person that stared back at me in the rearview mirror. My mind was becoming stronger. I had come to rely on it more. Believing in my thoughts was giving me the boost I needed to confront Childress. This feeling was so new to me. It was a sort of high that I never knew a person could feel. I guess this is what peace feels like. I felt so bold that I took a detour on the way to Nacio's home.

I found my way into a dress shop not too far from an older part of downtown. My eyes journeyed through the store to find the loveliest red dress that had ever been made. The dressing room was adorned with a three-way mirror. This hot little red number was sleeveless and cinched at the waist. My breasts were hoisted up to make them perky and attractive, instead of looking as if they were apart of my waist needing to be corralled in a girdle. I had an hourglass figure that was being silently complemented by making such a loud fashion statement.

The sales associate complimented me as I continued to look at myself in the three-way mirror.

"You look gorgeous! He must be a special man!" she said.

"Thank you. What a nice thing to say," I said, finally able to accept praise from someone without shooting it down with a negative statement. It had always been difficult for me to accept compliments or praise from someone. I had always been made fun of and thought that any praise given to me was a joke.

"I'll take it!" I told the grinning sales associate. I looked at the price tag and slapped a crisp one-hundred-dollar bill into the woman's hand. "In fact, I want to wear it now."

"Would you like for me to bag your things for you?" she asked. The woman looked all too pleased with the commission she had just earned.

"I certainly would," I said, grabbing my things to continue on to Nacio's house. I didn't want to keep my sweetheart waiting, let alone my own heated desire.

The journey to Nacio's home yielded answers to questions that I would ask myself early on in our relationship. The old neighborhood near the Alamodome and library had gang markings all over it. The savage Treemounts had been marking their territory like dogs. They acted live primitive people. It was awful to see just how well the graffiti made the little neighborhood look like a foreign country war zone.

I turned down the narrow alleyway leading to Nacio's home. A beautiful champagne-colored Rolls Royce was parked behind the waterfall that sat in front of the mansion. My curiosity was sparked. I didn't recall Nacio or Bose mentioning this vehicle, yet here it sat.

Feeling a little embarrassed by my old clunker of a car, I parked as far from the beautiful Rolls as possible. In fact, I probably should have parked my car out on the main road from Nacio's house, that's how bad my car looked compared to this beauty.

Nacio was standing at the front door waiting for me. He was wearing another tropical-looking ensemble, a brown linen pant suit. His shirt draped his frame loosely, yet still highlighted his rock-hard physique. He was smiling at me with his eyes. I knew I was looking good as well. My saucy red dress whipped around my hips as I moved in the direction of the gentle southern wind. He had always told me that he enjoyed watching me walk, so I let him get an eyeful of my strut. If I'd had theme music, it would have started playing just as I walked into his arms. Watching him watch me was a show in itself. He licked his lips, either from thirst or hunger—possibly both.

When I made it up to the threshold of the door where he stood, he reached for me and scooped me up in his arms. He kissed me so deeply that I thought time would stop and the world would go away.

"My body is responding to you in a way that is dangerously near the edge of submission," he said. "You are so beautiful. You look like a queen walking towards her king. I will always remember this day for all the days to come," he said as he kissed me again.

"I feel beautiful in your eyes," I said. "I want to go over the edge with you."

"Someday we will, my dear. For now, we have visitors in our home," he said, making me tingle at the fact that he said 'our home.'

"My dear friend Armando Caraway and his family have come to help us break the curse of the Treemounts. He and Bose have pinpointed the location of more family members," Nacio said.

"I'm coming with you, and I am not going to argue with you," I said, putting my foot down and standing my ground. To make myself abundantly clear, I turned towards the door of the mansion. Focusing on the door handle was as easy as blinking. With a soft clicking swoosh, the front door opened, slamming into the wall behind it.

"Whoa! You've been practicing!" Nacio exclaimed. "You think you're bad now, huh?" he said teasingly.

"Doesn't the dress say it all?" I fired right back. "I'm ready, Nacio. I will not have you go alone. Childress is my problem and I am ready to solve my problem."

"Well, we have help now; so that helps me feel a little better about you being involved in this. Armando will help you refine your abilities. He also is a telekinetic and can move objects with his mind. You will also meet his wife, Patience, and their twin children, Basrick and Basira. Those two are truly dangerous. I'm glad they are for the good guys, because I would hate to battle them. They have control over time. They can alter events in the blink of an eye. In doing so, they are able to wipe clean the memory of any human, causing a perpetual state of confusion for a time. They are tough to beat."

"Wow! I can't wait to meet them."

We went inside, and to my amazement, there stood the entire Caraway family. Armando was the first to make my acquaintance. He stood tall and lean. He was not as muscular as Nacio but still strong in a more marathon-runner type of way. His eyes were the color of diamonds. He was dressed in jeans, a T-shirt and tennis shoes, and his lengthy blond hair was tied back behind his shoulders.

"Greetings, Mistress!" he said as he reached for and kissed my hand. "I am Armando Caraway, and it is truly a pleasure to meet the woman who has captured the heart of my dearest friend."

"Pleased to meet you," I said as I smiled, still trying to take in the fact that he addressed me as 'Mistress.' Patience was next in line as she stepped from behind her dashing husband.

"Oh, you are a beautiful young woman!" Patience said as she hugged me. Patience was stunning herself. Standing about 5 feet 8 inches tall with an hourglass figure that would make movie stars shudder with envy, Patience was truly a showstopper. Her eyes were sky blue, and she had long, curly spiral ringlets of hair that looked like springs as she walked over to me.

"Thank you so much," I said, blushing from all of the compliments. Last, but not least, the twins came down from the staircase. Basrick and Basira, looking every bit the male and female mirror images of each other, spoke at the same time.

"Hello, Solis! So nice to meet you," the twins spoke. I don't know why I was expecting little kids. These two heartbreakers were adults, closer to my age to be exact.

"Hello! How are you?" I said, trying to cover the surprise on my face. The twins had violet-blue eyes and jet-black hair. These twins truly had a gothic appearance to them. I had so many questions but knew that there would be a time and place for inquiries soon enough. Bose was the last to make his appearance, and he did so with his usual announcement.

"Hello, Mistress," Bose said. "Your dinner is served." I felt like a queen in her castle. Once again, Bose had outdone himself with his menu. He had prepared shrimp brochette, dirty rice, beignets, and my favorite, oatmeal and raisin cookies. The aroma of the meal beckoned us to come into the kitchen. I would be the only one really partaking in the meal. The vampires had their usual: warm blood. There were six settings at the table for dinner. Five of the settings had beautiful China plates with tall, fluted champagne glasses filled with rich red plasma, which was the blood menu. My food was exquisitely laid out in front of my place setting. Shiny cutlery and a thick terry-cloth napkin were within my reach to make the meal an enjoyable experience.

We all sat down at the table to enjoy the hospitality. The conversation was light and pleasant. As usual, I ate as much as I could, and then had to have Bose prepare a "to-go" box for me. The vampires sipped their pleasure quietly as I took my last bite. I wanted a refill on my blackberry wine. Bose had set the bottle directly in front of my plate. I started to reach for it but was interrupted by Armando.

"Use your mind, Solis," Armando said, prompting me to begin my telekinetic exercises.

I soon lifted the bottle with my mind with ease. I felt accomplished and ready. Then the true test came when Armando asked me to lift the entire dinner table. I began to panic, but he cheered me on.

"Go ahead, Solis. Don't be afraid. Remember this is something you have to do," Armando's words encouraged.

I went ahead and concentrated a little harder, and soon the table began to levitate. Nacio sat to my left and flashed his sexy smile. I continued to have the table float silently in the air, just below our chins. I lowered the table just as easily. Gently, I placed the table back down on the tiled floor. Proud, but also with my guard down, I noticed a pirate's sword spiraling through the air, just over our heads. The strange ghostly sword boomeranged through the kitchen and back into the eating area where we sat at the table. The sword had come from one of the guest rooms in the mansion. Obviously, it wanted a dual. I was scared, but then realized this too was one of Armando's exercises. So let the games begin.

Trying to remember the layout of the lovely mansion, I tried to recall what room the sword's twin was in so that it too could be summoned to champion me in this dual. I closed my eyes and used my mind to quickly journey through the hallway and into the suites of the mansion. Ah, there it is. The twin to this ghostly sword hung high on a wall in the library. I summoned the sword from the wall and had it fly in to dual this nuisance of a sword that levitated over our heads, all of Armando's doing of course. My sword clashed immediately with Armando's sword. The clanking and clashing sound was loud, yet it was exciting to see the battle.

Armando's sword was trying to slice the handle off mine, but I squeezed my mind to make my sword try to cut his sword in half. I was unsuccessful at this feat. The dual soon left the kitchen and ventured to the backyard in the garden. We both jumped up from the dinner table and followed the deadly weapons as they continued their dual outside.

The aggressive sword that was Armando's had my sword pressed up against an oak tree out in the backyard. It was then that an awful feeling of defeat washed over me, and I called on my inner strength to annihilate the sword. I let the overwhelming feelings from the loss of my friends push my mind to the point of raising my sword and slamming it down on Armando's, shattering it with one final, loud, metal-crunching clank. The aggressive sword that was wielded by Armando's telekinesis was snapped in half, and now lay in the grass just below the oak tree in defeat.

"That's my girl!" Patience shouted. "That's how you do it!"

"My love, are you alright? You did wonderfully!" Nacio said as he held me in his arms.

I didn't realize how much effort it would take out of me to perform this exercise with Armando. Over the next few hours, we studied strategies to infiltrate the Treemount family. Nacio explained to his guests that he had already begun and wanted to continue until the world could have some peace from the criminal family.

"There are several of the family members left. The males tend to have less common sense and, therefore, are easy prey for us," Nacio said. "These family members will soon be vanquished, and then we can move on to the women."

"All females in this family have some of the knowledge of voodoo and black magic. This is where your abilities will be utilized the greatest Solis, and why your mind must be up to strength to successfully get rid of them," Bose interjected. "The curse travels mainly through the blood of the females. Once they have stopped reproducing, then the curse should be broken."

"Armando and I will venture out tonight so that we might continue our quest. I would imagine that Childress has her suspicions now and soon will want to strike," Nacio said.

"This is true, Hefe," Bose said. "We don't have much time. It is critical that this quest be completed soon."

"We will leave at once," Nacio said, giving the command to his visitors. "Are we ready?"

"I will be in a second, I need to change," I said, dashing out the front door to get my jeans and T-shirt that were in the car. I changed and kept my sandals on.

I rejoined the guests. "Ready," I said.

Everyone present in the room gave a nod of confirmation and soon headed out the front door. Each vampire had his or her preferred mode of nighttime travel. Nacio gathered me in his arms, preparing to teleport us to the next unsuspecting Treemount victim.

Preparing themselves for night travel, Armando and Patience each shape-shifted into mist that blanketed the front of the mansion into a thick fog. Basrick and Basira chose a more stereotypical form of travel for themselves, by shape-shifting into two extremely large bats. With a wingspan of ten feet, Basrick and Basira were bats the size of two condors. Their wings sounded like propellers slicing through the wind as they flew away into the night.

Tucked safely underneath my beloved's arms, Nacio and I jetted across the San Antonio nighttime skyline. Floating and feeling the wind in my hair, I knew that I would definitely catalog this night into my mind as one that was unforgettable. I was with my soul mate and he was with me, and we were one. Since he was flying me across the sky, I made a mental note in my mind to ask Nacio if, when we finally made love, we could make love in the nighttime sky on a cloud. It sounded crazy I know, but I still wanted to try. With him, anything is possible.

We were soon making the descent to the home of the next mark, Hastings Treemount. A bishop in one of the most successful churches in town, Hastings Treemount was a man of the clergy. Sermons on Sundays and stealing the money from the church's building fund, Hastings Treemount had given a new twist in robbing the Almighty.

Any tithes that were paid by parishioners to the church were having a huge cut off the top by Hastings. There had been a rash of church monument vandalism and statue beheadings on church grounds. This was done all at the hands of Hastings Treemount.

Hastings lived in one of the premiere subdivisions in Northeast San Antonio. With the largest Mercedes on the market parked in front of his home, Hastings got out of his car. He stopped to bend over to get the newspaper and was walking to the mailbox. Nacio hid me in some bushes several feet away in his backyard, giving me a side view of what was to occur. The vampires proceeded with their positions and took their places to strike.

"Stay here, Solis," Nacio warned. "I agreed for you to come along, but I did not agree for you to be a participant in this."

Frozen in place, I could only nod my head as a confirmation to his command.

Unaware of the impending doom that awaited him, Hastings continued to be distracted by the day's headlines as he slowly approached his front door. I watched anxiously from behind the bushes. I heard Hastings open his front door to his home, and close it. I quickly ran to the back window and found the blinds drawn up, enabling me to have a clear view of Hastings as he walked into his living room.

Nacio and his vampire clan entered the home at the same time as Hastings, using their supernatural speed. Hastings finally returned his attention to the inside of his home environment. He sat down and removed what looked to be several thousand dollars out of a briefcase he had laid on his table. He greedily began to count the money, licking each one hundred dollar bill as if they were chips being dipped in a bowl of salsa. I watched as the vampires materialized right before my eyes. Hastings picked up on the heavy presence in the room. He stopped counting the money to look up and find all five vampires standing before him with fangs drawn and tornado black-colored eyes.

"Oh Savior!" Hastings shouted. "Oh Savior please!" he continued to cry out as his guilty conscience finally wore him down.

"Do you honestly think the Savior hears you after you have robbed him blind?" Nacio questioned.

"Or that he hears you when you have sex with underage parishioners?" Armando chimed in.

"Tsk, tsk, tsk. Such a shame—no redemption for you," Patience said.

"It's time for you to pay back what you have taken, with interest," Basrick and Basira spoke simultaneously.

With having heard all of that, Hastings jumped up and reached for the crucifix he had as a tie clip to hold in front of the vampires as a means of protection. This pitiful effort bought him a few more seconds of life. Nacio reached out with his hand only to snatch the beautiful accessory from Hastings. Toying with the man, Nacio passed the crucifix to Armando, and it continued to be passed amongst them as they made comments on the craftsmanship of the jewelry.

"Beautiful piece of work," Patience said. "I have one similar to this that I wore with my dress on the day of our wedding, don't I dear?"

"Indeed you do, dear!" Armando interjected.

"You must pay back what you have taken—times five!" the twins said.

The vampires positioned themselves around Hastings; the twins each grabbed a leg; Armando and Patience each grabbed an arm. Nacio stood over Hastings and put his hands on his shoulders. Fangs drawn and with one smooth motion, each vampire made a huge bite into the claimed limbs that each one of them held in their hands.

I immediately turned around from the window to close my eyes. I had just figured out that dismemberment was to seal this Treemount's fate. After they fed, several loud snapping sounds confirmed my suspicions. The next thing I knew, I was being picked up by Nacio. Armando and Patience quickly shape–shifted, and we began our journey again. The twins remained behind to dispose of the body, never to be found.

"It is done," Nacio said as he licked a drop of Hastings's coppery-smelling blood from his lips. I thought I would be afraid to see Nacio like this, but I did not find myself afraid. He still seemed to be the same person that I had fallen in love with, not a monster like those that are afraid would make him out to be. I now believed in vampires and their existence. Maybe I just had a false sense of well-being because I was under the protection of a strong vampire. I've often thought of what it might be like to be a vampire, but I have found myself putting those thoughts to the back of my mind for the moment; my only focus was avenging Affinity.

I thought to myself, one less Treemount and closer to ending the curse. Revenge had a bittersweet taste, and vivid smell.

15

We continued to carry out our plan, traveling across the night sky, on to our next victim. Duboc Treemount was the next unfortunate soul to meet his demise on this night. I could feel myself changing with each drop of blood that was spilled. I didn't feel sadness for the loss of each Treemount life force. Instead, I felt relief. That might be an awful thing to say, but I truly felt that there was no hope for any members of that rotten family. I wanted it to continue on until each had been eradicated.

As we neared Duboc's hangout, Nacio knew that he would find Duboc hanging out on a street corner near a convenience store. Duboc was a child molester and had been for sometime. Conceit was one of his more negative attributes. Stunningly handsome, Duboc had milk-chocolate-colored skin. His hair was full like a lion's mane, and curly. A goatee graced his chin. A well-endowed man, Duboc also had dense musculature covering his 6 feet, 1 inch frame.

His endowment often made sexual resistance from the women he dated difficult. Beguiling as he was, he would lure women with children into a relationship with him. A slothful man, Duboc would move in with a woman he was involved with. He then would offer to babysit her children while she went to work. This was an opportunity to establish a rapport with the children, grooming them into trust. Offering special treats and privileges to the children in exchange for sexual favors was how he preferred to indulge himself.

Multiple children had been victims of horrendous sexual abuse at the hands of Duboc Treemount. The threat of death to their mother would be the promise Duboc made to the victims should they ever divulge the secret that was kept between himself and them. Duboc was walking down an alleyway between the corner of Houston and Olive streets. A combination of drugs and alcohol ran through his blood and skewed his senses as he staggered to the rundown duplex shack that he occupied. Once again, Nacio placed me in a position to watch his clan strike. No sooner was Duboc about to step on the porch of the hovel he occupied than Basira stepped out of the shadows.

Basira had shape-shifted her appearance to that of a 14-year-old child, dressed in a blue tank top and black miniskirt. She became much shorter, and thinner. She called to an intoxicated Duboc to draw his attention to her.

"Can you help me?" Basira said. "I'm trying to find the bus stop. I don't want to miss my bus home. If I do, I'll have to get a ride home. Can you show me where it is?"

Sobering up for just a moment to take delight in looking at what he saw as a pubescent Basira, Duboc tried not to slur too much.

"Sure, I can help you find the bus stop," he said, smiling with arousal.

The vampires had taken positions in the bushes on either side of the alley as I watched from across the street. It was pitiful to watch this sorry soul actually take no discretion in gratifying his sexual needs with someone who appeared to be a child. All I saw before me was a primitive savage.

Basira moved in closer to Duboc. By this time, the other vampires were beginning to materialize behind him. With her eyes fixed on him, Basira reached out for Duboc's belt buckle sending shudders of anticipation through the lecherous man. Too entranced to feel

Patience slip her hand up the spine of his back, Duboc closed his eyes in ecstasy and tilted his head back. Without any combativeness, he surrendered to the sweet pleasure of Basira's hand massage. Patience took her finger and sliced Duboc's throat diagonally, making a zipper sound as the flesh peeled back.

A plasma waterfall sent the vampires into a feeding frenzy. For only a brief moment, nausea visited me. A southerly breeze relieved me of my ailment by clearing the air and allowing me to continue to witness the event to fulfill my purpose of revenge. Headlights turned down the alleyway. Nacio called an order of retreat for the vampires.

"Shift and fall back!" Nacio hissed. The vampires instantly turned into mist, carrying Duboc's corpse for disposal. All of them shifted except for Basira. She fell on the ground a few feet away from where Duboc's pool of blood had been.

"Go ahead, I will be fine!" Basira commanded. "I will catch up later."

Nacio grabbed me with superhuman speed while the other vampires fell back and flew away. A young vampire, and still subdued from her feeding, Basira pretended to be in distress as the car came to a stop next to her. The door to the vehicle opened and out jumped Justice Treemount. Justice was in the neighborhood looking to catch up with some of his gang members and decided to swing by his cousin's house along the way, unaware of what he had just stumbled upon. Justice immediately went to Basira's aid, kneeling beside her to check to see if she was hurt.

"Hey, baby, you alright?" Justice inquired, looking at the tank top and miniskirt that barely covered Basira. "Are you hurt?" Justice continued.

Basira slowly opened her eyes and was about to strike when she looked at Justice. Totally taken by surprise at her attraction to the face she saw before her, Basira answered her would-be champion. She knew that she had crossed into forbidden territory, knowing that this Treemount was on the list to eventually be exterminated.

"I'm okay. Just a little tired," she said with her continuous gaze on Justice. Making time stop and only the two of them for the moment, Basira kissed Justice. Without saying a word, Justice and Basira continued their embrace for what seemed like hours. Surrendering to their passion, Justice and Basira became intimately acquainted with each other. Although she had just fed, Basira flashed her fangs and plunged them deep into the carotid area of his neck, flooding him with a pleasure he had never known. This was an experience of a lifetime for him, and he knew that he had found the love of his life. Basira drank from Justice causing a sexual imprint between the two of them.

Careful not to kill her newly found consort, Basira released Justice who was now out of breath and ghastly pale.

"I have to see you again, because whatever you've done to me, I need you to do it again," Justice said, spellbound and dizzy. "What's your name?"

"I'm called Basira," she answered. "I'll call you."

Justice handed her a piece of paper with his cell number on it.

Having said that to him, Basira reset the time, and all of the events fell back into sequence as time rolled on. This slight adjustment would have normally wiped her victim's mind clean as a slate, but her desire for her consort would allow her to do no such thing. But even with the slight adjustment, Justice appeared to have forgotten that he was at his cousin's house for a visit. He had no concern at all for Duboc's absence, leaving no reason for him to inquire about him. Justice was only concerned about feeling the unexplainable pleasure with Basira once more.

"I'll contact you tomorrow, sweetheart. Now go!" she said to him.

Justice turned for only a moment to get Basira's number, but when he looked up to speak to her, she had literally vanished into thin air. Feeling as if he had truly accomplished something, Justice started to grin and dance in the street as if he had just won the lottery. He was holding the spot on his neck as blood continued to seep from the wound. Trying to steady himself, he returned to his brother's car. Justice found an oil-stained car-wash chamois on the floor underneath the driver's seat to wipe his wound with. He flipped through his satellite CD jukebox and found the old school song "I'm in love." He blasted the stereo, nearly blowing out the speakers and his eardrums as the bass line in the song rattled the subwoofer in the trunk, vibrating the entire back end of the vehicle.

We arrived back at Nacio's home, a little shaken from the unexpected arrival at Duboc's home. Nacio questioned Armando about Basira being able to handle herself.

"Will she be okay? We weren't expecting anyone to appear," Nacio asked.

"Basira is more than capable of handling herself in any situation," Armando reassured Nacio. "She is a young vampire, but a vampire nonetheless. She will be alright."

"Is someone looking for me?" Basira said, materializing right before my eyes, looking beautiful. No one would ever suspect the life-threatening danger she is capable of.

"What took you so long?" Her twin Basrick inquired about his sister's tardiness.

"I don't ask you about your business, don't inquire of mine," Basira whipped back, trying not to give herself away. She knew that Basrick would be able to detect even the slightest change in her. She knew Basrick was capable of smelling the residue of intimacy on the surface of her skin, so she diverted her attention to me.

"Are you okay, Solis?" Basira asked innocently.

"Sure, I'm fine. Just a little tired," I responded. "Sweetheart, I think I'm ready to go home now," I said to Nacio.

"Yes, honey, until tomorrow," he said sweetly.

We sealed our embrace with a kiss, and I started on my way home. I was shaken at all the blood I had seen tonight but rationalized that it had been no different on the day blood was shed at the Texas Taste Tease. Sadly, people fear vampires, but the true monsters like the Treemount family walk freely amongst us each day. They are the monsters. With Nacio making the Treemounts disappear, he was making the world a better place one fewer Treemount at a time.

My drive home was so uneventful that it was as if I had blinked and was turning up the street that led to my cul-de-sac. All I wanted to do was get to my bed. It had been a long night. Just before I turned onto the street to my cul-de-sac, I noticed a tinted, late model, black two-door Mustang sitting at the corner. The lights of the parked vehicle were off, so I guessed our neighbors were having company. I pulled my clunker into our driveway. While I got out and headed up the walkway to the front door, Chase happened to pull up as well. He quickly parked his car behind mine, secured it, and ran up the walkway to get to me. I didn't feel like having a conversation with him, but here we go.

"Hey, Lou Lou! Where you been?" Chase said.

"I've been out, Chase," I said. "Nacio and I had dinner, and I met some of his friends that are like his family."

"What did ya'll do?" redundantly Chased asked. I know I just told him, yet he insists on asking again.

"Chase, we ate. I met his family. End of story," I said, now getting irritated from being exhausted.

"But what did ya'll do?" he said. Uuggghhhh! He makes my head hurt.

"Never mind, what did you do tonight, Chase?" I asked, trying to redirect him from what was beginning to be futility in my attempt to communicate with him.

"I just went and hung out—no big deal," he said, looking as tired as I felt.

"Alright then, Chase, I'm going to bed. See you in the morning," I said quickly so that I could get to my room and crash. I had no intentions of encouraging anymore merry-go-round conversation with Chase that night.

I turned off the light in the living room and noticed that the Mustang that was parked at the corner of our cul-de-sac mysteriously cranked up. Whoever was sitting in the car drove away. Maybe it was my imagination, but the car was rather loud, and it made me wonder if someone had been watching our house. Whatever the case, I did not have the energy to stand there and wonder what or who could be staking out our residence at this late hour. I needed to sleep.

The sun was shining brightly giving the city a clear horizon. Grandma Olvignia was awake and sipping her coffee as usual. She had the house smelling wonderful with the beckoning aroma of Luling sausages and scrambled eggs for my Grandpa Leonine. I actually caught a glimpse of him. He had a mouthful of the sausage and eggs with toast bulging on the left side of his face as he chewed with delight. As usual, his eyes were glued to the television, and he was enthralled with the CNN newscast.

"Hey, Grandpa Leo!" I greeted him.

"Hey, baby," he said, eyes unblinking from the television screen.

I made my way into the kitchen and sat with Grandma Olvignia. She slid a plate of sausage and eggs over to me right away, bent on me not having another spell of skipping meals.

"They've been busy, haven't they?" Grandma asked. "The news is full of missing Treemounts. At this rate, this curse just might wither and go away sooner than we had planned."

Grandma could sense that the Caraways had joined Nacio as a task force to stop Childress. She knew that it would take great skill to accomplish this feat, and she had total confidence in Nacio's plan and in me as well.

"You did well yesterday, Hammer. I could feel your success," Grandma said. "Your abilities are stronger than I had anticipated. As your mother and I had expected, you will succeed over Childress. You will need to be clever though, and not underestimate her, for Childress knows no boundaries, and she takes from those who are weak. You can't be weak, Hammer, you have to strike first!"

"I will, Grandma," I said. "Don't worry, I won't let you down. I will see Nacio today. Soon we will be confronting Childress head-on. I know it won't be easy, but I plan to face my lifelong bully, and then move past this roadblock in my life."

Running the siren lights on his Mustang, Detective Mathis Bouvier drove like a bat out of hell with its wings on fire over to the Treemount home. He found it difficult to contain his arousal from the mere thought of Childress. Even a simple gesture like sitting in his car led to a rock-hard erection that was more pain than pleasure. Getting to Childress was cause enough for him to run traffic lights in pursuit of apprehending his runaway desire for her. Detective Bouvier hoped to be rewarded for the information that he was bringing forth.

He brought his cruiser to a slow halt as he turned down the

driveway of the Treemount home. Desperately trying to compose himself without brushing against his manhood that was painfully pressed against his thigh, Detective Bouvier slowly opened the door to the vehicle. Needing an adjustment to his current state of arousal, Detective Bouvier took his right hand and situated his manhood to the left, giving himself only momentary comfort.

He reached the front door, taking care not to fall through the porch that was missing a floorboard. The mother cat and her litter were tucked deeply underneath the porch to the right of an intact floorboard. Detective Bouvier rang the doorbell in anticipation of seeing the object of his desire. Instead, he was greeted by a rooster-strutting Justice who sang and whistled as he opened the door.

"I'm in love!" Justice shouted as he opened the door. "Oh hey, Detective!"

"Justice, where's Childress?" Detective Bouvier said.

"Childress! Your maaannnn is here!" Justice shouted, still clucking around. Justice was fully dressed today, sporting a shirt with an actual collar. Oh sure, it looked in good taste, but the truth of the matter was that he was hiding his "passion mark" that he had received from Basira.

Justice left the living room, retreating to the kitchen to continue his high pitched off-key yodeling that could have given coyotes a headache. The detective was becoming anxious, and his erection was getting no smaller by the second. It had now begun to snake down his thigh, with the head as hard as an arrow tip.

"Where is she?" he questioned as he began to tap his foot restlessly. Movement from down the hallway in the small home caused him to react with excitement by spinning around on his heels, hoping it was Childress. He was disappointed as a stumbling Erland had just rejoined the conscious people in the home. Coming out of a rather catatonic state, Erland was hitting the streets looking to score a hit.

He barely acknowledged the presence of the detective as he shuffled passed him and out the door.

"I see you had a rough night, huh, Erland!" Detective Bouvier exclaimed.

"You're lucky you're the law, or I would answer that question in a totally different way!" Erland exclaimed.

"Go ahead and answer the way you want to. What's stopping you?" Detective Bouvier egged Erland. "Where's Childress?"

Erland didn't answer as he left the home. Once again, Justice reentered the room with his eldest sibling in tow. When Detective Bouvier placed his eyes on Childress, his manhood was attempting to race to his knee.

Justice had gone to his room to change his clothing, completely forgetting to dress in another shirt that covered his passion mark. The mark had gone unnoticed by any of the other siblings in the home until now. Childress caught sight of the two puncture wounds that could have passed for mosquito bites had they not been crowned with bloody scabs.

After seeing this, Childress instantly knew what the markings were. Her green eyes began to glow as she screamed her brother's name with rage. Childress was hot as fish grease!

"Justice! Did you let that damn vampire bite you?" Childress shouted. She grabbed her brother's arm and turned his face to the left with such force it could have snapped his neck. In doing so, she revealed the two scabbed wounds.

"So this is what your crazy ass is singing about!" she exclaimed. "What happened?"

"Aw Childress, you don't know what you are talking about," Justice said in his defense. "This girl is the love of my life. She is beautiful, and I'm seeing her again today."

"Get the hell out of here, Justice, before I hurt you," she snapped.

"I'll deal with you later, you damn fool!"

"You'd better have better news for me than these fools around here," Childress said, flaring up at Detective Bouvier. "Did you bring me what I asked for?"

Without a moment to spare, Detective Bouvier slithered over to Childress, trying to steal a kiss from her. He pulled her in close, hoping to entice her with his hardness.

"Yes, baby, I have what you asked for," he said. The desire mixed with the bass in his voice almost made his response incoherent. "Can we talk about it in private?" he asked. His desire was now unleashed and the aching that hung between his legs was unbearable.

Childress grabbed Detective Bouvier and lured him to her bedroom like an arachnid webbing her prey. He willingly allowed himself to be led to her lair. Desperately wanting to be overcome by Childress, Detective Bouvier uncontrollably kissed her, grabbing her while she walked backward. His advances continued until they reached the threshold of her bedroom. Childress abruptly pulled away from the detective.

"We're in private now! Give me what I need, now!" Childress demanded. "You've kept me waiting long enough." Dismayed, the detective dropped his shoulders.

"Solis Burkes lives about three miles from here. She has an uncle named Chase Henderson," Detective Bouvier continued.

The name "Chase" struck a chord with Childress. She recalled the night that she and her brothers had gone out to Santa Ana's. The lame simpleton that had come over and asked her to dance had slipped his name and number on a piece of napkin and handed it to her. *Chase Henderson* was the name scrawled on the napkin.

"She lives with her grandparents, Leonine and Olvignia Henderson. Her mother's been deceased for a number of years, and her father has been in prison for several years also. She attends school at San Antonio

College. She doesn't move in a large 'girl clique'; so she was relatively easy to find. What is it that you want from her?" the detective asked.

"Don't worry about that! What I want from her is my business—you just take care of yours. Now get out!" Childress shouted.

"Please, Childress, baby, I can't. I need you. Touch me. I can't walk out of here without touching you. Please, Childress!" he said.

Without heeding her warning, Detective Bouvier reached for her hand and placed it on his belt buckle. Prompting her to unfasten it, he couldn't wait for Childress to take a handful of his manhood. She fulfilled his request, taking pleasure in watching him moan, yet she hated to hear a man beg.

Childress pushed Detective Bouvier onto the bed. As he fell on the bed, he stretched out his arms in ecstasy. He closed his eyes, moaning with pleasure and waiting for her to finish what she started.

With a demon-like grin on her face, Childress grabbed another handful of his manhood. Once her hand was full, she yanked upwards as if she were pulling on a lawnmower string. The Detective screamed in agonizing pain. Childress grabbed another handful, and with all her might, she yanked again…and again…over and over.

This sadistic behavior tickled Childress to no end. She laughed louder and louder with every yank. Detective Bouvier looked up at the ceiling as he lay flat on his back. Tears of pain and pleasure streamed down his face, but seeing this agony was not enough for her. Childress took her talon-like fingernails and made sure to yank hard enough so that her nails cut into his skin, heightening his pain.

"Aaaaaaawwwww, aaaaaaaawwww!" Detective Bouvier winced without any discretion. "Please, Childress, baby! Stop! No, don't stop! I can't stand it!"

Childress had hexed Detective Bouvier with such a powerful spell that it didn't matter what she said or did to him, he would not leave her.

"Shut up, cop!" she hissed. "This is what you wanted, and this is what you get!"

With one last yank that nearly dislocated her shoulder, Childress sent Detective Bouvier shuddering to a pleasured end. Too ashamed to look her in the face, he rolled off the bed and crawled to her bedroom door. He wept uncontrollably as he tried to get to his feet.

"The next time I tell you to leave, you leave! Do you understand me, cop!" Childress shouted. "Now get the hell out of here!"

"What have you done to me?" he asked. "I can't stand to be without you."

"If you know what's good for you, cop, you'll leave," she laughed.

"I need to be with you, Childress, please," he begged.

For one moment, Childress softened her eyes and walked over to the statuesque, yet pitifully pride-broken man. She took his face in her hands and kissed him. Then in one smooth motion and a last humiliating gesture, she slapped him as hard as she could. She didn't break the skin but landed the blow hard enough to cause a deep contusion that would surely show up tomorrow. Childress let out a sidesplitting diabolical laugh that sent the detective racing for the front door.

Once he sat inside his vehicle, Detective Bouvier sat in silence weeping softly. With his pride hurt and feeling confused, he backed out of the driveway wondering what he had gotten himself into. With a sore and burning sensation like hot coals, Detective Bouvier's arousal started over again. Torn between whether or not to go back to Childress or continue on, Detective Bouvier sat at the corner before he could make a decision. Finally, he drove on knowing that he would return the next day.

Childress went to the bathroom and wiped Detective Bouvier off her hand. She placed the toilet tissue she used in a cup, conjuring another spell to subdue the detective.

"Bring me your weapon tomorrow. Come back to me with it. Bring it to me. Obey me," she whispered. Childress knew that she would see her hunky beefcake man tomorrow. She glanced at herself in the mirror with praise.

16

Childress had her thoughts shift to her discovery of the bite marks on Justice. She quickly ran to her room and opened the book of spells. She had become intrigued with her ancestor's legend of vampirism and knew for sure now that her relatives were disappearing at a rate too quickly to be your everyday gang retaliation.

She opened the book of spells, perused the ancient chapters, and found something of interest written on beige parchment.

Vampires

...the undead, bloodsuckers, seekers of plasma and organ fluids, immortality is the source of the youth, death of a vampire can occur by beheading with a weapon made of pure silver or by stabbing the heart of a vampire with a weapon made of pure silver. Should a vampire ingest any other form of silver, it would cause death by agony. Should someone be bitten by a vampire more than once, it can bring about the change to the undead, perpetuating the curse, and bringing on immortality.

Childress continued to read, making her eyes widen with interest as she plotted against her enemy. She knew that whomever Justice had gotten himself involved with had to be connected with Solis and her vampire. Childress set a plan in motion that would deliver that vampire to her and kill whomever Justice was involved with.

While the wheels of evil turned in her head, Childress rolled in her bed with a sinister grin splashed across her face. She jumped up and left her room. Childress joined her brothers in their living room.

"Ya'll know that Hastings and Duboc are missing now too?" Childress blurted out.

"What?" Klein said. "When did this happen?"

"Aunt Jenny called asking if we had seen either of them," Childress explained. "She's worried and asked for ya'll to stay close to home," she said.

"I'm ready to hit those Inner Circle Cannibal fools. That goes down tonight!" Klein said, pacing the floor.

"I told ya'll that it's not those Cannibal punks!" Childress shouted. "Solis has teamed up with vampires and they are sweeping us off one by one. Just ask Justice."

"What's Justice got to do with this?" Klein questioned.

"Yeah Justice, tell us what you know," she said as she lured him into a verbal trap.

"Quit playing, Childress. I told you that you don't know what you are talking about!" Justice shouted.

"I don't? Oh, well, that's too bad," Childress said as her voice was sweet honey laced with poison. "Look at his damn neck!"

Klein reached for Justice and snatched him up by his shirt. Klein slammed him against the wall and turned his head to the side. Erland soon jumped into the skirmish. A lamp was broken in the scuffle as well as a mirror that dropped from the wall, shattered, and broke, which meant seven years of bad luck.

"What the hell are you doing, Justice?" Klein barked. "Now look what you did! We are cursed for seven years now!"

"Are you trying to play us, fool?" Erland shouted, half-coherent but always near a state of disorientation.

"Explain yourself, Justice, and make it quick. If you don't, don't worry about that vampire biting you again, because I will slit your throat for you myself," Childress said, fanning her deadly talons in his face.

The other Treemount siblings released their hold on their brother and gave him an opportunity to explain himself out of the current matter at hand. Justice knew that he had to choose his words wisely, and convey them with care.

"I was out cruising last night after I dropped Erland off for a minute. I went over on Houston Street. I can't remember where exactly, but I met this chick. Her name was Basira," Justice said with a high-wattage smile.

"Man, she put her lovin' on me, and I haven't been right since. You know what I mean?" Justice continued. He reached out and did a fist bump with Erland in agreement with how good the mysterious Basira made him feel.

"Where did she come from? Do you even know dumb ass?" Childress said, bursting his bubble. "Or had she clamped down on your neck by then?"

"I just know that I love her, and that's that. No more questions," Justice said.

"So you are choosing to take sides with your enemies rather than your family?" Childress inquired.

"Look, it's not like that. You don't even know if she is tied to them," Justice said in her defense.

"You'd better know where your loyalty is Justice," Childress said. "Don't be a fool. We are obviously on the menu for these vampires, so watch your back—because if you go with her, you will be watching it on your own!"

"Yeah, without us!" Klein interjected.

"Don't say anything else to him, Klein," Childress stated. "We'll find out where his loyalty is. Ya'll stay here, and don't leave. I'll be right back! Don't leave."

Childress grabbed her keys to her Beetle and made a mad dash out the door. She jumped into her car and did her usual rubber-screech shifting as she tore up the streets. She jumped onto Loop 410 weaving in and out of traffic, making other drivers slam on their brakes to avoid rear-ending the car ahead of them. A red Porsche cut in front of Childress. That caused her to slam on her brakes, nearly causing the little black Beetle to cut off right in the middle of the fast lane.

"Oh, man—you've done it now, bastard!" Childress said in road rage as she pursued the Porsche. Childress waited until she got right behind the driver of the vehicle and whispered a chant in a low and steady voice. What happened next not even Mother Nature could explain. The driver of the Porsche continued to speed ahead weaving worse than Childress. As she continued to chant on, the driver of the Porsche ran over a broken piece of a wooden plank. This caused the Porsche to flip on its side at a speed of at least 102 miles per hour. As the flipped Porsche continued skidding in the lane, it slammed into a guardrail. The car went careening out of the northbound lane of the freeway, landing 50 feet below on top of an 18-wheeler cab traveling in the southbound lane.

Childress looked in her rearview mirror and watched the mayhem unfold while it faded from her view. She continued to her destination and made it there in one piece. Childress arrived at the Sun Meadow vitamin store. She went in and summoned a rather nonchalant-looking clerk for help.

"Do you sell silver that a person can eat or drink?" Childress asked, sounding halfway sincere.

"Yeah sure," the clerk said. She took Childress down an aisle that was shelved with every elemental metal that could possibly be absorbed by the human intestine.

"Here you go!" the clerk said. "This is colloidal silver. You can put a few drops of this in your tea or on your food. It helps by supporting your immune system."

"How much is this bottle?" Childress inquired.

"This bottle is twenty-three fifty," the clerk said.

"Damn, for this little bottle?" Childress said. "Is this the strongest you have?"

"No, this forty-five dollar bottle is," the clerk said. "This is the best we have."

"Alright then," Childress said.

As soon as the clerk turned her back, Childress slipped four bottles of the colloidal silver in her purse. The clerk turned around after sensing what Childress had done.

"Hey, you can't do that!" she said to Childress.

Childress glared at the clerk with her green eyes ablaze.

"Yes, I can, and you're going to pay for it, bitch!" Childress hissed. Having taken command over the clerk, Childress sashayed right out the front door. The clerk didn't so much as let a breath of air escape her lips about what had just transpired.

Childress hopped back into her car and hightailed back home. Her brothers were just as she left them, in a state of confusion. She plopped down on the sofa and continued her inquisition with Justice about the new company he was keeping.

"So have you made up your mind about what you're going to do about your little problem?" Childress asked her middle brother.

"Listen, Childress, I'm happy. Can't you be happy for me?" Justice said.

"Damn fool, do you hear yourself talking? You are going to get eaten!" she shouted. "If that's the case, we could just skin you, freeze you, and roast your ass for the next family reunion if it's any of us left!" Justice didn't answer her.

"Alright, let me make it easy for you," Childress said. "The vampire can be killed with silver. When you see her next, you are going to do just that."

Childress pulled from her purse the four bottles of colloidal silver and began to explain its uses to her siblings.

"This is what we are going to keep handy until we can get some pure silver knives and bullets, preferably knives," she said. "But for you, Justice, I want you to rub this across your neck. Hell, put it in her drink—but I want this bitch dead by the next sunrise. You got it?"

Justice knew the circumstances of his disobedience would truly cost him his life should he choose wrong.

"Alright, Childress, I'll do it," Justice said as his other siblings sat in silence.

"I knew you weren't stupid!" she stated.

17

The Caraways were becoming quite cozy during their visit with Nacio. When I arrived, Basira happily greeted me at the door. Her beautiful eyes were sparkling, and her jet black hair was neatly draped over one shoulder.

"Hi Basira," I said, smiling at the beautiful vampire.

"Hello, Solis, come on in," she said as she welcomed me. Basrick had just walked into the foyer and greeted me along with his sister.

Since their arrival, the mansion had come to life with laughter and activity. It was nice to have the massive square footage of the home somewhat occupied. I know Bose enjoyed it. He had certainly been busy, doting over Basrick and Basira. The twins appeared to have a loving sibling relationship with each other.

Basrick was the more introverted of the two, while Basira was the mouthpiece of the sibling duo. They were always giggling during conversations with each other, and always seemed to speak in unison when addressed. Although, this evening, the conversation appears to have taken on a more serious tone as they whispered in secrecy with each other. I could only catch bits and pieces of the dialogue between the two. Whatever it was, Basrick was furious with his twin.

"Do you know what you've done?" Basrick hissed. "How could you have imprinted with him? He is to be killed. You have put Solis and the rest of us in danger, not to mention your own existence!"

"I love him!" Basira fired back. "I will not kill him! He's mine, and we belong to each other now. There is nothing that you can do."

"Are you crazy?" Basrick questioned. "He is evil. If he were to be turned, it would not only perpetuate the curse, but he would make youngling vampires more evil than himself. We've got to kill him! I am going to tell Mom and Dad! I won't let you do this!"

"I'm leaving!" Basira said as she spun on her heels and exited out the front door leaving her brother standing there dumbfounded. It could only be guessed as to where she was going. Basrick looked at me as I tried to pretend that I wasn't eavesdropping.

"Solis, Nacio and my parents have gone over to Puente Masonry and should be back shortly," Basrick stated. "Please make yourself comfortable. Bose has prepared something for you to eat in the kitchen."

"Thank you, Basrick," I said. As I watched the handsome vampire disappear down the hall to his suite, I went into the kitchen. My curiosity was piqued as to the heated subject the twins discussed. Whatever it was, I'm sure Nacio will clue me in when he returned. I waited patiently for my honey to return.

Irritated with her twin's interference, Basira quickly called Justice and made plans to see him this evening.

"Hello Justice? It's Basira. Can you meet me somewhere?" Basira said with heavy desire in her voice.

An overheating Justice was impatiently waiting on her call, all day. His smiled widened when he heard the silky satin voice of his vampire seductress.

"Hey, baby, I've been waiting on you to call me all day," a smiling Justice said. He was so happy to hear from her as he lay in his bed. "Meet me at Mission Park on the south side."

"I'll be there in a few minutes," Basira said.

"Cool, I love you," Justice said as he sprang from his bed and readied himself to see her again. Justice felt his desire escalate as he reflected on his intimate encounter with Basira. He ran his hand across his puncture wounds. Drawing in a few deep breaths to steady himself, he couldn't wait to be joined with her again.

Nodding and slipping in and out of consciousness, Erland stood propped up in back of the bedroom door with his mouth agape. Klein and Childress were nowhere in sight, making it easy for Justice to escape. He snatched the keys right out of his dribbling brother's hand and headed out the door.

He was eager to see his beauty and wanted it to be a special occasion. He stopped at Timmy Tom's on the Southside to get a bottle of strawberry wine to share with her. He looked in his glove compartment and took out the bottle of colloidal silver that Childress had given him. Shaking the bottle of silver, he carefully poured the entire bottle of silver in the wine, watching it dissolve and mix in with the alcohol. Justice was so revved up it seemed as if it only took seconds to arrive at Mission Park.

Justice parked under a huge oak tree that swayed gently in the southerly breeze. He turned the engine off and looked in his driver's side-view mirror to make certain that he had parked close enough to the curb. As he turned back around, Basira was seated in the passenger's seat, sending a jolt of terror through him, heightening his arousal.

"Hello, Justice," Basira gave a raspy greeting to her consort.

"Hey, baby," Justice said as he looked into her eyes.

Within a fraction of a second, Basira and Justice grabbed each other and began kissing wildly. Justice closed his eyes and let Basira have her way with him. She moved so quickly he could not anticipate her next move from moment to moment.

Basira straddled his lap and removed her blouse. Justice allowed his hands to freely roam as she took his head in her hands and angled it upward. Basira tilted her head back with her fangs drawn and plunged down on his neck, striking like a pit viper.

Justice moaned and moved in time with her as she quenched her thirst and he satisfied his desire. Justice rode each wave of pleasure over and over again. Basira drank until she reminded herself to release him. He was weak but still alive.

Reaching for the bottle of wine, Justice took a swig to get some energy back. He coyly offered a swallow to Basira.

"To us!" he toasted, swallowing a large gulp of the spiked drink. He passed the bottle of wine to an unknowing Basira and encouraged her to toast in celebration of their love. Basira took the bottle, turned it up, and swallowed.

"To us!" she said. Basira took a small drink and then followed it up with a huge gulp. Smiling as she wiped a drop of wine from her lips, Basira reached out and kissed Justice again.

"I have to go," Basira whispered. "My family will be looking for me soon."

"I don't want you to leave," Justice said, feeling buzzed from the cheap wine he had guzzled down.

"I'll call you soon," Basira said as she licked his lips one last time. Before he could sit up straight, Basira had vanished. Justice sat, gripping his chest. Gasping for breath as sweat trickled down his temple, Justice allowed regret to settle in on him. Soon two tears escaped his eyes. Feeling as if he had no choice, Justice had carried out the cruel and deceptive wishes of his sister. He had poured silver in the wine, which was the poisonous elixir to slowly kill the person who was the object of his desire.

Trying to start the car, Justice found that tremors had begun to race up and down his arms. He drove the Chevy out of the park and started down the road when he noticed his skin had scaled over. The scales of skin were raised and cracked. Pieces of his skin began to fall off. This was happening slowly at first, but as he drove with the windows down, the wind seem to carry pieces of flesh off his bones.

When Justice saw that his veins were the only thing that covered his body, he screamed and swerved off the road. He crashed the car into a ditch. He hit his head on the steering wheel after the car came to a stop. The rearview mirror had popped off and lay in the seat next to him. He grabbed the mirror and looked at himself. He could hardly recognize his own reflection.

Patches of his sandy-blond hair were missing from his head. He appeared to have a faded and milky aura in the mirror as if his face were fading right before his eyes. His veins hung like string draped across the remaining tissue on his body. Justice tried desperately to look at his eyes. The jade-green jewels that were once the windows to his soul were now filled with white cataracts. As he looked at his face from side to side, he took notice of his ears. What was once a normal Treemount trait of attached earlobes was now gone and replaced with elf ears that were sharply pointed like church Steeples. His once hairless face was now hosting a waist-length blonde moustache that was starch stiff. The fading reflection that stared back at him was that of a monstrosity that was pure evil.

Not being able to stand the sight of his unsightly reflection, Justice continued to lie in the front seat of the vehicle as convulsions set in. He had no clue that the person he once knew himself to be was rapidly becoming the undead. He listened to his heartbeat slow down. The rhythm that once signified life would no longer be heard from within his body. He would soon become a night child, one that was the feared subject of nightmares.

Alone, Justice took to the streets in search of a place to retreat from the burning in his veins.

18

Basira had vanished into the night as soon as she took pleasure in her last embrace with her consort. She shifted into her usual winged preference of travel. She knew she had to return home before her parents and Nacio did. There were more Treemounts to terminate tonight, and the agenda would be no different than any other night. There was no way she could kill Justice. She was in love with him. Her thoughts raced through her mind as she continued to fly through the night air.

She knew that there must be a way that she and Justice could be together. She had planned to tell her parents, and together they would figure out what to do next. She was not too far from the mansion when she felt her wings begin to harden. Without the graceful movement of her wings, Basira automatically began to lose altitude. With her wings now in a state of paralysis, Basira saw Basrick, Nacio, and her parents standing out on the front lawn of the mansion estate. Like a fallen angel, Basira's limp body fell from the nighttime sky.

Basrick could feel the distress his twin was experiencing and took immediate action. Within the blink of an eye, Basrick caught his falling sibling. When he looked upon her face, Basira was turning to silt soil, dissolving with each step he took.

"Nacio! Dad! Come quickly!" Basrick exclaimed. "She went to see Justice. I believe he has made an attempt on her life!"

I heard all of the shouting and ran to the front lawn. Patience was right behind me.

"What happened?" Patience shouted.

"Basira went to see Justice," Basrick told his mother. "She said that she was in love with him. I warned her not to go!"

"Why didn't you tell us before she left?" Patience shouted.

"Give her to me!" Armando shouted. "She has been poisoned with silver!"

"Silver?" Patience inquired. "How can we stop it?"

I ran into the mansion and screamed for Bose to come quickly.

"Bose, please come quickly!" I shouted.

Without a moment to lose, Bose came running out onto the front lawn. He rushed to the circle that had been formed around Basira. She was fading into dust particles with every second that passed.

"Do something!" Patience shouted to her husband. Armando stared in shock at his child's rapidly disappearing body. Out of desperation, the doting father sliced open his wrist to try to get Basira to feed from him. Bose knelt beside the now weepy-eyed Armando.

"It is too late, my friend," Bose said. "The degeneration process has set in and is now irreversible. I am sorry," Bose said regrettably.

"No, please, no!!!! It can't be!" Patience wept. "How could this have happened?"

The wind blew gently, carrying away with it the silt soil that was the remains of Basira's body. The beautiful vampire was no longer in existence.

Nacio stood silent. His face was beginning to take on the frightening appearance that I had only seen at the Texas Taste Tease and the night Hastings had been terminated.

At that moment, my flesh began to crawl at the terror I felt as Bose and all the rest of the vampires stood and let out a grief-stricken roar. The sound shook the trees, frightening sleeping birds from their nests.

Childress sent Justice out to meet up with his vamp tramp in hopes of striking back at them for executing her extended family members. As the evening went on, Childress rummaged through her purse in search of the napkin that Chase had written his number on. Careful not to split one of her fingernails, she found the napkin crumpled up down on the bottom of her handbag. She quickly picked up the phone and dialed the number. Chase answered the phone after two rings.

"Who's this?" Chase answered.

"Hey, cher, this is Childress," she said with her voice oozing sweet-honey poison once again. Childress began to work her magic to lure the unsuspecting suitor to his tragic fate.

"What's up, lady?" Chase said. "I didn't think I would ever hear from you. You blew me off too good that night in the club. So what made you call me?"

"Well, I figured maybe I was a little mean, and I wanted to check you out," Childress said.

Chase grinned from ear to ear while he was on the phone. The phone call from Childress made his day. He knew that she thought that he was someone who was weak and a simpleton. This was his chance to woo this beautiful woman and make her his. He was truly feeling like a man.

"I was hoping that we could get together tonight, cher. You think that's possible?" Childress asked. "I live at 525 Bayou Bank—come and get me."

"I'm on my way!" Chase exclaimed as he jumped up.

"Come on in. The door will be open!"

Chase left home driving like the law was after him. He had been thinking of Childress over the past few days and was waiting to finally make a connection. Chase had spiffed himself up, and he looked presentable. He had no clue that he was headed into the very arms of a descendant of the devil himself.

Chase turned down the street that led to the Treemount home. He could feel the anxiety build within him as he parked in the driveway. He got out and made his way to the front door, ushering himself as a guest into the small wooden-framed house.

"Childress, baby, where are you?" Chase asked.

"Come on back here! Herrrreeee I am," Childress melodically serenaded Chase down the hallway with the falsetto of her voice.

"Here I come," Chase said. He was beside himself. Tiptoeing down the hall, he stopped in the frame of her bedroom door. He saw Childress lying on her stomach across her bed wearing a pair of her favorite face-towel-sized shorts and tube top. She slowly rolled over, turning on her back. When she made it onto her back, in the blink of an eye, she opened a gray canister filled with a spell potion mixed with crushed glass and black pepper and threw it across the room into his eyes and face.

Childress sprang from her bed and delivered a double kick to his groin as he choked a bloodcurdling scream in agony. Using her arms like a violent windmill, Childress came at Chase slicing his skin with her finger nails on contact.

"Welcome to hell simpleton!" Childress laughed. "You are going to stay here with little ole me until that pitiful dog of a niece comes looking for you!"

"Screw you, bitch! You're not going to hurt my niece!" Chase said as he kneeled doubled over on the floor, blinded by shards of glass.

Naturally, this agony wasn't enough for Childress. This extreme sadistic behavior tickled Childress, and it excited her. She wanted more blood, more pain, and more torture. She walked over to him, and taking her fingernails, she dug deep cuts into his face, gouging out chunks of flesh that flew across the floor.

"Klein and Erland, come and tie Simple Simon up!" Childress shouted. "He's going to be here for a while."

Klein and Erland came and did exactly what their sister had asked of them. Erland was actually sober enough to maneuver through the home to find some duct tape. He and Klein taped Chase up and sat him in the middle of the living room.

"Ya'll heard from Justice?" Childress asked.

Both goons shook their heads and shrugged their shoulders in confusion. Chase was placed in a chair that had springs sticking up out of the seat. The springs make it nearly impossible to sit still in the chair.

"Get ready to say bye-bye to your precious parents, Chase!" Childress said. This was the next phase of her diabolical plan.

"Ya'll go on over and blow their house up," Childress barked. "Make sure that the old folks are blown to smithereens!"

"Shouldn't we wait for Justice?" Klein said. "We are going to have to leave here and hide out for a while, Childress."

"We don't know where number two is. We need to do this thing tonight!" Childress said. "I want Solis Burkes gone, and everyone in her life gone!"

Klein and Erland were about to leave to carry out their sinister plan that their sister was bent on carrying out. They were just about to leave when it dawned on them that they had no transportation.

"We need the keys to your car, Childress, or else how are we supposed to do all this?" Erland said. "Justice took my car, and now we can't find him."

Just as she was about to speak, Childress looked out the living room window to see Detective Bouvier's black Mustang pull up in front of the house. Chase still had his Lincoln parked in the driveway.

"Dammit! Here comes another simpleton!" Childress exclaimed as she saw the detective making his way up to the front door. The detective rang the doorbell. Childress and her brother's froze.

"Shit, Childress, what are we going to do?" Klein said, pointing to the bloody-faced Chase sitting duct-taped in the chair. "I don't feel like getting locked back up again."

"Shut up, Klein, and calm down," Childress hissed. "Get the door, Erland."

Erland opened the door and allowed Detective Bouvier to enter their home. The detective cautiously entered the home. He immediately caught an eyeful of the bound guest that sat tortured in the middle of the living room.

"Childress, what's going on here?" Detective Bouvier said as he stood looking at Chase.

"What the hell does it look like, cop?" Childress snapped at the statuesque detective.

"This is why you wanted me to investigate where Solis Burkes and Chase Henderson lived? So you could kidnap him and bait Solis out?" Detective Bouvier exclaimed. "You used me! Why me, Childress? Why?"

"Because I could make you do whatever I wanted!" Childress shouted. "It's too late for you too, cop! You are now apart of this. You led me right to them, and there's nothing you can do about it now!"

Detective Bouvier stood in the middle of the Treemount living room with a cloud of regret hanging over him. He knew that he had been implicated as an accomplice in several felony charges that had just killed his law enforcement career. Getting involved with the Treemount family was as bad as being involved in every criminal offense they had ever committed. Tears filled his eyes, eventually streaming down his face. His desire for Childress still had not subsided.

Reaching out to kiss her, Detective Bouvier walked over to Childress, trying to embrace her. She threw her arms up and pushed away his affections, leaving him with hurt pride. Detective Bouvier was crushed. As all of the Treemounts stood in the living room laughing at him, Detective Bouvier reached for his .45 automatic service weapon. He took two steps forward toward the door, and turned and looked at Childress.

"I love you, Childress!" Detective Bouvier said. Those were the last words Detective Mathis Bouvier spoke as he aimed the .45 automatic at his right temple and pulled the trigger, blowing every thought he had ever had in his head all over the sheetrock.

"Damn! Did you see that?" Klein inquired as he stood to his feet after ducking when Detective Bouvier pulled the trigger. "Ooh that's nasty!"

"Yeah, we can see what's on his mind!" Erland said, laughing inappropriately.

"Shut up, fool! Clean this mess up!" Childress barked. "Erland, you and Klein get this dead dog cop out of here. Make sure to take his gun and put it on him. Don't touch the gun, and take his car. Klein, you follow Erland in my car. Find a spot in the hill country and drive the car off a cliff or something!" Childress commanded.

"Drive his car around back and load him in it, and then get rid of him!" Childress said, now looking at Chase.

"I want Solis to know that I have 'Uncle Chase' here with me," Childress hissed in Chase's ear, licking it with her tongue like the reptile she is.

Klein and Erland were busy hauling Detective Bouvier's body through the house. Blood dripped and brain matter dropped all along the wooden floors leading through the kitchen to the back door.

"He's a messy booger, isn't he?" Erland said, grinning inappropriately at the deceased man's remains.

Klein and Erland had made it to the back door. Erland fished the keys out of the detective's jacket. He ran through the house and out the front door to drive Detective Bouvier's Mustang around back. The two brothers loaded the detective in the trunk and slammed it shut.

"When you two finish, come in here and clean all this blood up with bleach," Childress continued. "In fact, clean the walls in this entire room with bleach. Make sure to clean the room from top to bottom. Remember to wipe off the ceiling, the door, and the table too."

"Alright, we will," Klein said. "We need to find Justice since we are doing all this, Childress. We need to get out of town after all this goes down. I say we hit the road and keep going," Klein stated. "Forget about that tramp, Solis. This damn fool cop has shot his head off, and more cops are going to start showing up here! We need to make a move, now!"

"Klein, shut up!" Childress shouted. "I say what we do, and when we do it! Right now, you need to make sure that this house is cleaned up. Let the damn law come. If we bleach this house down, they won't find a thing. Now do it!"

Childress took Chase's cell phone from the holster on his belt.

"Well Chase, looks like things are heating up," Childress said to Chase. "It's time to even up the score!"

Childress went in her room and pulled out a canister of crushed vines for her spell. She also had taken a small canister of hydrochloric acid out of the refrigerator in the garage. Childress reached for her book of spells. She found the little plastic bags with her mother's blood flakes in one and her ancestor's blood flakes in the other. She took the blood flakes, mixed them both in a cup of water, and swallowed it. She began chanting a spell of protection. As she spoke the chants, silver knives appeared on her bed along with a black cat o' nine tails whip. Childress gagged violently as the age-old plasma hit her stomach. She walked over to the mirror and gasped at her final reflection.

Childress saw that in the back of the green color of her eyes burned the fires of hell. Her eyelids were retracted, and her eyeballs were bulging. Her tongue had narrowed and was now lizard-like. She was becoming an upright, walking serpent.

Bringing all the material out into the living room, she stopped her brothers in the middle of their cleaning duties, causing them to jump with terror. They attempted to retreat from their sister's reptilian-looking features.

"Damn, Childress! You look worse than the dead fool we just carried out of here!" Klein exclaimed.

"Are you high?" Erland asked, wishing he was at that moment.

"Stop worrying about me, and do what I say," Childress sniped.

"This here is acid. It can kill you, so don't touch it directly," she said. "I want you to take this acid and sawdust and make a Molotov cocktail and blow up Solis's house, you two understand?" Childress questioned. "I know Solis's friend is coming with her, so use these silver knives if you have to."

"Yeah, we can do that," Klein affirmed.

"We could use a Molotov cocktail when we dump this dead fool," Erland said, pointing outside in the backyard to Detective Bouvier's car.

Klein and Erland quickly finished cleaning up the mess that the gunshot had made. Childress had come up with another alternative.

"We'll all go together and get rid of all the evidence," she said.

"What about this simpleton here?" Klein pointed to Chase.

"He ain't going anywhere—hell, he can't even see," Childress said. "He's no threat to us," Childress said, drawing back her hand and slapping Chase out of the chair onto the floor.

"Alright then, we're ready!" Klein stated. "Erland, let's go."

Childress waited until her brothers drove the detective's car around front. She waited for them to get in front of her so she could follow in her little car. The Treemounts headed west on the interstate.

"Drive to Kerrville, Erland," Klein said. "Let's dump him where we dumped those other Inner Circle Cannibal fools three years ago."

"Oh yeah, I remember that place," Erland confirmed. "No one will ever find him there."

The deadly brothers were talking about an underground cave that was on the side of a mountain. Klein and Erland made it to the hill country. They started their trek off road, nearly hitting two deer in the process. Childress stayed on the road, for her little car could not stand the trip.

Klein and Erland found the entrance of the cave. Erland rigged the car so that it would continue to roll straight into the cave. They lit a Molotov cocktail with a long fuse that would burn as the car rolled into the cave. If anyone were to find the car, the Treemounts would be long gone by the time they did. The brothers turned and ran as far as they could. They made it back to the road just in time to hear a big bang in the distance. The task was complete.

Childress sat in the little black Beetle waiting impatiently for her brothers. She saw their two figures in the darkness and knew they did what they were supposed to do.

"Let's roll," she said. Childress reached for Chase's phone that she had taken with her. "It's time to hit Solis's house and burn it to the ground," she said.

Leaving Chase behind was a huge mistake that Childress had made. Childress had no clue that Chase kept a backup cell phone because he always lost one. With glass fragments falling from his eyes,

Chase stumbled around until he took out his cell phone from his boot. He immediately called 911 and sent for an ambulance and the police. Chase gave the 911 operator an earful about the Treemounts, letting the dispatch person know that they had planned to dump the detective's body.

The Treemounts would now have to go on the run. They would have to live their lives as fugitives.

19

After the wind finished blowing away Basira's remains, the vampires stood grief-stricken before me. Patience wailed as Bose comforted her, Basrick was stone-faced, Armando rubbed his hands in the silt that was merely residue left on the ground, and Nacio's eyes were red with anger. The ringing of my phone snapped me out of my frozen stance. It was my Uncle Chase's number on the phone I.D. log.

"Hello, Chase, what do you want?" Solis said, still shocked at the events that had just occurred.

"Why hello, cher, but this ain't your 'Uncle Chase,'" Childress said, rolling her words off her tongue slowly. "It's, Childress, bitch! I know you and your plasma-drinking boyfriend have been killing people in my family. Well, it's time to even the score!" Childress threatened.

"Did you think I would be so stupid as to not know that someone or something was trying to get to me?" Childress sniped. "I should have killed your ass at the Texas Taste Tease when I had the chance."

"You could have, witch, but we all know that you don't have good sense or you wouldn't be the criminal you are today," I fired back, trying to subdue my own blood from boiling over.

"You've always been a simple bitch!" Childress jeered. "You were always crying, always whining, always weak."

Her words cut through me like the edge of a sharp tin can. She had always known what to say to me to get me off balance and to make me think that I could never be safe. She knew just what to say to make me feel confused and terrified.

"You are still the same sorry soul you always were, Childress," I fired back. "Your mother didn't love you enough when you were younger. If she had loved you enough, she wouldn't have dropped you flat on the back of your head to make you so senseless and evil," I jeered back, knowing that would only aggravate her more.

"There you go again, thinking you are better than everybody else," Childress started when I cut her off.

"I am better than you, Childress, and you know it. Only someone like you would be a bully as a child and then grow up to be a criminal as an adult!" I sniped. "A criminal tramp is all you are worth being!"

"Well, I can tell you what I am now," Childress shouted. "I'm holding your Uncle Chase hostage. I met him out at the club the other night. He came to me today willingly, and now I have him, slut! So what are you going to do about that?" Childress taunted.

"You'd better not hurt Chase, Childress," I said, shocked and praying that she didn't have him, but I knew she did.

"There's nothing you can do, Solis, because you are weak," Childress said as if she were smiling over the phone. "You have a choice to make, Solis. You see, I know where you live, and I know that your grandparents are there right now by themselves," Childress continued. "You need to decide to save either Chase or your grandparents. Choose carefully, Solis. If you don't make your mind up by one o'clock, you will be crying at two more funerals," Childress threatened. "Make sure to have plenty of tissues for the occasions," she said as she ended the call.

Nacio heard every word of the conversation, and before I could speak another word to him, Armando and the surviving members of his family had already shape-shifted and were manned up to go after the core members of the Treemount clan.

"Nacio, this is it—let's go," I said. "She has my uncle and she has threatened to kill my grandparents as well."

"This ends tonight," Armando said as he wiped the rest of the silt that was Basira's remains from his hands.

Nacio did not dispute my commands of following him into battle. He teleported us to the street corner of where the Treemounts live. We all positioned ourselves to storm the Treemount home.

"On my signal," Nacio said. "Now!"

With superhuman speed, all of the vampires surrounded the home and entered, ready to attack. I came in through the front door, only to see my uncle with his hands loosed from duct tape lying on the floor.

"That's my Uncle Chase!" I screamed.

I ran to my wounded uncle. Angered at what Childress had done to him, I tried to keep myself composed.

"Chase, I am so sorry you got mixed up in all this!" I cried. "Childress is after me! She always has been. She's hurt you to get to me! Childress is the one who killed Affinity, but I couldn't prove it!"

"Don't worry, I have already called the police," Chase said. "They should be here any minute."

The vampires checked the inside of the home, looking for any sign of the Treemounts.

"None of them are here," Nacio said.

"I need to know where Justice is," Basrick said. "We need to crush him first!"

"I heard them say that they are waiting for him, but they don't know where he is," Chase said. "Right now, we need to get home! They are talking about blowing up the house. I tried to call home to tell Mama, but she is not answering! You have to get home—please, Solis, go!" Chase said.

In the near distance, the sound of sirens filled the night. Without a second to spare, Nacio and the rest of the vampires shape-shifted, ready to get me to our subdivision as quickly as possible.

"I hear the police coming, Solis, please get to Mama!" Chase said.

Nacio secured me under his arms as we teleported away once again into the night. The Caraways followed closely, equally thirsting for blood and revenge, whichever came first to their satisfaction.

Nacio set us down at the corner by my cul-de-sac. The entire block appeared eerily quiet and still. There were no porch lights on, which was strange. I began to walk up to my yard when I saw two tiny lights that shined in the pitch-black darkness, and a raspy voice called to me from the night.

"What's your hurry, Solis?" Childress hissed as she slithered in my direction. Childress looked at me with her eyes literally on fire. Even in the dark of night, her skin was pale. Her hair looked as if it were a wild, windblown bush. She wore a tight black, low-cut spandex dress.

"You are still a weak crybaby," Childress said. "Were you going inside to tell your grandmamma?" she said. "Guess that's the only one you can tell since your mama's dead and gone! No one can hear you, because they've all been drugged! So scream all you want!"

Childress brought her cat o' nine tails from behind her and cracked it in my direction towards my face. I blocked the attack with my mind, sending the whip cracking backwards with one of the silver-tipped fringes slicing Childress in the face. Childress turned her face and winced in pain.

Before I could turn to call out to Nacio, the brothers appeared on the street. They were walking slowly towards the now-visible vampires. Each vampire took position to battle the Treemounts. Klein and Justice continued to walk willingly towards the vampires. Once close enough, each vampire grabbed hold of the Treemounts.

Upon touching Klein and Erland's skin, the vampires each screamed in horror as they were chemically burned by the colloidal silver that they had rubbed on their skin. The vampires hissed as they lay on the asphalt. Squirming in pain, Nacio warned his clan.

"Fall back!" Nacio called as he lay on the ground in agonizing pain.

At that moment of retreat for the vampires, the Treemounts charged forward with the silver knives. Klein and Erland moved with stabbing motions towards them. The vampires tried to crawl away to safety, but the brothers continued forward in their assault.

Meanwhile, Childress and her hellfire eyes never left me. She continued to talk her trash as she kept swinging her cat o' nines whip.

"Look at you, you can't even save your family," Childress laughed as one of the silver tips from the whip cut me on my shoulder. Her words were starting to wear on me once again. She continued to move forward. She cracked her whip again, wrapping it around my left ankle. She then yanked my leg out from under me. I fell to the ground. Trying desperately to crawl away, I remembered my mother's words.

...You will succeed child. You are not alone, Solis...get up, Hammer. You have the strength to defeat this demon—use your strength, Do it! Do it! Remember the tie that binds...the tie that binds...

As I recalled words that my mother and grandmother had spoken to me, I called on my strength and forced my mind open. I propelled myself back to my feet, loosening the cat o' nines whip around my ankle. I used my mind to unleash my fury on Childress. Using my abilities when she tried to crack her whip on me again, I stopped it in mid air, and made it reverse. Using my telekinesis to spin Childress around, I used the whip to bind her arms behind her.

Once Childress was secure, she was pushed forward and she fell flat on her face. When her face hit the asphalt, she fell on her teeth, shattering them right in the middle of the cul-de-sac. Blood splattered in all directions from her fall. It felt good to stop her in her tracks.

"Childress, since causing pain is what you like most, it's time you experienced some of your own!" I shouted.

I grabbed Childress by her ankles and dragged her face down on the asphalt. The sound of her skin skidding over the rock fragments and gravel only made her laugh.

"Is that all you got?" Childress egged me on. "I told you that you are weak."

Totally enraged now, I grabbed her by the hair on her head and dragged her to the curb of the sidewalk and banged her head as hard as I could. I turned her bloody face over and punched her nose, making sure to hear the snapping of cartilage. I punched her face again, making sure to land a punch right in the eye. I punched and punched and punched, harder, harder, and harder. The years of emotional bondage that I had been enslaved to were being represented with every hit I delivered.

"Do you like it, Childress? You like pain, don't you?" I whispered in her ear. "Surely, this is not enough."

Childress couldn't mumble a word due to her nose being smashed in. She rolled over on her side, still laughing psychotically. She lay there on the cement laughing louder and louder. The vampires were going crazy over the smell of blood but were unable to move due to the colloidal silver that was burning through their skin from attempting an attack on Klein and Erland.

Knowing that the vampires were minimally subdued, the Treemount brothers took out the knives they each held. Klein walked over to Patience and stabbed her. He thought he put the knife in her heart. Luckily, the knife made a mere flesh wound in her chest just below her heart. Nonetheless, Patience was down and unable to move. Feeling a sense of success, Klein moved away from Patience towards his brother who was now moving towards a subdued Armando.

"Stab him, Erland! Stab him in the chest!" Klein shouted. "Move back once you get the knife in him!"

Knowing that Erland was not too bright, he stabbed at Armando, landing his silver knife more in the groin area. This caused Armando to curl up on his side, giving the appearance that he had killed him.

"I did it!" Erland shouted. "Let's go and get Childress from that bitch!"

"Wait man!" Klein said. "We have to get the big bastard over there!" Klein said, pointing to Nacio lying on the ground.

Both of the brothers walked towards Nacio who was panting for breath on the ground. Erland had the last knife that Childress had given them. Wielding the knife high over his head, Erland lunged towards Nacio's fallen body!

With what little strength remained, Nacio swiftly kicked Erland's feet from under him, making him tumble to the ground. Attempting to break his fall, Erland loosened his grip on the knife sending it flying into my neighbor's yard! Nacio was still attempting to retreat to a safe distance away from the two murderous brothers.

I was still punching Childress. I couldn't stop! It felt so good to direct my anger at the person who caused it. I was beginning to like it a little too much.

Now caught in a frenzy of my own, I began to tear huge patches of hair from Childress. I enjoyed the sound that it made. Hearing the hair ripped straight from her scalp and knowing that it was hers heightened my pleasure of inflicting pain on her. Revenge finally! It felt so good!

I took one last punch to her face. Chanting the words that Grandma Olvignia had said, I started to finish Childress.

...With the tie that binds, Childress, I bind your mind—you will not harm me again, you will not harm us again, with the tie that binds, I bind your mind, Childress, you will not harm us again, in our Savior's name, you will not harm us again...

Childress continued to laugh. Bloody and beaten, she managed to look at me with the flames still burning in her eyes.

"You can bind me, but you can't stop me!" Childress said, shouting to her goony brothers.

"Klein, do it now!" Childress screamed.

Klein came up behind me and covered my mouth with something. Down I went onto the ground with my eyes only seeing a few images as I fought to keep them open. Klein carried me to the porch of my home.

I saw that Nacio managed to stagger to his feet, stumbling his way to my yard to get to my grandparents. Setting foot on the fringe of the yard, Nacio staggered up the driveway. Out of the darkness, Erland took his knife and plunged it into Nacio's back!

Nacio screamed in pain. He threw Erland off his back with one powerful thrust. As Erland fell to the ground, Klein threw the Molotov cocktail laced with acid, sawdust, and other poison into the front window of my home.

Windows shattered inside the home, and upon contact, there was an explosion that seemed as if it could be heard on the other side of town. The explosion shattered windows of the houses across the street and two blocks away!

After he threw the cocktail, Klein ran and brought the Beetle to the corner. Erland grabbed his still psychotically laughing sister and threw her in the backseat. He jumped in the front seat as Klein burned rubber, making their escape into the night.

"Where do you want me to head?" Klein asked his sister who sat in the backseat a bruised and bloodied mess.

"Hit Interstate 10, and let's go to New Orleans," she said. "Maybe Justice will catch up to us later wherever he is."

"Yeah, we can hide in the swamps and marshes until things blow over," Klein said.

"Awww, man, I need to get my medicine," Erland said.

"Damn fool, we can't go back to the house now," Childress said. "The law might be there, and I ain't going back to the pen!" Childress shouted. "Just drive, man!"

Klein drove east towards the swamps and marshes, home to New Orleans.

20

I finally regained consciousness from the blast of the explosion as the fire burned the frame of the house in front of me. The front door of our house was blown off, and smoke poured out into the night sky. I couldn't see through all of the thick smoke and sludge that was in the air, but the flames continued to roar.

"Nacio, where are you!" I shouted.

Disoriented and staggering, I tried to find my beloved. The last thing I remembered before I lost consciousness was Erland wielding a silver knife and plunging it into Nacio's back. I didn't get a response from him. This can't be happening!

Klein slipped a towel over my nose and mouth that had something on it to make me pass out. I guess he must have doused the house with gasoline, because the smell of those distinct fumes was undeniable. I needed to get to Grandma Olvignia.

Childress had planned to kill my family and all the vampires once we were in the same place. I found the strength to stagger through the front of the burning house. The flames were searing my face as I tried to look for Nacio and my Grandparents.

"Grandma! Grandpa!" There was no answer. I continued looking through the house but began to crawl. The heat was unbearable. Finally, I saw her small feet sticking out of the front bedroom. Grandma was lying unconscious, next to my grandfather. I gathered all my strength and dragged her and me out of the inflamed house. I was too late. Childress put crushed vines into the Molotov cocktail that was thrown in the front window of our house causing the explosion and the acid to splatter everywhere in the house. Some splattered on my grandfather and ate away at his skin. I grabbed my grandmother and held her in my arms.

"Grandma, please don't leave me! Please!" I said as I continued to rock her gently. With her dying breath, she whispered to me what I did not want to hear.

"You are Mistress now. You will continue to protect those in harm's way. Hold your head high, and be proud."

"Stop saying that, Grandma! You will be fine, just hold on, please!" I screamed.

"It's okay Solis—you can let me rest, honey," she said. "My work here in this world is through now. You will succeed."

I dragged her outside into the yard. Nacio was lying facedown. I ran to him and saw the knife sticking out of his back. Without thinking, I pulled the knife from my beloved's wound. He coughed, and I knew he would be okay.

"Sweetheart, you need to take the others and leave!" I said. "I'll call Bose to meet you at the lake two blocks away!" I said, kissing his lips.

"I'll gather the others," Nacio said. He was weakened, but he knew what needed to be done.

"If you can stand, let's go!" Nacio called to the other vampires.

I saw the other vampires. I ran to remove the knives from Patience and Armando. Basrick was still lying on the ground in agony.

Armando and Patience stood and walked over to lift their son onto their shoulders. Still wounded, they all began to head out of the cul-de-sac, following Nacio to the lake.

Grabbing my phone, I quickly called Bose to come and pick up the weakened vampires that were lying in the street.

"Bose, please come and get Nacio and the Caraways. They've been hurt!" I said. "The Treemounts caused an explosion at my house!" I said. "Please pick them up at the park at the lake. They will be waiting in the shadows."

"I'm on my way, Mistress!" Bose said as he ended the phone call.

I phoned for the police and fire department next. Nacio and the Caraways needed to leave the scene before the police and fire department came.

I went back to Grandma's side and held her. She continued to speak as loudly as she could, which was no more than a whisper.

"You will be happy now, child. Be wise, and strong. I will speak to you in your dreams. You will never be alone. I love you, Solis," Grandma Olvignia said.

And with that, my Grandma faded away.

A sneak peak at the next book

Embellish 2: Justice served

1

Itching and scratching is how Justice awoke. With his mind clouded with confusion, his thin, clammy skin was as white as snow. Blue veins squirmed just beneath the surface of his skin. Justice couldn't understand what all the pain was from. He had come down off of being high before, but this particular state of mind was intense and nothing seemed to help the pain go away.

He had the shakes and thought maybe if he had a joint or some alcohol it would enable him to calm down a bit. Justice had no idea how much time had passed or where he was. All he remembered was how he had met the love of his life and the deep passion that they shared between the two of them. Basira was her name. Holding her was like holding an angel in his arms. Her eyes were sky blue, and her hips were full and round.

Justice remembered the taste of her lips as his tongue slid in her mouth. The pleasure she gave him was like no other.

Oh, how he wanted to be near Basira. Justice jumped to his bare feet, still confused. He did not know which direction to head in to find the object of his heart's desire. He didn't care which way he was headed, for he knew he would find her.

With every step Justice took, he began to smile, because he knew he would find her. Faster and faster, he quickened his pace—Basira was all he wanted. She was the only one that could make him feel safe. He needed Basira.

"My Basira," Justice said out loud to himself. "My Basira."

Justice continued his pace but soon found his legs and feet slowing down, having to acknowledge the sledge hammering pain he felt in his chest as reality came crashing in on him. His pace reminded him of his last encounter with his beloved.

Deception sealed his beloved's fate. He had mixed colloidal silver in a bottle of wine that he had tricked Basira into drinking after they shared an intimate moment with each other. Unknowingly, she consumed enough of the spiked wine that could have been fatal for her.

Justice recalled doing this upon the request of his hateful sister, Childress. How he hated his sister at times. Now he's all alone. He's aching, in pain, and thirsty—so very thirsty.

It was nightfall, and Justice was underneath a bridge. He had been hiding in a drainage pipe next to the San Antonio River. He had to get something to drink. He couldn't stand the dry burning in his throat. It was driving him insane. He checked his pockets and found that he had a few dollars in them. He started walking on a trail in a grass meadow towards a convenient store that he saw in the distance.

Coming down the trail from the opposite way towards him was a drunken young woman. A set of apartments was on the opposite side of the meadow. The trail must have been one that is frequented often by the apartment residents. The woman had what looked to be a beer can in her hand. Justice looked at it with anticipation.

The young woman looked to be twenty-one years old. She had on a miniskirt and halter top. Justice was thirsty, but he also wanted something else from the young woman. Startled, she stopped in her tracks and looked at Justice.

"You want a sip of my beer?" the young woman asked.

She was careful not to make any sudden moves in front of Justice. She stared at him in shock. Justice had a wispy-looking blond moustache and pale white skin. His eyes were milky white, and he had lost all of his blondish, curly hair, leaving him totally bald.

"Yes, please, I would like a taste if you don't mind?" Justice said in a heavy seductive voice that he did not recognize as his own.

The young woman raised her arm to hand him her beer. Justice looked at the beer can and walked toward the young woman. He reached for the beer can and took it from her hands. Catching her off guard, Justice embraced the young woman. His fangs lowered and he plunged them in a warm spot on her neck. He drank from her neck like a glutton as the thirst-quenching blood plasma revived him.

Drinking deeply, he thirsted no more.

Lightning Source UK Ltd.
Milton Keynes UK
15 August 2010

158464UK00003B/1/P

9 781432 740337